WHAT YOU DON'T KNOW

"Riveting and terrifying! The very definition of a thriller! This is what I call, "an all-nighter." Once you start, you won't be able to stop! Chilling all the way down to your bones! *What You Don't Know* is what nightmares are made of."
–@Elizabeth.Ness.56

"[*What You Don't Know*] was a 5/5 for me ... Brilliant."
–@Momfluenster

"It was pure joy to read and edit *What You Don't Know* by Bianca Sloane. Alternating between the violence unfolding at the Gilbert's and investigative interviews with their friends and family, Sloane transports us into a terrifying, brutal home invasion while constructing a brilliant plot that reads like an episode of Dateline. I was mesmerized and petrified through every page. Masterful and gripping, this is a suspense novel that any thriller lover will devour."
–Samantha M. Bailey, #1 bestselling author of WOMAN ON THE EDGE

"Sloane creates complex characters within multi-layered plots that will have you flipping pages to the very end."
–Cindy Reads & Writes

"I read [*What You Don't Know*] in roughly 24 hours, and when I was near the end I was carrying my Kindle around the house so I could sneak in a page or two because I had to get to the end, I had to know

what happened. I actually turned the shower on and stood in the bathroom so I could read the last few pages. This book is that good."
–@The_Towering_TBR

"[What You Don't Know] . . . [was] such a thrill to read . . . We have been looking for a thriller that captures our attention from the first page and holds it until the last. Bianca Sloane's ability to plot and pace such a universally scary event was masterful. We were absolutely petrified reading this book. . ."
–@**audioshelfme**

"My favorite thing about being a book reviewer is discovering new authors and Bianca Sloane was a new to me author who has me ready to read more of her books after devouring this one in just two nights. I was quickly hooked on this story [and] Sloane's writing style is fast-paced and totally gripping."
–**GripLitGrl**

THE LIVE TO TELL SERIES

"Bianca Sloane sure knows how to make a page turn."
–**Whatisthatbookabout.com about TELL ME A LIE**

"...Once again, [Bianca Sloane's] fast-paced, nail-biting, on-the-edge-of-your-seat style of suspense had me gripped from the first page to the last."
–**Goodreads Reviewer about LIVE TO TELL**

"...You will sail through these fast-paced thrillers."
–**Ashley Gillan, eBookNerdReviews.wordpress.com about LIVE TO TELL and TELL ME A LIE**

EVERY BREATH YOU TAKE

"Once you start reading this book, you won't want to stop."
—Ionia Martin, ReadfulThingsBlog.com

"...Will have you chewing your fingernails down to the quick. The author has a deftness for building suspense and tension, leaving you wondering what's coming next."
—The Haphazardoushippo.Blogspot.com

"The character buildup ... is beyond perfection. Highly recommended."
—San Francisco Book Review, 5 Stars

SWEET LITTLE LIES

"It is impossible for a reader to relax their grip on *Sweet Little Lies*. The story elements are crisp and exciting with multiple twists and turns."
—Night Owl Reviews

"The mystery [of *Sweet Little Lies*] deepens from the very beginning and comes to a satisfying but shocking ending. I feel that anyone looking for a good thriller would be hard pressed to find a better one."
—Green Embers Recommends

"From the first few pages, you get instantly hooked. When you first read about the premise ... you think you know exactly how the story might unfold. There is no amount of predictability that would have foreseen all the twists and turns that came from reading [*Sweet Little Lies*]."
—Whatisthatbookabout.com

"Once again, Bianca Sloane has written a fast-paced mystery that is the perfect choice for some exciting reading escapism."
—SheTreadsSoftly.Blogspot.com

"I could not put this down until ... I found out what would happen. The ending was a big shock. I loved this and would recommend it to any thriller fan."
—WiLoveBooks.Blogspot.com

KILLING ME SOFTLY

Thriller of the Month by www.e-thriller.com (May 2013)
"2013 Top Read" by OOSA Online Book Club

"[A] cross between 'Sleeping with the Enemy' and a superb murder mystery."
—a CrimeReadersBlog.Wordpress.com

"[*Killing Me Softly*] is a book that will leave the reader scratching their head trying to figure out the villain. And, just when the reader thinks they have it all figured out - think again - AND AGAIN!"
—Examiner.com (New Orleans)

WHAT YOU DON'T KNOW

BIANCA SLOANE

BOOKS BY BIANCA SLOANE

WHAT YOU DON'T KNOW

A NORMAL SATURDAY

Elena York, True Crime Writer, Author of _Terror in the Suburbs_: It was Saturday, April first—April Fool's Day.

Bridget Johnson, Blair Gilbert's Sister: Two days before my birthday (Scoffs and shakes head) My birthday.

Lani Jacobs, Blair and Malcolm Gilbert's Neighbor: It was a beautiful day. That's probably what I'll always remember. What a beautiful day it was.

Guy Sledge, Friend of Malcolm Gilbert: The four of us—Malcolm, myself, our friend, Don, our friend, Kip—had a standing golf date—weather permitting—every Saturday at twelve fifteen at the club. Had been that way for years. Malcolm was usually there around ten forty-five, eleven, as he liked to chip and putt beforehand.

Lani Jacobs: It was one of those beautiful warm spring days. Blair and I went jogging early that morning, like we usually did on Saturdays, then we'd stop for coffee on the way home. It was just a normal Saturday.

Elena York: Blair and Malcolm Gilbert had lived in Highland Park, Illinois, one of the cornerstones of Chicago's tony North Shore, for over twenty years. The North Shore is a cluster of suburbs north of the city that represents some of the highest per capita income in the country. Highland Park is affluence defined—the cream of the crop, a gated community with no gates. It's home to CEOs, singers, actors, philanthropists, doctors, attorneys. Athletes in particular flock to Highland Park because the practice facilities for the city's football and basketball teams are in neighboring suburbs. It's also a popular locale for movies and television shows.

Guy Sledge: What came later that morning—well, yes, it was a bit odd. Nothing worrying necessarily, but ... well, knowing what I know now, I wish I'd called him, maybe even gone over to the house. My wife says it's a good thing I didn't—I might have been there. Still, you can't help but wonder what if.

Loretta Robinson, the Gilberts' Neighbor: I've lived in Highland Park fifty years and I've never seen anything like this here. Ever.

Bridget Johnson: What I've never been able to forgive or understand is the brutality of it. To this day, I ask myself, "How could someone be this cruel?"

Skye Stafford, Reporter, Channel 4 News, Chicago: Can you imagine? Your doorbell rings and the next thing you know, you've opened the door to a nightmare.

Cassie Wexler, Blair and Malcolm Gilbert's Neighbor: You know what's dangerous about the suburbs? The false sense of security. It's so easy to buy into this notion that nothing bad can happen to you when you live in a beautiful mansion or behind a gate. Bad things happen in other places. Bad things happen to other people. So, you let your guard down. Which is the biggest mistake you can make.

That's the thing about evil. You can't escape it. It's like water. It manages to find its way into the smallest of cracks.

PART 1

SATURDAY, APRIL 1
HIGHLAND PARK, ILLINOIS
THE RESIDENCE
OF
MALCOLM AND BLAIR GILBERT

10:20 A.M.

Malcolm adjusted the collar of his peach Polo in his bathroom mirror before running his index finger along the crease of his khakis, almost disappointed he didn't slice the skin open. He was just playing golf today, but it didn't matter. He still had to be *Malcolm Gilbert* and that meant expectations. A role to play. A flawlessness to maintain. A massive gold Rolex had to rest at the end of one lean, muscular fore-arm. An expensive Polo was expected to drape his flat, sixty- (almost sixty-one-) year-old abs. His khakis were meant to hang just so down the length of his legs, still two pillars of concrete. The money clip was supposed to bulge obnoxiously. And of course, that *other* thing—one of six—was expected to be on display at all times for those in its presence to notice, fawn over, revere.

Downstairs, Blair thrashed around the kitchen. He scoffed softly as he squirted toothpaste onto his toothbrush. Hurricane Blair. Right on time. The requisite slamming of cabinet doors soon commenced. He'd endured her tirade on the way home from dinner last night. Had tolerated her cursing and mumbling into the pages of the Metro section at breakfast while they ate scrambled eggs and fruit salad. He didn't take the bait either time, knowing it would irritate her. He'd calmly slurped his coffee, ate his eggs, enjoyed his sweet and juicy strawberries and kiwis, while he read the sports page. He wasn't ashamed to admit it gave him a measure of satisfaction. After what she'd pulled at the bank yesterday, she'd had it coming.

Another crash erupted as he spit blue mouthwash into the sink. He could see her now, whirling around the kitchen, righteous indignation at full tilt. Muttering under her breath about what an asshole he was and how she wasn't going to take his shit, and this was a marriage, not a fucking dictatorship, and how dare he, how *dare* he.

Funny how she was the one who was wrong, yet *she* was the victim.

Malcolm stepped into the bedroom as he glanced at his watch. He'd need to leave in the next ten minutes at the latest. From the corner of his eye, he could see the table on the balcony outside their bedroom. He noticed the flapping pages of the crossword puzzle book he'd been working on earlier that morning. He stepped outside to grab the book, stopping a moment to drink in the view. Lake Michigan was serene today. He stood with his feet slightly apart, his hands on his hips, relishing the warm wind threading across his body as he took a deep, cleansing breath. Sunlight danced across the lake's glassy surface. Seeing the magnificent expanse of water stretching into infinity every day was one of his favorite things about the house.

It was a beautiful house, of course, what one would expect from a man of his stature, his wealth, his name. And he had enjoyed showing it off over the years, watching those granted access into the inner sanctum oohh and ahhh over the clean lines of the contemporary-modern mansion awash in crisp white, slate gray, soothing beige, and sea glass green. A marked change from the dark wood panels, ornate oil paintings, and heavy Oriental rugs his mother favored or the black leather couches, glass top coffee tables, and oversized cubist paintings of his once-upon-a-time bachelor pad. Watching visitors marvel over the uninterrupted sweep of glass offering panoramic views of the

lake, as though you were teetering on the edge of the world, was titil-
lating. He loved all of it—the wine room, the cigar room, the indoor
swimming pool, the private movie theater, the steam showers, the
sauna, the library.

But the lake. The lake made him happy. Even in the winter, nothing
gave him greater pleasure than to sit outside, the wind slicing through
him, the tips of his nose and fingers burning bright red, and watch the
choppy, ugly gray waves capped with specks of foam, swirl and
churn. Even the ugliness of the water was beautiful to him.

He took one last inhale and closed the balcony door behind him, the
digital lock beeping as he tossed the book of crosswords onto his
nightstand and grabbed his keys, wallet, and phone before heading
downstairs. He frowned as he took a cursory look at the cameras on
his phone. It looked like a few of them were glitching.

Blair's phone trilled from the kitchen and he rolled his eyes, already
knowing who was on the other end, so there was no point in asking.
She shook her head slightly and rolled her eyes as he stood at the
threshold of the kitchen.

"I can't talk right now," she said. "I'll call you later."

She ended the call and threw the phone down, along with a dirty look
in his direction as she picked up her tube of wipes to clean. Again.

It struck him again, as it had earlier, that she looked like hell. Blair
had one of those curious faces that often had trouble deciding
whether it was stunning or hideous. At any given moment, she was
the exotic looker whose unusual features had deepened into "God,
she looks great" forty-eight-year-old beauty; the silky swells of long
black hair spilling across her shoulders. The burnished cola brown
skin. The pink pin cushion lips. The large, molten brown eyes
simmering beneath spider-leg lashes. The check-mark chin. The sky-
high, knife-edge cheekbones.

It was the angles that usually did Blair in. She could cock her head just so, squint her eyes at the wrong moment, or scrunch up her mouth and the beauty would vanish, replaced with dry, cracked lips in need of ChapStick, tight wrinkles puckering around her mouth like a drawstring. The deep luminous eyes dwarfed by the dark half-moons of flesh sagging underneath. The glossy ripples of hair morphed into a ragged nest of straw held together by a careless pony-tail holder.

Blair the Beauty had been missing in action since yesterday. She stood at the stove, scrubbing maniacally, her back drawn tight as a corset, even through her pink sports bra tank.

"I'm leaving," he said.

"Oh, you're talking to me this morning, Malcolm Gilbert?" she asked, whirling around, a clump of wipes still in her hand.

"Seeing as how you slept in the guest room after we got home last night, I couldn't exactly talk to you, could I?"

"Why the hell would I want to sleep next to you?"

"Here we go—"

"You didn't bother to say two words to me during breakfast."

"Who could say anything with you mumbling to yourself the whole time?" Malcolm laughed, equal parts frustrated and incredulous, as always, at the ridiculous zigzag of her logic.

"Oh, you think you're funny, huh? You got jokes, 'Mr. Big Man,' hiding behind a telephone?"

"I'll say the same thing to your face that I said to you on the phone yesterday."

"Nothing but a fucking dictator," she said as she gave the stove a final swipe before grabbing a mop bucket and filling it with bleach and hot water.

"You don't like it, you don't have to stay."

"Shut up," she said over her shoulder.

Even after twenty-two years of marriage, the hurricanes came fast and stayed as late as ever. There were times he wished volatility weren't her vocation, that outrage didn't permanently simmer on her lips. Then again, if she were sugary sweet and docile, lapping up after him like a desperate groupie, she wouldn't be Blair—ridiculous, funny Blair. The woman so completely unimpressed by his slick attempts at seduction when they'd met, that she'd laughed and told him not to bother, a first for his ears. The woman who didn't want to be wined and dined, but who drooled when he put pepper and extra butter on her popcorn when they went to the movies. The woman who sang him to sleep and giggled at his jokes, corny and otherwise, until tears streamed down her face. The woman who was the first person to tell him it was okay if he didn't like his father.

Sometimes, the hurricanes were a fair price to pay.

This time, though ... this time was different. He was on the right side of this one.

He watched Blair, on her hands and knees now, swiping the floor with a big yellow sponge.

"I'm heading out," he repeated. "I'll pick you up at six."

"I'm driving myself."

He closed his eyes and shook his head. Making everything more of a hassle than it needed to be. As usual. "Fine."

"That's it?"

"You want me to say something else?"

"Oh, you've said plenty."

"Jesus Christ." He sighed as he pinched the bridge of his nose between his fingers. "All right, you know what ... I'll see you tonight."

She resumed pushing the sponge against the floor, like a demon. "And then you're going to spend all day badmouthing me, making yourself look good—"

"Okay, Blair, you want me to treat you like a child, keep it up."

"You know what, Malcolm Gilbert? Just go." She threw the sponge to the floor. "Go and play your precious, stupid golf."

"You're acting like a lunatic. You know that, right?"

"Fuck you."

"Yeah, okay, fuck me," Malcolm said, turning toward the front door.

"That's right, fuck you!" she yelled to his back.

He rolled his eyes, waving his hand behind him in an "I don't care" motion before stopping and pivoting for the stairs, cursing himself for forgetting he planned to shower at the club. He darted up to the bedroom for his toiletry kit and tux, checking his pockets and the balcony door once more before heading back downstairs and straight for the front door. Just avoid Blair altogether.

He swung the door open, then jumped back, startled.

Shit.

MALCOLM GILBERT, THE GREATEST OF ALL TIME

Bob Boswell, the Voice of the Bruins, 1962–2000:
Malcolm Gilbert's the best to ever play the game, period. Don't let anybody tell you different.

Autry Stevens, Sportscaster, ABS Network, 1965–2007:
Well, I don't think the boys in that family were allowed to be anything but football legends, were they? I mean, when Admiral Gilbert's your daddy, you don't got too many other options, do you?

Elena York: Malcolm Gilbert grew up in a storied football family, the son of Eldred "The Admiral" Gilbert, a college football star at UCLA and the first black quarterback to come in as a starter in the old Pacific Coast Conference. He later played ten seasons with various teams in the NFL before going to work for the Rams as a defensive coordinator, creating the legendary Brigade Defense. Malcolm's mother, Delores, worked in the banking industry and together she and Eldred had five sons, all of whom went on to some form of success in football. However, Malcolm is the one who became an icon.

Mitch Gilbert, Malcolm Gilbert's Brother: Daddy had us out running drills and doing suicides as soon as we were out of diapers. I think he would have started us earlier if Ma had let him (Laughs). Yeah. It was definitely hammered into us pretty early that we were Gilberts, which meant we were football players.

Autry Stevens: Now, the Admiral is a legend in his own right and Mitch is one of the greatest tight ends in the league. Terry's about the best damn offensive coordinator you've ever seen, and if there's a coach that can turn things around at Ole Miss, it's Nate. Those years Ricky had in Seattle, he's going into the Hall. But Malcolm? Boy, I don't know if we're gonna see anything like him again.

Halsey Perkins, Head Coach, UCLA Bruins 1970–1976: Malcolm was just so quick, so powerful—he could have thrown the ball to himself. Just a monster athlete. He could play—and win—any sport you asked him to. You want him to set a ping-pong record? Hand him the paddle.

Elena York: Continuing the Gilbert legacy, Malcolm, like his father and brothers, attended UCLA, quickly becoming the starting quarterback for the Bruins. He skipped his senior year to enter the draft, going as a first round pick to the Chicago Bears in 1977, playing twenty seasons with them, his entire professional career. He was renowned for his powerful arm, versatile athleticism, and uncanny ability to read plays. Smashing and setting quarterback records all became a part of the Malcolm Gilbert lore.

Bob Boswell: You've never seen anyone who just fundamentally understood the game, even at an early age, like Malcolm Gilbert. He was the kind of guy you held prayer vigils for, hoping to God or whoever, that he stayed healthy.

Autry Stevens: All-State. Heisman. Led UCLA to two National Championships. Two-time MVP. Nine-time Pro Bowler. Six Super Bowl rings. So, yeah, he stayed healthy.

Halsey Perkins: Besides being so naturally talented, he was just so *prepared*, you know? Just so God-danged prepared. Night before the Super Bowl, what's he doing? Film, film, film, playbook, playbook, playbook. What was Joe Namath doing the night before a Super Bowl? A blonde.

Autry Stevens: I hated to see him retire, but I understood it. He was forty, way past the age you normally get put out to pasture. But you know, his knees were starting to give him problems, shoulder was acting up a little. When you've shattered as many records as Malcolm did, defied so many odds, and proved everything he proved, you don't need to play to the bitter end.

Alex Martinez, Left Tackle, Chicago Bears, 1979–1984: There's just not enough clichés, adjectives, or whatever to describe what a phenomenal football player Malcolm Gilbert was, so I'm not even going to try. He was just the best. End of story.

10:45 A.M.

Blair dragged the sponge as hard as she could against the shiny black limestone of her kitchen floor, assaulting nonexistent dirt and grime with her usual fervor. The bottom of her necklace swayed in front of her, the delicate chain brushing against her cheeks. She swung the pendant behind her so she could concentrate on the task at hand. She'd done this last night before she went to bed, so the floor hadn't had time to collect dust or footprints. Despite the kitchen's square footage, she'd be finished in no time. The power of having a system.

She loved her floors. It was her reminder she'd made it. These floors would always be clean. These floors would never resemble the wretched cracked and moldy linoleum floors of her childhood. No matter how many times a day she used to drop to her knees on those peeling plastic floors and attack them with a frayed scrub brush, they would never sparkle like they did in the commercials. The dirt would be back before the sun set. Those floors would never, ever be clean.

But her floors now? Even if they were filthy—not that she ever let that happen—even if they *were* grimy, they still *looked* clean. That was the thing about *nice stuff*. *Nice stuff* could be decaying, falling apart at the seams, grubby, held together with nothing more than tape and a prayer and would still look better on its worst day than cheap shit did on its best day.

As she emptied the bucket out the back door, she had the fleeting thought that her rugs were due for Scotchgarding next week, her customary every-three-month endeavor instead of the recommended six. She kept her ear cocked for Malcolm's departure, wishing he'd leave already. For him to try to pull that dictator shit on her yesterday about the money ... it made her hot all over again. Him and his ridiculous Monday morning deadline. So much for what's yours is mine and mine is yours.

Fuck him. No way, no how, was she doing what he wanted about that. *She* was the wife. *She* was standing on the right side of this one.

Blair looked at the clock on the stove as she picked up her phone and double checked her Scotchgard reminder for Monday before glancing up at the ceiling, Malcolm's footsteps still shuffling above her. She rolled her eyes. He was always so eager to play golf with his cronies, yet always puttered around the house, taking his time leaving. There was the checking for his phone and keys a hundred times, then double checking doors and locks and windows.

And when he wasn't doing that, there was always a story, some anecdote, some *thing* that popped into his head like a thought bubble in a cartoon, that he just had to tell her all about right then, at that exact moment. Stories she'd heard a million times. Tedious details that spilled forth in a torrent of words and sentences, as though his brain were a keyboard, his mouth the screen. One of the many and varied quirks of Malcolm Gilbert. Most of the time, she found it charming, these rabbit trails he meandered down. Other times, she found it annoying.

And today, it was annoying. Annoying as fuck as Bibi would have said. In spite of herself, she laughed a little at the memory of her mother's voice. That whiskey-soaked, nicotine-scarred voice, strad-dling the blurry line between come-hither seductiveness and unintel-ligible slurring. The voice that, when she was so inclined, slipped into clipped precision. Flawless enunciation. The voice that mimicked the theatrics of Bibi's idol Elizabeth Taylor in *Who's Afraid of Virginia Woolf* doing her best Bette Davis in *Beyond the Forest*. What a *dump*! Annoying as *fuck*! A cigarillo in one slender, veiny hand, a smudged, crusty tumbler of pungent beige liquid in the other. Holding court from the dilapidated orange Barcalounger rooted to the corner of the cramped cube that did triple duty as a living room, dining room, and bedroom. Annoying as fuck. What a dump.

And there it was. Her mother could be funny. Her mother could be charming. It startled Blair to realize she could look at her mother through clear and focused lenses and ascribe a descriptor like "charm-ing," or "funny" and not "albatross," or "embarrassment." "Horrible."

But for whatever reason, today, right now, Blair could have a fleeting thought of Bibi Johnson and smile oh-so-briefly.

Had time sealed the wounds shut? Perhaps, like so many survivors of bad childhoods, Blair had learned to live with the scars. Or maybe, she'd forgiven her mother all her trespasses without even realizing it. After all, her mother, like all bad mothers, had probably done the best she could with what she knew.

Blair ran her hands under the scalding hot water of her shiny chrome faucet, pumping the foamy meringue of lemon verbena soap into her palm and scrubbing her skin raw. As she dried her hands on a dish towel and retrieved her wedding ring from the small ceramic dish next to the faucet, she heard Malcolm open the front door. A murmur of voices followed. She rolled her eyes. Now he'd never leave.

Malcolm's voice raced into the kitchen ahead of him. "Blair? Blair, it's—"

"Felice. Well. This is a surprise. What brings you by?" Blair asked her neighbor who lived across the street a few houses down, who trailed behind Malcolm. Blair didn't hate many people. Felice, however, occupied slots one through five on her very short list of five.

"Oh, hellooo, hellooo. Good morning. Oh, I am so sorry to barge in on you like this. I nearly scared poor Malcolm to death when he opened the door and saw me standing there. We almost collided with each other—"

"Oh, what a disaster—"

"—but I was wondering if I could trouble you to borrow your mixer. The KitchenAid?"

Gossipy, petty, rude Felice with her ash white, Mary Tyler Moore flip, slash of fluorescent orange lipstick throwing a useless lifeline to her sinking, puckered lips, rhinestone-studded librarian glasses perched on her hook nose, was always doing this. Dropping by at all hours. Quick to request a favor, always slow to return it. Hold her mail. Water her plants. Walk her dogs. Collect her packages. Give her the name of their lawn service. Who serviced their cars. Could she borrow fill-in-the-blank. Ask her to do the same, she acted like she was being subjected to water torture. Blair would loan her the gleaming, spot-free mixer and it would come back a greasy, crusty mess.

Because Felice was too self-absorbed, too thoughtless, to return it in the condition it was given to her. Felice, who'd ordained herself the moral authority on everyone she crossed paths with, deeming most women fat, ugly slobs—that is when they weren't stupid, vapid, and trivial—and men as pathetic boors. Except for her own lecherous oaf of a husband, who Felice thought, for reasons Blair couldn't quite suss out, hung the moon.

She suspected half the time Felice dropped in unannounced on them so she could catch them swinging naked from the chandeliers, ushering out the last of their late-night harem, or wiping powder from their noses. It was almost as if she wanted to be the whistle blower, the one who exposed the "dirty" dealings of the staid, quiet Gilberts. To be the one *who knew all along* they weren't as perfect as they seemed.

"Of course," Blair said as she dragged the mixer across the counter next to the sink, plopping it down on the island, making a mental note to purchase a new one next week. "You keep it as long as you need," she said as she took a paper shopping bag from the pantry and placed the mixer inside.

"Oh, I do appreciate it. Mine just went on the fritz and if I don't get started on the four dozen cookies for my grandson's bake sale next week—I mean, his mother should really be doing this, but she is absolutely *worthless* in the kitchen. How my son ever wound up with her, I couldn't even begin to tell you. Anyway, as usual, I have to put on my cape and save the day, and if I don't start today, I will just shoot myself."

"Well, now, we can't let that happen, can we?" Malcolm said, the wink barely disguised in his voice.

Blair twitched as she tried to suppress the fit of laughter rumbling in her stomach, while Felice erupted into her high-pitched cackle, exactly what an awful old woman would sound like, a horrific clank that wobbled between screeching peacock and nails on a chalkboard.

Felice adjusted her glasses. "Oh, no, we can't let that happen. Oh, dear me, no. Though, I'll tell you that half the women in this neighborhood would descend, I mean just *swoop* down on Horace, my goodness. These vultures would just *stack* casseroles on my front porch." She sniffed. "Do you know that just the other day that *harpy* Jan Custer—or should I say whale, because the woman is as big as one. Bigger. She's not like you or me, Blair."

"How's that, Felice?"

"Oh, you're so funny." Felice smacked Blair's arm. "You know. You and I both have these tiny little waists."

Blair snorted to herself. Felice easily had a good thirty pounds, if not more, on her, not to mention missing about five of Blair's inches.

"I mean Horace and I were at Highland Park Library the other day—you know we're part of their canasta group—and Jan, well, she just *threw* herself at poor Horace. I mean, she would be first in line with some monstrosity of cheese and noodles and God knows what else, that Horace wouldn't even be able to eat. You know we're watching his sugar—"

"Felice." Malcolm placed a hand on the woman's shoulder and looked deep into her eyes. "I was on my way out to the club to play golf, so I can walk you out. I'll even drop you at home."

"Oh, noooo, noooo. I don't want to keep you. Blair and I will have a quick cup of coffee." Felice snapped her fingers. "Here's a thought. Why don't you come over and help me with the cookies? Then we can catch up. It's been so long since we've caught up. In fact, I can't really remember the last time. You would think as neighbors we'd—"

"Sorry, Felice. Can't. Hair appointment, errands after," Blair said, fingering the pendant of her necklace. "I'm running so late and I still have to take a quick shower before I motor on out of here."

"Oh. Of course. Errands. A hair appointment. Now, tell me again where—"

"Felice, it was great to see you as always," Malcolm said, handing her the bag with the mixer as he gently pressed his palm against the small of the woman's back and steered her in the direction of the front door. Blair followed slowly behind them, her arms folded across her chest, her gaze pointed to the floor to hide her smile.

"Well, it's great to see you, too—"

"Make sure to save us some cookies," Malcolm said. "Now, what kind are you making?"

"Oh, nothing special, just chocolate chip."

"Chocolate chip. Did you hear that, Blair? She's making chocolate chip cookies."

"Yes, I heard," Blair said.

"Chocolate chip cookies are my favorite. Did you know that, Felice?"

"Well, no, I didn't."

"Oh, Malcolm Gilbert loves chocolate chip cookies," Blair said. "Can't live without them."

Malcolm swung the front door open. "Truly. I can't wait to try them. And you make sure I get a nice, big cold glass of milk to go with them."

"You know, the four of us should get together sometime for dinner. You and Blair, me and Horace. Like I was saying, you'd think for neighbors, we would socialize much, much more. I mean, Blair, I see you and Lani out together all the time. And you two girls *never* call me—"

"Getting together for dinner is a great idea, Felice. We'll call you. We will definitely call you. Set something up," Malcolm said, edging the door closed. "Give our best to Horace."

Malcolm shut the door on the woman before she could say another word. He glanced at Blair.

"You're horrible," she said. "Chocolate chip cookies. Give me a fucking break."

"She doesn't have to know I don't like cookies," he said, a knowing grin tugging at the corner of his lips. "That I *hate* cookies."

She didn't want to, but she melted, got lost in that smile. That every-thing. The velvety russet of his skin, stretched taut over sinewy, head-to-toe muscles. The polished dome of his head, the end result of taking a razor to his head at twenty-two to hide the premature bald-ing, a gift from the Gilbert men. (She had to keep from laughing out loud the first time she met her future father-in-law and brothers-in-law. One bald head after another. It had to be a joke. Five bald heads. See how they shine.) The gold-green eyes, the first black man—black person—she'd ever seen with eyes that color. The cluster of three flat black moles on his cheek, drowning in his dimples. The surprise of finding out he was twelve years older than she was (He could be that old and look that good?) Even the jagged scar slashing his chin, cour-tesy of a tumble from the handlebars of one of his brothers' bikes when he was ten, faded to near invisibility, was beautiful to her.

She found herself smiling back in spite of herself. He could always make her smile. Could always make her laugh until tears spilled out of her eyes. Until her sides screamed for mercy. Until she couldn't remember if she'd been sad or mad or what when he waged his campaign of hilarity. The first time he'd pulled that belly-aching laughter from her, she fell in love.

Right now, though, she didn't want to laugh, even though really, she did. Sometimes, for motivation, when he was really irritating her, she conjured up slights and hurts, real and perceived, from years past. Let yesterday's wounds fuel today's anger. Like those awful early years. The fairy-tale marriage that went sour in almost the blink of an eye. That left her wondering what the hell she'd gotten herself into.

Today, though she didn't need to imagine any hurts, his words from yesterday looping in her memory. She promptly let her mouth recede into a hard, concrete line

"I think I feel a migraine coming on," she snapped, pivoting toward the kitchen, Malcolm following her.

"If Horace wasn't such a prick, I'd almost feel sorry for him."

Blair picked up her tube of wipes and extracted one, swiping it across the kitchen counters a final time.

"They deserve each other."

"True that," Malcolm mumbled as he palmed the outside of his pants pockets. She knew he was feeling for the familiar bulge of his keys and phone. Again.

"Aren't you going to be late?" she asked. "I mean, shouldn't you get going?"

"Yeah, I just—" He pulled his phone from his pocket, tapping the screen.

The doorbell rang.

Blair's hand dropped to the counter, smacking the granite. "Oh God —I can't. I can't deal with her."

"Jesus, Blair, when are you getting the video doorbell fixed? It's been a week already."

"Don't start."

"And it looks like a few of the cameras are glitching—"

"They're coming on Tuesday, all right? Jesus. I'll have them look at the cameras too, okay?" She rolled her eyes. "My God. It's not the end of the fucking world."

"One thing I ask you to do, one thing I ask you to take care of right away," Malcolm grumbled more to himself than Blair. "And if I try to do it myself, I never hear the end of it, because you're always right, everything has to be what you—"

"Are you through, Malcolm Gilbert?"

He sighed. "You know what? I just won't answer the door. You go upstairs, do your thing, and I'm going out through the garage."

"You parked out front last night. You put your golf clubs in the trunk last night. And you were going out the front door when Felice showed up. Remember?"

"Ah … that's right." Malcolm smacked his forehead with his fist as the doorbell chimed again. "Shoot."

"Knowing Felice, she wants a cup of sugar and all my eggs." She headed toward the staircase. "You deal with her. I have to take a shower."

"What if she really wants—?"

The doorbell pealed a third time.

"Just answer the door, Malcolm."

FEAR IN HIGHLAND PARK

Lieutenant Dimitri Cora, Highland Park Police Department: With cases like this, you have to look at two things. One, what was the marriage like, what was the family situation like. Was there any tension between them? A financial motive of any kind? Infidelity? Two, you have to look at the circles ... who's in the family circle—their friends, their family. Who's close to them? On the flip side, you have to ask, who's outside the circle that maybe wants to *be* in the circle? Or maybe it's someone who used to be in the circle and they want, you know, revenge of some type because they're on the outs. The Gilbert's knew a lot of people. A lot of people knew them. And that's a lot of potential suspects.

Skye Stafford: From the beginning, there was a lot about this case that didn't make sense, a lot that didn't add up.

Elena York: Initially, the media speculated this was a burglary gone wrong, except that didn't really jibe with what was found at the crime scene. There was no sign of forced entry. There was a fair amount of jewelry stolen from Blair Gilbert. All the cash they had on them was taken, but none of the electronics: TVs, iPads, laptops.

There was a garage full of cars, the keys all hanging on hooks in the kitchen. This couldn't possibly be a burglary gone wrong. The evidence just didn't point to it. Quite honestly, if anything, it was more like an afterthought burglary.

Lieutenant Sharon Donahue, Highland Park Police Department: Contrary to popular belief, burglaries typically *don't* happen at night or on the weekends—they usually happen between ten a.m. and three p.m. on a weekday, when most people are at work. So, because of that, something happening on a Saturday or Sunday morning is highly unusual—unless they've been casing your house and know you're out of town.

Felice Patterson, the Gilberts' Neighbor: Well, I had just popped over that morning to borrow Blair's mixer to make cookies for my grandson's bake sale—she was always letting me borrow things, because of our close friendship. Well, anyway, I missed the whole thing by minutes. Minutes. I mean if I had been over there, just two minutes—even a minute later ... I mean, it really goes to show you that everything happens for a reason. I was spared for a reason.

Cassie Wexler: God, I hated looking over there. I had to start looking the other way every time I drove by the house. Especially knowing that we weren't a hundred feet away when everything was happening ... it ... it gave me nightmares.

Lani Jacobs: I'd be lying if I said deadbolts weren't turning all across Highland Park afterward. People were beefing up their alarm systems, hiring private security, contracting for panic rooms. I heard gun ranges got a major uptick in business. We were all terrified. If it could happen to the Gilberts, it could happen to us. We were all thinking, "Maybe we'll be next."

Lieutenant Dimitri Cora: We ruled out burglary gone wrong right away. Now we have to look at, was it random? Well, there hadn't been any other crimes of this nature committed either in the neighborhood or in Highland Park, in general, quite frankly. So, we had to either view this as the beginning of a possible string of similar attacks, or an isolated incident.

Lieutenant Sharon Donahue: I've been an investigator for over twenty-five years. Seen a lot of crime scenes. Thousands, probably. This was no burglary gone wrong. This was no ordinary home invasion.

11:00 A.M.

Malcolm squinted at the freakishly tall young man standing in his doorway.

Basketball player.

"Can I help you?"

The guy hesitated, staring at him, his jaw slack. He stepped back a bit to look up at the doorframe before smiling at Malcolm. A big, bright smile full of yellow pebbles masquerading as teeth, protruding from dark pink, almost black, gums. The pads of his fingers all touched each other, forming a triangle that rested in front of his stomach, elbows jutting away from his waist. His faded black suit was cheap and shiny, imprinted with the metal grate pattern of an ironing board. Loose threads dangled from the hems and the cuffs flopped over his wrists. The white button-down underneath was rumpled and dingy. Brown loafers scuffed and peeling. Fuzzy, matted dreads swept the bottom of his earlobes and fluffs of lint burrowed inside the frayed ends.

Malcolm narrowed his eyes at this bizarre-looking kid, the hairs dancing frenetically across the back of his neck.

Something was wrong.

"Yessir, I uh, I was wondering if I could come in and use your phone. You see, my car, my van out there, broke down outside your house and my phone died, and I need to call my friend to ask him for directions to get to his crib—I mean his place."

Malcolm slowly ran his tongue across his bottom lip, the hairs jitterbugging now. "Where does your friend live?"

"I think it's uh, uh … Dobson! That's right, that's right. He lives on Dobson."

Malcolm gripped the doorknob. "No Dobson around here. No Dobson anywhere in Highland Park."

"You sure? Cause my friend told me—"

"No, no, no Dobson."

"Okay, ah … shoot." The guy put one hand in his pocket and clamped his hand across his mouth. "So, like I was saying, my phone just died and if I could use your phone to call him—"

"No, sorry," Malcolm said, closing the door.

The guy's palm exploded against the door's wood panel and he rushed toward Malcolm, who threw his weight against the door to block the tackle. He grunted as he pressed against it. The guy had both hands planted against the wood and pushed just as hard.

The door started to give way. Malcolm's feet slipped beneath him on the slick marble floor, his heart beating a little faster than he wanted to admit. He just about had it closed when the barrel of a gun peered through the crack of the door and directly into his face.

"Stand back," a girl's voice said. "Stand back and let us in. Now."

His heart stopped as he contemplated whether to comply with the request. A gun pointing in his face. Hell of a choice. Malcolm eased back, his hands up. The door flew open, smacking the wall, as the owner of the pistol rushed into the house right behind the kid who'd rung the bell. In all his sixty years, he'd never seen the cold black hole of a gun staring back at him. His mouth burst with cotton. He gulped and took a shallow breath.

"Hey, look, listen—"

The girl, no more than sixteen or seventeen, snapped a wad of fluorescent blue gum between healthy pink gums and white teeth, her lips outlined with black pencil and filled in with shiny purple lipstick. She inched the gun closer to Malcolm's face, as he flicked his eyes up and down to size her up like he did all his opponents, a lingering habit from his playing days, the importance of imprinting memories even more important these days. Her ample breasts spilled out of the snug black tank top she wore beneath the brown pleather jacket, the zipper pull dangling above her belly button, her acid-wash jeans shrink wrapped around her sizable thighs.

He glanced at the third member of "us," a wiry young man with a massive case of BO. The boy followed behind her, his eyes darting around the foyer like rowdy pinballs. There was no pretense with a cheap, hand-me-down suit or stained button down dress shirt with this one. He wore the standard teenage uniform of saggy jeans—a black leather belt snaking ironically through the loops—and a faded black Hanes t-shirt, massive black Nikes weighting his feet to the floor. The shoes looked new to Malcolm. Were they stolen? It was doubtful any of these kids had much disposable income. No weekly allowance from mommy and daddy. Was that what this was? A bid for shoe money, TV money, iPhone money?

The smelly, t-shirt-clad kid continued to dart his eyes around the room as he slammed the door shut. Glossy drops of sweat blanketed his forehead. He, too, had a gun, though the weapon seemed clumsy in his floppy, puppy dog paws as he raised it and pointed it at Malcolm, the butt of the gun resting in a shaky palm.

Cheap Suit, as Malcolm had come to think of him in the short time they'd been acquainted, clutched his own piece as he paced in a semicircle, one wild, wary eye trained on him the entire time. The other two kept flicking glances his way, waiting for Cheap Suit to say something. Anything.

The ringleader.

He thought about his phone. Specifically, the panic button on his phone connected to the alarm system. He needed to get to that.

In the meantime, work with what you got.

Malcolm tried to catch Cheap Suit's eye. Bypass the minions, go straight to the head of the table to negotiate.

"Look, I don't want any trouble. I got about two thousand in cash on me and another—"

"Malcolm Gilbert, what—?" Blair sputtered behind him on the stairs.

His heart dropped. Blair the Bomb. The last thing he needed.

If I ask her to keep her fucking mouth shut, to, for once, be quiet, will she do it?

"It's all right, BJ."

She bounded downstairs and marched toward the three, a mix of irritation, confusion, and anger swimming across her face. "What—? Who the fuck are you?" she demanded as Malcolm caught her around the waist. As he sometimes forgot, she'd grown up with this. Boogie Down Bronx. Girl in the Hood. Blair from the Block. Staring down three guns was no big thing to her.

"Shut up, Blair," he said.

No, of course she won't shut her damn mouth. That's always too much to ask.

"Shut up? No, I want to know who the fuck these people are. Did you let them in?"

"Blair, huh?" Cheap Suit's eyes glittered as he regarded her. "You should listen to your husband and shut the fuck up ... *Blair*."

She blanched in Cheap Suit's direction. "Excuse me?"

He didn't have to look to know the lake was storming in her eyes. She was ratcheting up to blow any minute. He gripped her tighter, hoping she'd get the message to shut it.

"Listen, like I said, I got about two thousand in cash on me, with another ten in the house. Take it and whatever else you want," Malcolm said.

"Give him—what? What are you doing? Malcolm—" Blair was back to writhing, twisting around him in an attempt to free herself, to confront these intruders.

"I said, shut the fuck up!" Cheap Suit yelled, the black coals of his eyes flashing erratically as he waved his gun around. The trio looked scared. Unsure. The girl rocked from side to side, her gaze flicking between Malcolm and the leader, while her panicky companion licked his lips and hopped from one foot to the other, the sweat from his forehead now cascading down his cheekbones, damp patches of it gluing his shirt to his bony frame.

"Take whatever you want." Malcolm pursed his lips. "Take whatever you want and we'll call it even."

Cheap Suit pointed his weapon at Malcolm again, aiming directly for his head. Blair gasped.

"Oh, God," she whispered, finally, it seemed, having gotten the hint this wasn't another Tuesday on the block, that this was serious.

Cheap Suit's accomplices were now rooted to their spots, frozen in action figure stances, guns clamped in what Malcolm suspected were sweaty palms. The five of them stared at each other, three against two, each side unsure of who would make the next move or what that move should even be.

The room crackled with the sound of Blair's agitated panting. Malcolm's shallow breaths. The snap of the girl's gum. The nervous sniffing from Sweaty Smelly Guy. The clap of Cheap Suit's footsteps against the gleaming marble floor as he resumed pacing.

"What we gonna do?" the girl asked, shattering the impasse, her voice quivering.

"Yeah, what we gonna do?" Sweaty Smelly Guy echoed. "You said there wasn't—"

"Shut up, shut up, shut up!" Cheap Suit shouted again. "Stop all that noise so I can think about what I'm gonna do 'cause this shit is all fucked up now."

Malcolm narrowed his eyes as he watched the young man pace. What did that mean?

"T—" his smelly accomplice tried again.

"I said shut the hell up!" Cheap Suit thundered, rushing toward the boy, who cowered away from him and got shoved for his trouble anyway, before resuming his march around the room.

T. An abbreviation for a nickname or a full name? T for Ted? Tyrone? Tank? T for Trouble. Find out what it stood for. Build a rapport. Get chummy.

An odd sound escaped T's dark, crusty lips, an anguished cross between a grunt and a cry. The heels of his hands flew to his temples, the gun pointing toward the ceiling, as he slammed his eyes shut and took several deep breaths.

Malcolm licked his lips, decided to go for broke.

"Yo, T. What's the T stand for?"

The boy came to a dead stop. Eyelids popped open to reveal blood-shot eyes no more settled, no calmer, than they had been just moments before. Maybe he was high on something. Their menace though, as they focused on Malcolm, was clear.

"The T stands for T."

"Okay ... T. You go by T, okay. Okay. T—I got cash, a car—lots of cars —jewelry, electronics. Whatever you want, it's yours. Like I said before, we don't want any trouble."

T rushed toward Malcolm just centimeters from his face, his rank breath stale, wet, and heavy. Malcolm tightened his grip on Blair and put on his game face.

Don't move.

Show no fear.

Don't blink.

Don't even breathe.

Dominate your opponent.

Win at all costs.

"You about to be in a whole lot of trouble, you keep running your damn mouth," T said.

"Okay, then, you talk. You talk. I'll listen. I'm here, man." Malcolm shrugged. "What can I do for you? What do you need?"

The guy blinked. His lip trembled. His face drooped. Malcolm could see he was caught off guard by the magnanimous gesture. He felt himself relax. Despite the gun pointing in his face, Malcolm Gilbert was the one in control. Not this guy. Malcolm.

"What you think you can do for me?" he asked, drawing up.

"What do you need?" Malcolm repeated, his voice low yet confident.

The guy was silent and their stare-down continued, neither giving the inch required. Malcolm could smell the guy's fear. He'd inhaled that scent all his life. The vapors flooded Malcolm's nose, wove their way into his own pores.

He knew how to conquer that fear.

T opened his mouth.

"Oh my God, what—!"

All five heads snapped toward the sound of Farrah Gilbert's voice from the top of the stairs.

UNEXPECTED GUEST

Lieutenant Dimitri Cora: The daughter, Farrah, wasn't supposed to be home that weekend, which, of course, raised suspicion right away.

Elena York: Farrah Gilbert was a freshman at Indiana University in Bloomington, double majoring in education and English, with a minor in creative writing. She was a literacy tutor, wrote for the school paper, contributed short stories to a student anthology, Dean's list.

Lieutenant Sharon Donahue: We had to examine Farrah's relationship with her parents. Did she have a plan, was she in cahoots with someone, did the plan go awry somewhere along the way?

Elena York: She came home late Friday night, surprising Blair and Malcolm, as they hadn't expected to see her until she came home a month later for her summer break. A high school friend was having a surprise birthday party at a club in the West Loop on Saturday night and at the urging of her friends, she decided at the last minute to join the festivities.

Skye Stafford: According to Farrah's friends, the only real blemish on her record was an ex-boyfriend, Theo Tillis, who she'd met shortly after coming to Bloomington and had dated on and off over the course of the school year. He was a native of Bloomington, a few years older, high school dropout, a couple of kids by a few different women. He and Farrah were light-years apart in terms of education, socioeconomic status, and just about everything else, so their relationship was a bit of a mystery to her friends.

Chloe Marston, Farrah's Best Friend: He was a loser.

Laila Amari, Farrah's Roommate: You know, I could never really figure out what the attraction was there. He couldn't hold down a job, wasn't terribly cerebral. A total pothead. He wasn't even all that good-looking.

Bridget Johnson: Farrah never introduced us to him. I mean, we heard about him, but only snippets. And the snippets were … not good. I guess he'd been in jail a few times for battery and assault. He definitely didn't sound like a good guy.

Chloe Marston: A volatile relationship? Oh, yeah. Totally. They'd break up, get back together, break up, get back together. She said he never got physically abusive, and I never saw him hit her or anything, so I can't speak to that, but he was definitely verbally abusive. I absolutely saw that.

Laila Amari: Farrah was confident in just about every aspect of her life. Incredibly intelligent and kind, a loyal friend. But when it came to relationships, she had zero self-esteem. Totally insecure about guys and her looks. She'd dated a little in high school, but nothing serious, nothing long-term. A black girl from the lily white suburbs of Highland Park with no real experience with guys. Fresh meat for a thug like Theo.

Chloe Marston: If a guy can be a gold digger, well, he was it. Theo was obsessed with Farrah's money, her background, her lifestyle, how she grew up. Talked about her dad. All. The. Time. She'd loan him money. Buy him things. Sometimes, and I don't know why, she'd let him drive her car. A brand new Range Rover. He'd brag to people about how she'd let him do whatever he wanted, how he had her under his control. He was trash. Absolute trash.

Laila Amari: Finally, thank God, Farrah broke things off with him. She'd met someone else. A really, really great guy. And this did *not* sit well with Theo. He viewed her as his property. His meal ticket, his gravy train. She belonged to him. No one was going to take Farrah away from him. No one.

Bridget Johnson: He was the first person I thought of and I told the police they should take a look at him.

Skye Stafford: Theo shot to the top of the suspect list right away.

Laila Amari: When I heard what happened, I said, this had to be Theo. This was exactly the kind of thing he would do. Round up some of his boys and show up at her house. No, from the moment I heard about this, I definitely believed Theo was behind the whole thing.

11:10 A.M.

What the fuck?

That was the first thought to slam into Farrah's brain upon seeing three strangers standing in the foyer, pointing guns at her parents.

It was still racing through her mind as she darted down the hall toward her bedroom, her cell phone clamped in her suddenly drenched palm, her heart pounding, blood pulsing in her ears. From downstairs, one of them yelled something about "that bitch." That must be her.

Her bare feet slipped a little on the shiny wood floor just outside her room and she gripped the doorframe to keep from tumbling. Behind her, she heard one of the guys yell out for her to stop as he came running down the hall after her. Not the same one who called her a bitch.

She flew into her room, flinging the door shut behind her. She leaned against it, wishing, as she sometimes had growing up, the door had a lock. Her mother didn't believe in locks.

Farrah's fingers trembled uncontrollably as she tried to unlock her phone to hit the panic button, the screen freezing. *Damn it.* It was doing that a lot lately. It was time for a new phone.

How long would it take for the police to get here? Surely the alarm company would have them on some kind of priority list or something.

Theo flashed across her mind. Was he behind this? He was always bragging about how his boys would fuck people up for him if he asked. Would he try to come after her parents to get to her? He'd never explicitly threatened her or her parents.

Still. It was possible.

The door exploded with a wallop and the phone jumped out of her hands, sailing across the room. She screamed, scrambling to escape the guy—sickeningly skinny and muscular all at once—as he charged toward her, sweat and irritation blurring his face. She ran across the room, searching for where the phone had landed. Her eye fell on the plastic desk chair. Without thinking, she hoisted it up, grunting as she did so, and hurled it toward him. It bounced against his shoulder and he grumbled, briefly stumbling backward and falling.

She flattened herself against the wall, tears clouding her eyes, her breath now coming in gasping, shallow gulps, as she tried to get her bearings. She dropped to the floor, spotting the phone under the desk, and scrambled toward it, breathing a sigh of relief as her hand closed around the hard plastic.

This time, the phone unlocked immediately.

She scrolled through her mountain of apps, cursing herself for not putting the panic button right on the front screen.

With another grunt, he rose up from the floor and leapt toward her.

Right there.

Farrah jammed her finger against the bright red icon.

Screen frozen.

She whimpered and tried again.

Come on, come on, come on.

Still nothing.

She hit the screen with the heel of her hand, tears of frustration pooling in her eyes.

The screen leapt to life.

Farrah let out a cry of relief.

Just as her fingertip made contact with the button, he slapped the phone out of her hand, sending it soaring across the room once more. She screamed again as he wrenched her up from the floor, his fingers pinned around the tiny, delicate bones of her wrist.

"Get the fuck up," he said, a cloud of something rotten wafting from his body. "We going downstairs."

11:15 A.M.

A scream erupted from upstairs and Malcolm's heart leapt out of his chest and stopped in mid-air. Breath stalled in his lungs. Mind blank. Ears ringing. He closed his eyes, unable to wipe away the image of a wide-eyed Farrah, clad only in a black tank top and blue-striped boxer shorts, phone in one hand, bounding innocently down the stairs, likely in search of breakfast. Stumbling into this catastrophe.

The second accomplice emerged at the top of the steps, a trembling, squirming, teary-eyed Farrah in his grip.

"I got her, Tree," the guy said, pride lacing his words. "See? I got her."

Tree. A nickname. Must be because he's so tall.

Tree's head whipped toward them, his mouth open to say something. Instead, when he looked at Farrah, he smiled.

No. He leered. This punk leered at his little girl.

Malcolm pursed his lips, his fists curled, ready to burst. His insides coiled. Anger ignited across his skin. His grasp on Blair went slack as he prepared to strike. She held onto him, pressing her palm against his back to hold him to her, as though she were now the one keeping him calm.

Tree puffed his chest out a little and knitted his lips together as Malcolm watched the boy's gaze roam across his little girl like an appreciative butcher appraising a cut of meat. Farrah grimaced under his lewdness and shut her eyes while he laughed.

"Tree!" Malcolm shouted. "Hey. Hey! We're talking here, you and me. My daughter doesn't have anything to do with this."

"Damn, you fine as hell," he whispered, ogling Farrah. "What's your name?"

"Daddy—"

The girl snapped her gum. "Oh, hell no. I know you not trying to step to Miss Bougie."

"It's okay, baby girl," he said, edging closer.

"Malcolm," Blair whispered as she continued writhing against his grasp, the unmistakable hiss of *do something* underscoring his name.

"Man, Cookie, shut the hell up. You always worried about what I'm doing."

Cookie. Another nickname.

"Daddy?"

He grimaced. It was hard not to hear the fear shaking in his daughter's voice. It was hard to *hear* the fear in Farrah's voice.

"You need to let my daughter go," Malcolm said calmly.

Sweaty Smelly Guy's eyes darted to his boss, seemingly torn. "T?"

Tree continued staring at Farrah, his eyes traveling down, up, and back again, while his girlfriend silently fumed.

"Tree. Tree! We were negotiating, remember?"

At the sound of Malcolm's voice, the boy's head snapped away from Farrah, almost as if he was coming out of a trance. Malcolm's chest tightened and red rage clouded his vision as Tree shuffled around until the two of them were facing each other.

"You know, man, I'm real mad you didn't tell me we had company upstairs." He flicked another glance in Farrah's direction. "That's, what do you call it, dealing in bad faith."

"Don't you touch her, or I swear to God, I will—" Blair rasped, flailing against his grasp once again.

"Man, bitch, shut up," Tree said. "You ain't about to do nothing."

"Tree." Malcolm pursed his lips. "I can't let you talk to my wife like that, man."

"I'll talk to her any damn way I want. You feel me?"

Malcolm took a silent inhale as he continued to hold Blair's quivering body closer to him.

"No need for name-calling. No need for anybody getting upset. I'm here, man. I'm still here. Ready to negotiate with you. I'll say it again. We don't want any trouble. What do you want? What can I do?"

Tree sniffed, nodding as he looked around the room, his eyes growing wider with each new object, each shiny new thing. Finally, his gaze pivoted back to Malcolm.

"Tell the truth. You got a safe full of cash up in here, don't you? Probably got stacks of gold and shit, just piled up to the ceiling, don't you?" He laughed. "Probably got a room just for stacking up your paper."

"Like I told you before, I got about two thousand in cash on me and another ten in the house. I'll give you that, whatever my wife and daughter have. I've got three Rolexes, my wife has jewelry, I've got cars. I—" Malcolm looked at his hand, his Super Bowl ring flashing in the light. He wrenched it from his finger and waved it around. "You see this? I got five more of them upstairs. You know what you can get for these?"

"That for real?" the smelly one asked, leaning a little closer to Malcolm for inspection.

"It's real, man, and it's yours. All of them. Just take whatever you want and we'll forget this whole thing."

"What kind of cars you got—?" the smelly one piped in.

"Man, shut up, Dio!" Tree shouted before looking at Malcolm again. He sniffed back a noisy lump of mucus. "All right, so since my boy asked, what kind of cars you got?"

And Dio makes three.

"Porsche, Mercedes, Range Rover, a Hummer—a brand new Hummer, only got a few hundred miles on it." Malcolm clicked his tongue against the roof of his mouth. "It's yours."

"What if I said I wanted two cars, huh? One for me, one for my girl?"

"I want the Mercedes." Cookie giggled.

"Done," Malcolm said. "What about you, Tree? Which one do you want?"

"What, I can't get no car?" Dio asked.

"Man, you ain't even know how to drive, what the hell you gonna do with a car?" Tree said, his eyes still locked on Malcolm.

"I could learn," the boy muttered under his breath before falling silent again.

"We got a deal?" Malcolm asked.

Tree was quiet, still staring at Malcolm. He exhaled a little. He was going to go for it. Throw a couple of cars his way, some cash, some hardware and that would be it. It'd be over soon.

Tree cleared his throat. Malcolm shifted a little, his palm damp with the sheets of sweat rolling down Blair's back. She had curled into him, her body quaking savagely, her heart thrumming against him. He held her closer. If he let her go, she'd do something stupid, something that would sign all their death warrants.

"Do we have a deal?" Malcolm repeated, aware of the mild tremor of impatience in his voice. "Huh? Tree?"

"Yeah, yeah, that all sounds good," the boy finally responded as he sniffed back another clump of mucus. "But it's not enough."

Malcolm pursed his lips. "Okay, what do you want? Tell me."

"I know you got more than twelve G's up in here."

"I told you, that's it—"

"I know you got more than that. I know it. I know you keep the paper *stacked*. So come on, *Malcolm*. Where's the rest of it?"

"Tree—"

"You know what? I've had enough of this. Lock they asses up," Tree said, flicking his chin toward his accomplices. "Lock 'em in those rooms upstairs. Separate. Keep them in separate rooms so they can't talk to each other, try to come up with some plan or something. Tie them up and lock 'em in until Malcolm feels like talking."

The two accomplices stood frozen until Tree barked, "Now!" causing them to scatter into position. Blair stood rigid in his arms as the girl yanked on his wife's ponytail. Blair yelped as her head jerked back. Malcolm pulled her to him and out of the corner of his eye, he saw Dio clamp his arm around the waist of a kicking and screaming Farrah in an attempt to drag her upstairs. Malcolm's head pivoted between the two disasters, his next move scrawling itself across the playbook in his head. Let the third one take Farrah upstairs—that would only leave two. Push Blair to the ground—send her sprawling so it would take some time for her to recover—and tackle the girl, turn her gun on her, force Tree's hand.

Hut-hut-hut.

"You let her go or I'm a blow a huge fucking hole in your head," the girl squeaked.

Malcolm grimaced at the gun suddenly snug against his cranium. Blair looked at him, terror shining in her eyes. He gave her the most imperceptible nod and reassuring smile he could manage. She returned her own tiny nod and smile.

He let her go.

Malcolm watched helplessly as Cookie snatched Blair by the arm and hustled her toward the staircase, with Farrah and the second accomplice halfway upstairs. He heard doors slam shut and he slowly turned toward Tree, his hands up. The two stared at each other, the boy still aiming the gun at him.

"All right, Malcolm. It's just you and me now."

THE GILBERTS

Isabelle Ryan, Criminologist: If there was a "template" for how to have a successful post-football career, Malcolm Gilbert is the poster child. He retired from the game and managed to avoid many of the pitfalls that seem to crush so many other professional sports players. He didn't go broke, suffered no career-ending injuries, continued to have very lucrative endorsement deals. His company, MG Enterprises, invested heavily in hotels and restaurants, becoming incredibly profitable. He did very, very well for himself.

Skye Stafford: Blair Gilbert was a stay-at-home mom and by all accounts, a fantastic mother. She and her daughter, Farrah, were exceptionally close. She was very much the "suburban mom," the "soccer mom," shuttling Farrah to dance classes, music and swim lessons, serving as room mom and chaperone for dances and other school activities. She loved every minute of it.

Bridget Johnson: It was so important to Blair that Farrah have a normal childhood, something that was totally opposite of what we had. She wanted her to have slumber parties and skating and pool parties and go to football games and play sports and go to dances and be allowed to be a kid. Be carefree.

Kip Sellers, Friend of Malcolm Gilbert: Did Malcolm have any enemies? I'm sure some of those guys he played against probably hated his guts (Laughs). But you know it's all trash talk, what you do on the field. Nothing serious.

Don Jensen, Friend of Malcolm Gilbert: People loved Malcolm. He was "that guy," Mr. Smooth. Mr. Charm. The guy who would send over a bottle of champagne to a table of strangers at a restaurant, because why not? The guy who would sometimes pick up the tab for an entire restaurant, just because. The guy who'd sign every autograph, pose for every picture, answer whatever question a fan had about some game from 1975, 1992, or whenever. Questions he'd answered a million times, games he'd talked about for decades. And it was always with a smile.

Cap Gleason: Malcolm could be tough on his teammates, sure. But it was borne out of competitiveness, out of wanting to be —*needing* to be—the best. Nobody held any grudges. Nobody resented him. If anything, it made them work that much harder not to just meet, but exceed his expectations.

Alex Martinez: Every season, when we'd get back to training camp, there'd be some electronic gift—a boom box, a brand new color TV. One year he bought everyone a car phone—even the wives (Laughs). That tells you how long ago this was. We won the Super Bowl, and everyone got a gold watch. After we broke the Dolphins' record by winning our second Super Bowl after a second perfect season, he bought the entire O-line a Mercedes—paid the taxes on them, too. He would always say, no man is an island, that we were all on that island together.

Felice Patterson: Well, you know Blair and I were more than just neighbors. We were really good friends. Quite close in fact. But I will tell you, she could be a bit of a cold fish at times.

Kim Fletcher, Friend of the Gilberts: Cold fish? No, no, I wouldn't say that. Bad temper? A hundred percent. She could snap on you in a minute. Act first, think later. It would blow over pretty quickly, but in the meantime, watch out.

Lani Jacobs: Blair? Oh, yeah, she could be a bitch (Laughs).

Kim Fletcher: Blair tangled with a few people—gardeners, servers, handymen, construction workers. I mean, she was always on Howl leaving these long, nasty reviews about service people, restaurants, that kind of thing.

Lani Jacobs: Exacting. That's how I would describe Blair. Eccentric. We would go to brunch and everything had to be on a separate plate. I'm talking cheese on one plate, eggs on another, and so on. And then she'd eat each thing one by one. (Laughs). Waiters definitely hid when they saw her coming. Of course, she tipped really well, so at least she knew she was a pain in the ass, which says something. (Laughs). I was just happy with my little bowl of oatmeal and coffee.

Kim Fletcher: Okay, sure, Blair gave whole new meaning to bat****, but on the other side of that, you wouldn't find a more loyal person. She volunteered at the food depository two times a week, volunteered as a mentor with a community arts organization in the city, and in addition to writing a pretty big check, she was always running 5Ks to raise money for a local children's cancer charity, and she volunteered in the pediatric cancer ward. She'd run errands for you if you were sick, brought donuts to the guys who serviced her car. Truly one of the most giving of people.

Lani Jacobs: It doesn't matter who they were or weren't. They didn't deserve this.

11:45 A.M.

"Get in there." Cookie sneered as she shoved Blair into the master bedroom, the door thundering shut behind her.

Blair grimaced as she stumbled, narrowly missing diving headfirst into the ivory shag rug. She whipped around in time for Cookie to grab her again and push her onto the California King. She trained the gun on Blair, her eyes flitting around the room as she swayed from side to side.

Blair racked the pendant of her necklace across the chain, before dropping the charm into her shirt to hide it as she let her own eyes zip around the room for weapons, an escape route, a way to overpower her captor. There were the two tall, clear vases of white roses, coffee table books stacked in the built-in bookshelves, decorative white ceramic bowls, the glass candle holders with the white pillar candles, the trio of heavy mirrored frames hanging on the pale gray walls. The floor lamps with the heavy metal bases.

Lots of glass. Lots of metal. Lots of ways to inflict damage.

"Hey!" the girl snapped at Blair. "I'm talking to you."

"Don't yell at me—"

The girl narrowed her eyes. "What did you say?"

"I said, don't yell at me. I'm sitting right here."

The girl cocked her gun and rushed up on Blair, the cold, black hole mere centimeters from her temple. "Bitch, you don't—"

"And stop calling me a bitch."

The girl reared back. "Bitch, I will—"

"Stop it. Stop it! Just calm down, all right? Calm down."

"You got a death wish?"

"All I'm saying is to calm down, okay?"

"I'm gonna show you how calm I am—"

"Okay, okay, just..." Blair gulped. "I'm sorry for screaming."

The girl blinked and the gun wavered a bit in her hand before she lowered it, gum still snapping, eyes still narrowed.

"That's better," she said, straightening up, her eyes jumping around the room. "Tree said I got to tie you up. He said—" The girl patted herself down and pulled a roll of duct tape out of her jacket pocket. She cocked her head toward the straight back chair at the dressing table. "Get over there."

Blair hesitated, her gaze flashing in the direction of the door.

"Don't even think about it, bitch. You'll be dead before your body hits the ground."

Blair swallowed hard and eased her way to the chair, the dark barrel of the gun watching her. She sat down, looking up expectantly at the girl, who, instead of bullets, shot daggers into her.

"Put your hands behind your back," the girl commanded, waving the gun around. Blair obeyed and the girl undid a strip of tape, tearing it with her teeth. She grabbed Blair's hands, chuckling.

"What's so funny?" Blair asked, her back tensing, more unease settling over her.

"You live in this big house, your husband say you got a Porsche and Mercedes and whatever in the garage and you ain't got no ice?" the girl asked as she let Blair's hands drop.

"Ice. What do you mean, ice?"

"Your rock, your piece, your ice?" She scoffed and shook her head. "I knew it. Your old man was lying before when he said you had a whole bunch of ice. Just trying to distract us."

The heat of her necklace, hidden beneath her top, burned against her skin.

"Cookie—is that your name? Cookie? I have no idea what the hell you're talking about."

The girl groaned. "Jewelry. Where's your big rock, your big ring? You live in this big-ass house. Ain't you supposed to have diamonds on every finger?"

Blair blanched as she rubbed the pad of her thumb against the thin, barely perceptible band of diamonds encircling her ring finger. She preferred this simple ring, what Malcolm jokingly referred to as her weekday ring. He'd bought it for her when Farrah was two, tired of seeing her wear her wedding ring only on occasion. Flashing the twenty-carat, square-cut stunner he'd slipped on her finger on their wedding day made her self-conscious and just this side of nervous, feeling it made her a target, the irony not lost on her at all in this moment. She reserved wearing the ring for special nights out—date nights, charity events, the endless football obligations that came with being a legendary Hall-of-Famer's wife—any time she'd be on Malcolm's arm. She'd planned to wear it tonight.

"I do have jewelry. Lots of it."

"Yeah, right." The girl folded her arms across her chest, her eyes fluttering over the dressing table and the nearby dresser. "I don't see no jewelry box."

"Honey, when you have the kind of jewelry I have, you don't keep a jewelry box. You keep a safe."

"What? Where?"

"In the closet."

The girl's head whipped around to the walk-in closet, then back to Blair. She grabbed Blair's arm and leaned down until she was inches from her face. "You better not be playing me—"

"Oh, I'm not playing, trust me." Sweat drenched her armpits. Her shower. She'd taken a quick one this morning before her run, like she always did. She'd come upstairs for her post-workout shower then gone back downstairs for her phone from the kitchen counter.

Her phone. The panic button.

She wanted to smack herself. She should have stayed upstairs for that second shower. She would have heard the noise from upstairs. She would have run down the hall to Farrah's room, hit the panic button on her phone, called 911. Anything. They could have hidden in the closet or under the bed until the police came.

If only.

She took a shaky inhale and moved toward the closet. Cookie stepped in front of her, the gun hovering just inches from Blair's chest.

"Give me the combination."

"It's fingerprint activated. It will only open for me."

The girl seemed caught off guard by the steeliness in Blair's voice, blanching a bit.

"All right," she said, seeming to back down. "But don't forget I got a gun and I will blow your brains out, you make one move. Just one."

"Yeah, I got it."

Blair closed her eyes briefly as she walked toward the closet. She glanced at the balcony, the frenzied, reckless thought of bolting for it skipping across her mind. It was just far enough up that even if she were to somehow get over the balcony, once she made contact with the concrete below, she'd likely crush enough bones in her body to make the whole thing pointless. And she couldn't risk it. Not with Farrah in the clutches of that nasty punk, and Malcolm God knew where.

Blair sniffed as her fingers danced nimbly over the digital keypad of the Traum safe installed in her colossal walk-in closet. Blair could hear the girl's heavy breathing behind her, the gum chewing becoming quieter, yet somehow more pronounced, as she no doubt took in the plush surroundings of a closet that was likely bigger than the girl's own bedroom.

Blair pressed her fingers against the console and the safe popped open, revealing rows of shiny wooden drawers. Her hands shook as she removed a few of the drawers and set them on the island in the middle of the closet. All of the girl's bravado and belligerence was gone, as she hung back in the doorway, shyness and awe clouding her harsh features.

"Here." Blair plucked a sapphire and diamond ring, a birthday present, out of its snug perch and held it out toward the girl, who hesitated in the doorway. "It's yours. All of it. Take whatever you want."

With faltering steps, Cookie inched her way toward Blair, her eyes transfixed by the hunk of glitzy stones. She reached out a wobbly hand and tugged it from Blair's fingers, her gum chewing halted. She turned the ring over in her hands repeatedly, her eyes wondrous black orbs.

"Really?" the girl said, her eyes shooting up to Blair. "You'd really let me have this? Just like that."

"I already told you, yes."

The girl continued to stare as though she expected Blair to yank the rug out from beneath her. Finally, she slipped the ring onto her finger and let out a small cry as she admired the stone against her dark skin. She held up her hand to admire it before spinning around a few times like Cinderella at the ball. She laughed and came to a stop, never taking her eyes off the ring.

"Here, just—" Blair took out more drawers and plunked them onto the island: earrings, bracelets, necklaces, watches. She placed them side-by-side, like a jeweler hawking her wares. "Just take it. Take it all."

The girl's eyes lit up as she realized she was being given permission to raid the candy store. She moved in for the kill then stopped and frowned at something in the bottom of the safe that caught her eye.

"What's that?" She pointed to the pink Barbie doll box on the bottom shelf. "You a grown-ass woman. What the hell are you doin' with a damn Barbie doll?"

"Oh." Blair scoffed as she bent down to retrieve the box. She looked at it for a moment before glancing at the girl. "It's me."

"What?" The girl snatched the box out of Blair's hands. "What do you mean, it's you?"

"I used to be in a singing group. Back in the day."

"No way."

"I mean, Jesus, look at it. It's obviously me, my face."

The girl eyed the hot pink box, her gaze shooting from Blair to the smiling, plastic doll trapped behind a wall of cellophane. She held the box up next to Blair's face.

"Damn ... that is you. How you get to be a Barbie doll?"

"I was in a girl group and we each got our own Barbie doll."

"Which group?"

"It was called Captivate. We had a bunch of songs. Back in the day."

"Like what?"

"'Morning' was one—"

"Oh, wait, wait, wait ... that's you? 'Morning?' That Playa Brown remade and that—oh snap. Didn't Sharpie D just have it in that song from last year? Man. Damn near everybody done sampled that."

"Yeah." Blair shrugged wearily. "A lot of people like that song." She bit her bottom lip, her eyes flicking over to the jewelry. "Aren't you going to look through all of this, figure out what you want?"

"So you got all your money from singing then, right?"

Blair folded her arms across her chest and took a few deep breaths to calm down.

Malcolm would say just play along.

"No. I mean yeah, a lot of people made a lot of money, but none of us girls, the singers, really did." Blair shook her head. "Just a little bit, really."

"Come on now. You had all these hit songs, got a damn Barbie doll and you telling me you ain't make no money off of it?"

"You have to pay everybody else before you get paid—managers, agents, the record label—whatever is left over has to be split three ways."

Jesus. What the hell am I doing?

"I don't believe that," the girl said. "I thought you was gonna tell me you was a damn millionaire from that."

"I never made any money from it. I mean, I made some, but not like Madonna money."

Keep her talking, I guess. Is that how this works?

The girl leaned against the corner of the dresser. "So where's all your awards and stuff, huh? All your pictures and everything? I know you must got like a room or something with all of that."

Blair pursed her lips. "That's really the only thing I kept."

"So you don't have anything? Nothing?"

"I gave most of it to my sister."

The girl shook her head. "Man, if I was a big-ass star, I wouldn't be giving up any of it to be no housewife."

Blair rubbed her wedding ring, the metal slick and warm beneath her still-trembling fingertips, hoping the girl couldn't smell the fumes of fear and desperation she was certain rolled off her in unrelenting waves.

"Don't be so sure."

POP PRINCESS

Dreena Harrison Grace, Captivate, 1986–1987, Registered Nurse: I first met Blair at her audition for Captivate. Me and Gwen were already in and they were still trying to fill the third slot.

Gwen Majors, Captivate 1986–1990, President and CEO Manhattan Realty: Oh my God, we auditioned with like, I'm not kidding, hundreds of girls. Hundreds. Maybe even thousands. Blair was literally like the last girl to come in but right away, Dreena and I knew she was the one. She was kind of cool and a little edgy and the three of us totally hit it off.

Dreena Harrison Grace: For groups like this, you have to be the total package. The looks, a style of some kind, you have to be able to dance. And of course, you have to be able to sing. You have to have a personality—I mean you can't be like a robot up there on stage singing. Like I said, total package.

Bridget Johnson: Actually, not a lot of people know this, but Blair and I auditioned together on a lark. I saw a flyer somewhere and thought it would be fun. We couldn't believe it when Blair got picked. It was so exciting and the truth is, I don't think I could have handled all that traveling and everything. It was perfect for my sister.

Kiki Downs, DJ, Music Box TV (MBTV), 1982–2000, Host of Dance City, Video Live, and Club Dance, et al., Current CEO of Kick It Productions: Captivate came straight out of the beatstyle movement in New York City in the early to mid-eighties, which was hardcore electronic dance music with heavy bass. It kind of picked up where disco left off. Captivate was one of those producer-driven girl groups that were so prevalent back in the mid-to-late eighties. Skinny Ralph Gomez and Ollie "Slick" Parma were pioneers in the beatstyle sound and had massive club hits with one-, maybe two-hit wonders. Jo Jo Mars, Kenny X, folks like that. They were looking to crossover to the pop charts and hooked into this idea of a girl group with long-term, mainstream appeal, so they put Captivate together. "Keep Me" really is one of the classics of the beatstyle sound. I mean you can't talk about any "Best of Beat-style" or "Definitive Songs of Beatstyle" lists and not include "Keep Me."

Dreena Harrison Grace: We hit out of the gate. Like on Friday, Blair joined the group and on Saturday, they had us in the studio recording "Keep Me." Everyone knew it was going to be a hit. It was that good. First, the clubs started playing it, then radio. "Keep Me" went top five dance in the States and top twenty in the UK and Australia. But in Germany it was massive. Massive. Went to number one there for something like three months. When we got booked on a six-month club tour of Germany—none of us even had a passport—they had to rush that through. That tour was crazy. They loved those hot pink wigs we used to wear—that was Blair's idea—they loved everything about us. Our style, our voices, our personalities. Every-thing. Everywhere we went, people went nuts, like Beatlemania.

Gwen Majors: We were three nobodies and overnight, we were stars. We did all the dance shows, talk shows, radio shows, music video shows—everything. Photo shoots, red carpets, magazine covers, music videos. We worked six days a week and slept all day on the seventh for pretty much a year straight. It was insane.

Bridget Johnson: I actually worked for Blair a little bit during those early days. It was exciting and exhausting all at once. We traveled around the world, meeting all kinds of fans and celebrities—royalty, even. Like I said though, that life really wasn't for me, so I quit after a while.

Jenny Valentine, Captivate 1987–1991, Five-time Grammy Award-winner, Fifteen Billboard #1 Records as a Solo Artist, Named "Bestselling Recording Artist of the New Millennium": After about a year, Dreena decided to leave to become a nurse and get married and I got the call to be in the group. The minute I met the girls, it was just, *boom!* Instant. I mean, I was singing in a disco cover band and had one foot on the deck of a cruise ship for a six-month gig when I got the call. I was thrilled to be in the group. Got me the hell out of Miami and kept me off that cruise ship (Laughs).

Gwen Majors: We went on for three more years and really, that lineup of me, Jenny and Blair, was our peak, what's considered the classic lineup of Captivate. We had some amazing success—a string of top ten pop hits, more dance number ones, each one bigger than the last. Crazy popular overseas.

Then the endorsements came—we had a soft drink deal, a tennis shoe, and Barbie dolls. A frickin' Barbie doll. That all sounds great, and don't get me wrong it was, but the reality was, we were bringing in money for everybody but us—the record company, the producers, our management—*everybody* was making money off our backs. *Every-*

body. Our managers are living in penthouses and driving Jags and I could barely afford my little roach-motel studio in the Bronx—not that I saw it more than two months out of the year. I was driving a Toyota that the label leased for me. I've got the number one record in the UK, just came off a sold-out world tour where I'm opening for The Kids, the biggest boy band in the world at the time, and I'm driving a Toyota. Not that there's anything wrong with Toyotas (laughs)—I bought my daughter one for her sweet sixteen. But you know what I mean. Everyone thinks, "Oh, you're this big star, you must be making all this money," and that was just not the case.

Kiki Downs: It's the same thing that happens to so many of these groups. If we've heard it once, we've heard it a million times. Musical tastes change, the group wants more creative control, the producers and the label want to keep the formula going. And the money. The money is always a problem. Always. Bad contracts, bad management deals, bad royalty rates. Same song, different girls.

Jenny Valentine: Gwen left when her contract was up. Blair and I did one album as a duo, which sucked. I got a solo deal and I jumped at it. Blair stuck around and they brought in a new producer, two new girls, but to me it was just dead.

Gwen Majors: Blair was kind of funny that way, though. She was never what I would call ambitious. I mean, she wasn't driven by money, or fame or success or any of that. She wasn't like me and Dreena or Jenny, even. Singing, performing, that's all we ever wanted. But Blair, you know, she didn't grow up thinking she was gonna sing her way out of the projects. But she's loyal. I'll give my girl that. To a fault.

Kiki Downs: And to everyone's surprise, out of the box, this new lineup scores a number one pop hit with "Morning." First pop number one in Captivate's history. This thing sold millions upon millions upon millions. Was the number two bestselling song of the year. Won all kinds of MBTV Awards, USA Music Awards. Even got nominated for a Grammy.

Jenny Valentine: Yeah. Nobody saw that coming.

Chrissy Lennox, Captivate 1993–1996, Oscar-nominated Actress, President, and CEO, CL Entertainment: That was about the time Blair met Malcolm.

11:55 A.M.

Had she made contact with the police?

Farrah had hit the button. She *knew* she'd hit the button just as he knocked the phone out of her hand.

She'd replayed those dizzying seconds over and over and had convinced herself that, yes, she had most definitely hit the panic button and the police had been alerted and were on their way to rescue them.

She hoped. God, how she hoped.

One thing she *was* sure about was that she never should have come home.

Of course, then her parents would be here by themselves. She couldn't live with that.

Her captors legs were crossed and he was hunched over on his knees, one hand cupping his elbow, the other slung across the opposite shoulder. He gnawed on his lips as his bottom leg jiggled and he rocked back and forth in the chair. Panes of sweat glistened on his cheeks. That awful BO floated across the room, pricking her nose. She had to fight to keep an impassive face, to force herself to resist looking at him. She didn't want to make eye contact. She didn't want him or his creepy friend in that cheap ass suit staring at her. She didn't want them to get the wrong idea and think she was interested. She didn't want that seriously unhinged girl putting a bullet in her brain because she thought Farrah was looking at her man or something.

Farrah shifted her own weight a little, grateful for the barrier of the royal purple patch of area rug between her bum and the hard floor. He'd tied her hands around the doorknob of the closet with a belt he'd found hanging on a hook inside. He'd also stuffed her mouth with one of the pink and white checked bootie socks she'd discarded last night as she crawled into her king-sized bed, tired after the long drive, blissful over not having to be confined to the twin bed of a dorm room for a few days. She wanted to tell him it was useless to gag her. This was a quiet street, boasting a handful of soundproofed houses, shrouded in trees. No one would hear her screams.

No one would hear any of them.

All week, Farrah had looked forward to the weekend. For the first time in nearly a month, she had some time on her hands to catch up on life. Laundry! Cleaning! Groceries! Errands! That must mean she was an adult or close to it anyway. She'd actually *wanted* to do all that stuff.

She'd been in such a hurry to jet out of town Friday afternoon, it hadn't occurred to her until she reached West Lafayette that at the very least, she could have brought the laundry home this weekend—her mother would have done it. Her mother loved doing laundry. Anything domestic. Anything with cleaning, scrubbing, washing, disinfecting, or sanitizing—Blair Gilbert was your girl. Woman. She had to stop thinking of women as girls and men as boys. At least that was what her Gender Roles in Literature professor kept telling her.

Sheree had started harassing her about a week or so ago about this surprise party she was putting together for Phoebe's twenty-first birthday. It would be a night to remember. Epic. Something they'd be talking about in ten years. Farrah couldn't imagine she'd be talking about anything to do with Phoebe in ten years. Not if she kept acting like a stone-cold nutjob. The awesome girl Farrah had met in Jack and Jill when they were gangly nine-year-olds, existed now in fleeting glimpses. She cried about everything. Indecisive. Mopey. It was that boyfriend. He brought out the worst in her, though Farrah probably wasn't really one to talk. Except she hadn't let things drag on with Theo for years, so she could feel superior about that. And Farrah had a good guy now. Eddie. The kind of guy she should have been with all along.

Sheree had promised Phoebe's boyfriend wouldn't be there because he was on reserves duty this weekend, so it would be safe to come and wouldn't it be great for everyone to hang out together like the old days? The promise of spending time with Phoebe—the *old* Phoebe— had lured Farrah home. It would be fun. Laundry! Cleaning! Groceries! Errands! could wait until next weekend. They'd laugh, they'd dance, they'd remember, for a few drunken hours anyway, why they were friends, why they loved each other.

So, she hopped in the car last night and came home.

Out of the corner of her eye, Farrah watched her captor watch her from his perch on the plastic turquoise desk chair that only moments ago, she'd hurled at him in a wild, desperate attempt to slow him down. He just stared at her, leaning one elbow on the white wood desk that Farrah decoupaged with slivers of multicolored tissue paper when she was twelve.

She never should have come home.

Her arms burned. Prickles of pain shot down the sides of her neck and zigzagged across the top of her shoulders. She scooted closer to the door so she could push it against the wall and lean against it. He bolted out of the chair and rushed toward her.

"What you doin'?" he asked as he loomed over her like a giant stalk.

Farrah propped up her knees so her elbows could rest against the hilly surface, relief momentarily racing through her aching shoulders. She grunted a little to indicate the motion made her feel better.

His eyes flickered understanding and he cast his gaze to the floor. "Oh ... okay, all right ... well, don't try nothing. 'Cause I'll shoot you."

She didn't say anything, just stared at him.

"You hear me? I said I'll shoot you."

She nodded.

He stood, gawking at her a few more moments, waiting. Satisfied she wasn't going to make any sudden moves, he backed into the chair again, resuming his folded-over position, his gaze penetrating her. She focused on the wall in front of her and the ancient Adam Lambert, Lady Antebellum, and Kings of Leon posters splashed against the lilac walls—an altar to the experimental musical tastes of her adolescence, the embodiment of suburban teenage angst—the corners flopping and curling into themselves, the faces alternately scowling and smiling down at her with preening smugness. Every time she was home, she was seized with a frenzy to rip them down, paint the walls a soothing eggshell, and replace them with tastefully framed prints of flowers or boats, or arty black and white photographs. Anything to signal to herself that she was an adult. Then again, this room was probably supposed to stay a shrine to her childhood. Arty and tasteful might not belong in this room. Besides, she'd always prided herself on being the oasis of grungy color amid the island of white, gray, and watery sea green floating across the rest of the house.

Farrah bit her bottom lip and ventured a quick glance at him. His gaze pointed to her and only her. The chair squealed like a pig beneath the weight of his incessant rocking and a deep hum rumbled from his body. He dragged his forearm across his forehead and she could swear drops of sweat dribbled down to his lap in big fat plops. Under normal circumstances, she might have felt a little bad for him.

The humming stopped. The chair continued to squeak and his breathing became heavier. Louder. Deeper. His BO seemed to explode around him and she half expected to see vapors rising from his skin. Her head throbbed from the mixture of oppressive heat and his stench. Farrah stole a glance at the window, wishing she could open it to let fresh lake breezes waft into the room.

He continued to stare at her. She continued trying to look at anything but him. She strained her ears to hear anything from the other rooms. That Cookie girl had dragged her mother toward the master bedroom and Daddy—where was he? Farrah's own flop sweat pooled in her underarms. They shouldn't have left him with that other dude—T or Tree or whatever his name was. He seemed crazy. And it didn't seem like it would take much for that Cookie girl to pop off.

Still, if anyone could get them out of this, it would be Daddy. He was super smart and could negotiate with anybody. A charmer. Smooth operator. She'd seen him put what she called his "Malcolm Moves" on car salesmen, neighbors—police even—during the handful of times through the years he'd been stopped for DWB. Of course, if they didn't recognize him the minute the window came down, he'd just lay the Malcolm Moves on them and it wasn't long before panties and boxer shorts were dropping.

Daddy would figure this out. He'd save them.

Thank God he'd been here when this all happened. If her mother had been the one to open the door, if it had *only* been her mother here to deal with this ... well, the two of them would have been dead from the jump. She loved her mom, for sure, but she could be totally batshit sometimes. Talk about popping off. Too blunt for her own good. Overly sensitive and emotional about the dumbest shit. Her mother wasn't malicious. She just acted first and thought later.

Farrah wiggled around again, twinges of discomfort poking her knees, the skin behind them slick with sweat. She continued to squirm around in an effort to relieve the distress.

The piercing throb of her cell phone sliced through the silence of the room. They both gasped. The guy sprang out of the chair like a jack-in-the-box and instinctively, Farrah leaned forward to grab the phone wedged in the corner across the room.

He ran over and snatched up the phone as it chimed with a text message. Her heart leapt, revived. If this guy kept her from answering her phone, that could help. If enough time passed, maybe whoever was texting her would get suspicious or ticked off about why she wasn't returning the message. Maybe they'd call other people wondering what was going on with her.

What if it was Sheree? That would be awesome. She hoped to God it was. If Sheree didn't get a call or a text back within seconds, she'd start psycho-dialing, psycho-texting. She was exactly the type to sound an alarm and get everyone all worked up about "OMG, Why Can't We Reach Farrah?"

"What's your code?" he asked as he fumbled with the phone, trying to unlock it.

She gave him a dumbfounded look and it seemed to take him a few seconds to realize she couldn't say anything.

He hesitated a moment as his eyes flipped between her and the phone, as if contemplating whether it was worth yanking the sock out of her mouth to get her password. He glanced toward the door, panic washing over his face.

The phone rang. It had to be Sheree. Farrah groaned and began knocking back against the door and kicking her feet out in front of her. He licked his lips and hit the reject button, seeming to breathe a sigh of relief at having made a decision.

"Who's Sheree? Why she keep calling and texting you?"

She kept looking at him. He walked over to her, leaning down until they were eye-level. *Don't flinch at the stench. Don't flinch at the stench.* The rhyme almost made her laugh. Almost. She struggled to keep from inhaling. Inhaling made her eyes water. She gulped and shrugged.

The phone jingled again. An agitated groan pushed past his lips. He jerked the sock from her mouth. "Why does she keep calling?"

"I don't know," she panted, the lie slipping easily from her mouth. "If I don't answer, she might keep calling."

He blinked. "Shoot," he mumbled, standing up. "I need to talk to T." He shoved the phone in his pocket and undid the belt enough to slip it off the doorknob, but not enough to free her hands before he yanked her toward the door, flinging it open. Farrah inhaled the fresh, cool air of the hallway, taking in huge gulps.

He stood in the middle of the hallway, calling for Cookie, who swung open the door to her parents' room, irritation spreading across her face, her mouth open, ready to say something. He hustled Farrah down the hallway.

"Here." He shoved Farrah toward the girl. "Watch her. I have to talk to Tree."

"He said we should keep them separate. He said—"

"I ain't got time for this," Dio said, turning his back on her. "Do whatever you got to do."

Cookie scowled for a bit before pushing Farrah into the bedroom, slamming the door shut behind her.

PHONE CALL
SATURDAY, APRIL 1, 12:23 P.M., CT

Tree: Yo. Yo! Where you at? I been calling you, texting you—

Look, we got a problem. A big one. Malcolm was here. And that, uh, uh, Farrah, the daughter or whatever. Now, you said they wasn't gonna be here, that it was just supposed to be Blair and now everything is all fucked up.

So, listen, you need to call me back and tell me what you want me to do.

Okay. Call me back.

Call me.

SOMETHING'S WRONG

Lieutenant Dimitri Cora: Blair and Malcolm Gilbert were expected at a charity event in the city on Saturday night, while Farrah Gilbert had plans to meet up with friends at a surprise birthday party, also in the city.

Sheree Moore, Friend of Farrah Gilbert: Farrah was supposed to meet me at my boyfriend's apartment in Bucktown and we were all going to Uber to the party.

Bridget Johnson: My sister and I talked almost every day. Except that Saturday morning, we talked for literally thirty seconds. I'd meant to call her earlier that morning but got busy, so by the time we connected, she had to go to her hair appointment, run errands—plus it was always a chore to get Malcolm out of the house to go golfing, so she didn't have time to talk.

Guy Sledge: In seven years, Malcolm Gilbert never missed a tee time. Never. He'd be late on occasion. Malcolm was notorious for running late, but never so late they'd give our time away or anything

(Laughs). Of course, if that *had* happened, he just would have talked his way onto the course.

Sheree Moore: I texted Farrah on Saturday morning. Nothing. I called, left a message. I called her again later in the day and her phone just kept going to voicemail. I thought maybe she got sick or something.

Kip Sellers: We were all at the club by eleven thirty and no Malcolm. Eleven forty-five, still no Malcolm. I text him. No response. I call him. No answer. Don, I remember (sighs, shakes head), Don kind of joked, "Well, maybe he's dead."

Guy Sledge: We kept the tee time, played skins. I thought—well, I figured something important must have come up, like maybe Blair got sick and he had to take her to the hospital or something. I tried calling him a few more times on my way home from the club, but still, no answer. Eventually, it started going to voicemail.

Lieutenant Dimitri Cora: Blair Gilbert had a hair appointment at a salon in Evanston at twelve-thirty. According to her hairdresser, this was a standing, bi-weekly appointment and she missed it for the first time in fifteen years. In fact, even though this was a regular appointment, Mrs. Gilbert was in the habit of calling to confirm every Friday morning, which she did at eleven on the morning of March thirty-first.

Guy Sledge: I wound up showering at the club and meeting my wife and some friends for dinner, so I never even made it over there. I tried calling him again early on Sunday, but it went to voicemail. I got busy later that day and thought perhaps I'd try again on Monday.

Verona Scucci, Edge Salon, Blair Gilbert's Hairdresser: I start psycho-dialing her. Like redial, redial, redial. No answer. Just rings and rings. I go and stand outside the shop, see if I can see her coming down the street, running late. Nothing. I get on my phone, start

Googling her, Googling her husband. Maybe they've been in an accident or something. It'd be all over the news if they were. Nothing. I probably spent a good half hour calling and texting her and nothing. I gotta tell you, I went home that night feeling sick to my stomach. I was gonna call the police, but my girlfriend she says to me I'm getting too involved, stay out of it, whatever it is, it's her business, she'll call me on Monday (Shakes head). My Grandma June says, she always says to me, go with your gut. And normally, I do. Except this time. Except this one time.

Guy Sledge: I thought about going over there on Sunday, but … my wife convinced me I was overreacting. For the first time in my life, I wish I'd never listened to her.

12:25 P.M.

How am I going to get out of this?

The thought kept looping through Malcolm's brain as his captor returned from making a hushed phone call outside the study. He thought about his own phone, still trapped in his pocket. Tree kicked a pile of paperbacks out of his way as he paced the room, his anger and agitation seeming to swell with each step. Though he'd just been on the phone, he looked at it again, this time tapping out yet another text message, his fifth at least since they'd been in here, before shoving the phone back in his pocket.

Once Blair and Farrah were upstairs, Malcolm told him the ten grand was in the safe in his study. Even after Malcolm had handed over the crisp and tidy stacks of cash, and Tree stuffed it into the inside pocket of his suit jacket, it wasn't enough to satisfy him, convinced there was an even bigger stack of paper in the house. He'd commanded Malcolm to sit in one of the mission-style chairs and secured him to it with strips of duct tape from the roll in his waistband. Malcolm ran his tongue across the bloody ravages of his bottom lip, the remnant of the blow Tree had delivered with the butt of his gun after being told yet again the ten grand was it.

Of course, he'd wanted to get into the study for another reason. He hadn't counted on being tied to this chair, thought he'd have a few extra seconds at least to get the upper hand.

He'd have to wait.

The room lay in shambles. His laptop and scant papers from the desk swept to the ground. The shelves cleared of books, assorted pictures, and miniature sculptures. Glass from photo frames smashed to splinters. He winced at the photo from a golf event of him and his old commercial agent, Mark Monroe—long ago murdered by his wife—crumpled and muddy from the stomp of Tree's shoe. The small mission-style table, where he worked on his jigsaw puzzles, knocked to its side, the fifteen hundred pieces of the Eiffel Tower flung to the far corners of the room. Malcolm's heart raced when Tree crawled underneath the desk, ran his hands along the walls, flipped over the gray and black hand-tufted wool rug to tap the wood panels of the floor with the soles of his feet—afraid of what the boy would find.

"All right, Malcolm. Which room is next, huh? Which room has the safe—the real safe with the real money?"

Malcolm shifted in his chair, his wrists sweating against the duct tape binding them. "I can't tell you something that's not true."

Tree stood up, clearly frustrated. He punched a fist into the palm of his hand, pacing yet again.

Through the small sliver of the open study door, Malcolm could see the third member of this deranged little trio come bounding down the stairs, frantically calling for his leader.

"Yo, man, what you want?" Tree asked as he flung open the door.

"We got to get out of here, man," he huffed as he rushed over. "I don't like this. I don't like this at all—"

"Dio, calm down, what's all this noise?"

"The girl—her phone keeps ringing, and I gotta bad feeling about this. Real bad." On cue, the phone jangled from somewhere on Dio's body and he jammed his hands over his ears as he paced, as though that would get him away from the sound. Malcolm watched this agitated young man stalk the room, much like Tree had.

Dio. Jittery young Dio. The weak link.

"I'm serious." Dio extracted the phone from his back pocket. "What if whoever it is keeps calling or they decide to come over here because Ol' Girl's not answering the phone? What if they call the cops, T?"

"Man, ain't nobody calling the cops."

"For real, let's just take whatever money they got and get up out of here."

Dio jumped as the phone beeped with a message. "Give me that," Tree said, grabbing the phone. He sniffed and looked at it for a second before dropping it to the ground. He brought the heel of his shoe down onto the screen, smashing it. He stomped it a few more times before he kicked the remnants in Dio's direction.

"I just solved your problem."

"Forget the phone. Forget all this. Let's just get up out of here," Dio pleaded.

Tree turned around, rubbing his bottom lip with his thumb, and looked at Malcolm. He shook his head. "Naw. We not leaving. Uh-uh. I'm not walking out of here with just ten G's."

"You heard him, T," Dio said. "We can take the cars and the jewelry, so come on, let's just take whatever and go."

Tree stood still, his legs apart, his arms folded across his chest. He sniffed and cocked his head toward Dio.

"Grab his phone," he said. "And get Wifey's phone, too."

"No, please. I don't want to do this, for real."

Tree backhanded his accomplice, the slap cracking across the air. Dio grabbed his cheek with both hands and scowled at his friend while cowering toward one corner of the room.

"I said, get his phone, get Wifey's phone."

Dio stumbled backward, one hand clinging to his face. He nodded feebly. "All right, T. All right."

Malcolm watched as Dio crept over to him. The boy extended a shaky hand toward Malcolm's pants pocket, lightly tapping the outside, blanching at the jingle of his keys. He slipped his hand inside the pocket, quickly extracting the bulge of keys, and wrestling the wallet from his back pocket. Malcolm tried to keep his face from screwing up at how bad this kid smelled. Reeked. Like he hadn't bathed in a few days, or if he had, he didn't use soap.

The two made brief eye contact as Dio moved over to his other pocket. Malcolm's heart sank as the boy slid his iPhone out of his pocket and quickly backed away. He handed all three items to Tree, who gripped Dio's shoulder and grinned.

"See? That wasn't so hard, was it?"

Dio didn't say anything as Tree perched on the edge of the desk, thumbing through Malcolm's wallet, extracting the thick wad of bills. He threw the wallet on the desk and counted out the money, nodding in appreciation as the numbers grew. "Two G's. Just like you said. All right, that's twelve G's. That still ain't enough."

"I already told you. You can have whatever you want."

"What about my cut?" Dio asked, his voice shaking.

Tree's head whipped around. "Your cut for what? You ain't done nothing."

Dio's head drooped as he fell silent again. Tree clapped his hands twice in Dio's face, causing the boy's head to snap up. The whites of his eyes were shiny, like he was on the verge of crying.

"Hey. Hey! You want to earn something? See how much money Wifey and that fine-as-hell daughter got, and bring it back down to me. And don't try to play me, 'cause I'm gonna ask them how much they gave you."

"I won't. I won't try to play you."

"Better not." Tree looked back at Malcolm. "Me and Mister Quarterback got to finish conducting some business down here."

Dio quickly bobbed his head up and down as he backed out of the room and sprinted upstairs.

Malcolm's heart raced. His nose started to run. He watched as Tree reached into his pocket and withdrew a cigarette lighter. The tiny orange-blue flame shot to life as he depressed the little red lever over and over and over. He smiled. Malcolm inhaled, his mind sprouting with possibilities, each one more disturbing than the last. Another blister of sweat erupted on his forehead, crawled down the side of his face. He had an exceptionally high tolerance for pain, so that might work in his favor. Whatever the boy had planned, he could probably hold out for a good while.

Tree walked over to Malcolm, a maniacal grin spreading across his face, glints of light bouncing off the yellow pebbles of his teeth. He stopped his advance and flicked the lighter again, this time, holding his palm over the flame. Malcolm's stomach did a slow plummet as he figured out where this was going.

He waved the flame underneath Malcolm's nose, who flinched at the tiny surge of heat. A small plume of smoke rushed into his nostrils and his eyes watered. Tree laughed and walked behind him, sniffing again.

Malcolm closed his eyes and took a deep breath, bracing for the unpredictable, though expected gush of pain sure to ensue shortly.

The tip of his index finger on his right hand exploded. Malcolm jumped, the chair he was taped to skipping a little as it grated against the wood floor.

He took another deep inhale to steady his breathing, focus his brain. His freshman year at UCLA. He broke his wrist during the game against Tennessee. In all his years of playing, it was his first real injury. To that point, he'd somehow been immune to the tears, strains, twists, and pulls that football players were so prone to. The dodging of those bullets all through Pee-Wee League, junior high, and high school had fueled his father's speechifying and his own eventual belief that he was untouchable. Immortal, somehow. The hits didn't even really bother him. Sure, he'd had his bell rung a time or two, but nothing that warranted stretchers, tape, or casts.

But that wrist. It was the first time he experienced real pain. No one could believe he'd kept playing, like it was nothing. Of course, when you were Admiral Gilbert's son, pain wasn't an option. Stopping wasn't an option.

But it had hurt. Like a bitch.

He focused on that now. This pain was nothing compared to that pain. His wrist had hurt like hell. His wrist had hurt like hell. His wrist had hurt like hell.

His middle finger detonated, then his third. Behind him, Tree laughed as he zigzagged the lighter across Malcolm's fingers, the searing heat of the flame crawling into Malcolm's palms. He continued to breathe, to try to stay calm, not make a sound, not be alarmed by the acrid stench of burning flesh.

His wrist had hurt like hell.

The lighter flicked closed and Malcolm's eyes did the same.

"Boo!"

Malcolm's eyes popped open with the sound of Tree's voice booming in his ear, the sound echoing down his ear canal.

Tree walked around until he was facing Malcolm, laughing, his arms folded across his chest again. He leaned down, the two men nose to nose.

"Did that hurt, Mally-Mal, huh? Did I hurt your precious fingers?"

Despite his heart sprinting across his chest, Malcolm shrugged. "Pain's relative, man."

Tree cut the lighter on again and even though he didn't want to, Malcolm flinched.

And an idea shot through his brain.

"Wait," Malcolm said. "Hold on a minute."

"What, you don't want me to ruin that passing hand? Oh, wait, you don't need that no more."

"You said you wanted more cash. I can get you more. Lots of it."

The lighter clicked off.

"How?"

FALLING IN LOVE

Neely Smith, Captivate 1993–1996, 2011–Present: He was at one of our shows. The Hollywood Bowl. He came backstage. He was a big football star, so of course, we all knew who he was. Except for Blair. She didn't have a clue. We were all kind of flirting with him. Everyone was falling all over Malcolm, but she didn't pay any attention to him. That's probably why he zeroed in on her (Laughs).

Alex Martinez: I'm pretty sure they met in Vegas. Captivate was playing a show there, somewhere on the Strip. Anyway, he went backstage and met her and he was pretty much done for.

Willie Dalton, Running Back, Chicago Bears 1980–1989, Los Angeles Rams 1989–1991: Malcolm could have had any woman he wanted. And he did (Laughs.)

Terry Gilbert, Malcolm's Brother: Yeah, that all changed when he met Blair, though. He fell for her hard.

Willie Dalton: What was it about her? Well, come on, look at her. I mean, Blair is a beautiful woman. Also, I think she was a challenge, you know? She wasn't like that typical groupie, sending him panties in the mail or whatever. She was just kind of like, okay, who are you? I think he liked that he had to work a little for her.

Nate Gilbert, Malcolm's Brother: I remember Malcolm calling me and saying, "Guess who I'm going out with, you won't believe who I'm going out with." I mean, this was my brother we were talking about, so he could have told me he was going out with Madonna, Janet Jackson, and Whitney Houston all in one night and I would have believed it (Laughs).

Isabelle Ryan: Blair had a lot of trepidation about becoming involved with Malcolm for a number of reasons. He had a reputation as a ladies' man. There were rumors that the number climbed into the thousands.

Alex Martinez: They met at the right time. She was looking to move beyond her group and Malcolm was starting to think about retirement. Though, when you've got gridiron coursing through your veins like he does, I wondered how he would make that transition. But he was pretty adamant he was ready to settle down.

Mitch Gilbert: The first time he brought her home—I think it was Thanksg—no, it was for dinner. Just a regular dinner and we were all there. And Blair, you know I'd seen her in magazines and in music videos or whatever and she was pretty, but in person, my God she was stunning. I mean, Malcolm had dated some honeys, but Blair was about ten honeys rolled into one.

Neely Smith: Blair had a handful of boyfriends. She and Oliver Flitt, who was hot in the movies at the time, dated for a little while and they were semi-serious. This business is hard, though. You never really know if someone is trying to get close to you because of what you do or who you are. So when you find that one, you want to latch on and never let go.

Bridget Johnson: Malcolm was pretty low-key courting my sister.

I mean, yeah, at first, it was a lot of hardcore dinners and jewelry and over-the-top stuff like renting skywriters and crazy things. My sister didn't want all of that. Once he figured that out, he toned it down. He'd bring over a pizza. They'd sneak into a movie theater at noon on a Friday and share a box of popcorn. Go for a walk in the park at six in the morning when there wasn't anyone else around and they could just be alone and talk. He'd bring her a pint of praline ice cream, her favorite, and they'd split it. It was these little things that really made Blair fall for him. Ultimately all she wanted was a regular guy. Once she started falling, she crash-landed. I'd never seen her so happy.

Neely Smith: She took me and Chrissy out to dinner and told us she was leaving. She and Malcolm were getting married and she was moving to Chicago. And I got it. It's hard to maintain a relationship with that life, on the road all the time. If you want it to last, you prob-ably do have to step off the merry-go-round for a minute anyway. So, even though I knew it was coming, I was still stunned. And scared. I mean, Blair may not have been like the lead singer or the biggest star in the group, but she WAS Captivate. We were like, without Blair, there is no Captivate. And that's pretty much what happened. Chrissy and me, we tried doing it as a duo for that one album, but it just didn't work. The label dropped us not long after and no other labels were biting, so we gave it up. In a way, it was a relief, but still sad. The end of an era, you know?

Chrissy Lennox: I had a blast doing it and I think the timing was right with it ending. Sometimes you have to know when it's over, and it was definitely over.

Neely Smith: I resurrected the group a few years ago because, hey, a girl's got to eat. We weren't on the charts anymore, but we never really went away, you know? And people were always asking me, "Are you guys coming out with new music? When are you getting back together?" and there were some offers of shows and different appearances and I said, there's something there. People still want to hear from Captivate. I asked all the girls—I mean, Jenny and Chrissy were a long shot. And Dreena and Gwen, you know they'd moved on to other careers. I thought for sure Blair would go for it. She always liked being in the group and was good at it. She made it pretty clear she was happy being Little Miss Suburban Housewife, so I moved forward without them.

Bridget Johnson: Blair went to one of the shows a couple of years ago. The group was playing some street festival in Chicago and she promised to be there, to check it out. I think Neely even got her up on stage to sing "The Dream of You," which Blair sang lead on, for old time's sake. She told me later the show was just sad. Here was her former bandmate, fifty something years old, now a size sixteen tiptoeing around stage in a size four dress, with two girls not much older than Farrah behind her, lip-synching songs from the eighties. She said it hit her for the first time in all those years that Malcolm had saved her from that fate. That could have been her.

Neely Smith: Listen, we can't all marry some rich football player and live in a mansion. We can't all have that life.

12:35 P.M.

"Baby, I'm so sorry."

"Mom, stop."

"I'm sorry you came home this weekend. I'm sorry you're in the middle of all of this."

"It's not your fault." Farrah scoffed. "Blame Sheree."

"Don't worry. Daddy will figure something out."

Farrah bit her bottom lip as she took a quick glance around. "I hit the panic button on my phone," she said, her voice low. "I think."

Hope leapt through Blair. "You did?" she whispered.

"I think so." Doubt now seemed to tug at the girl's face. "I mean, I'm pretty sure I got to it before he knocked the phone out of my hand."

The elation snuffed itself out just as quickly as it had ignited. Blair smiled feebly. "We just have to hope you did."

Farrah nodded and they fell back into silence. Despite the instructions from her accomplice to tape their mouths shut, the girl—Cookie—had opted to quickly return to pawing through Blair's clothes in the closet instead. A wobbly musical note floated out from the closet as she racked the hangers across the metal poles in search of clothes to pilfer. She was a terrible singer. Her voice cracked and hissed as she tried to hit the high notes. An unnatural vibrato. No breath control. As Blair's Hungarian chorus teacher used to scream as she tapped her wooden pointer against the metal music stand, "From zee diaphragm! Zee diaphragm!"

Cookie was one of those girls who shouldn't be singing anywhere but in her car by herself, but thought she was the next undiscovered Mariah Carey or Whitney Houston. A superstar waiting to happen. Probably entered talent shows all the time and never won a single one. Thought everyone was jealous of her. No one understood how unique she was. Probably tried to start a group, visions of Destiny's Child and Fifth Harmony superstardom dancing in her head. Except she didn't have the chops. She didn't have what it took to ascend the ladder of pop domination.

Not that Blair was one to judge all that harshly. She had a pretty voice. Not especially powerful, but nice to listen to. A light lyric soprano, well-suited to the fluffy pop-dance confections that drove Captivate's success all those years. Her delicate little pipes had served her well. She would never have gotten out of the Bronx otherwise. A mind-numbing retail job or secretarial position, married to the type of losers her mother liked, the only future she saw for herself at eighteen. Captivate had been her salvation, taking her around the world and sweeping her away from the squalor of the roach motel she'd called home for eighteen years. From the chaos. The misery. Out of Bibi's clutches. For a sliver of time anyway.

"What's she doing in there?" Farrah whispered as Cookie attempted another high note.

"Looking for clothes."

Farrah wrinkled her nose. "Clothes?"

"I already gave her all my jewelry—rings, bracelets, earrings, whatever. Now she wants my clothes."

"She's disgusting."

Blair craned her neck in the direction of the closet. "Listen, none of it matters. You heard your father. Give them whatever they want so they'll leave."

"Do you think they will?" Farrah gulped. "Leave?"

"Of course, baby, of course. We'll give them whatever they want and they'll be gone. We don't know their names, we don't know anything, so ... everything will be fine."

"What do you think that guy's doing to Daddy?"

Blair gave her a feeble smile, the only thing she was able to muster. "I'm sure they're negotiating or something. You know Daddy. I'm sure everything's fine. This will be over soon."

"I don't think this was random, Mom."

"What do you mean?"

"I think it might be Theo."

Blair blanched at mention of the loser's name, glad once again that little romance had faded quickly. There had been talk this new boy, Eddie, might come for a visit this summer so she and Malcolm could size him up. All she knew so far was he was from Indianapolis and his parents had a podiatry practice together, and that he had played football in high school. That alone would get the boy Malcolm's approval sight unseen.

"What makes you think that?" she asked. "Has he threatened you? Did he say he was going to do something like this?"

"No."

"Okay, then why do you think he's involved?"

Farrah took a quick glance at the closet. "I don't know. Maybe he doesn't have anything to do with this. It's just ... who comes to rob a house on a Saturday morning?"

Before Blair could answer, Cookie sauntered out of the closet, a heap of dresses hanging over one arm. Black, red, blue, rhinestones, cocktail-length, floor length. *Help yourself, Cookie.*

"You got a bag?"

"Are you really stealing my mother's clothes?" Farrah asked.

"What you got to say about it, little girl?"

"I'm pretty sure you're the little girl. What are you, like fifteen?"

Cookie's eyes grew wide, her fists curling at her side. "Bitch, I will—"

"Farrah—" Blair's head swiveled between the two girls. "There's a garment bag on the top shelf. Just ... take it."

Cookie gave her a thumbs-up and threw a scowl in Farrah's direction before retreating back into the closet.

"Don't provoke her like that," Blair whispered.

"You're one to talk."

"I'm not going to do anything and neither are you, all right?"

Farrah rolled her eyes. "Okay, anyway, even if Theo doesn't have anything to do with this, it's still weird, right? Don't you think it's weird?"

"What?"

"Who robs a house on a Saturday morning? People usually rob a house during the day when they think no one is at home, or at night if they know you're out of town. Like they watch the house for a few days to see if anyone's home. What do they call it—they case the neighborhood, case the house."

Blair stopped and made a face, Farrah's words lulling a throwaway thought to the surface. Earlier, Cookie had referred to her as a housewife. Such a specific choice of words. *Housewife*. How would she know that?

"I'm going to ask them," Farrah continued. "About Theo."

Before Blair could respond, the bedroom door burst open and the damp, disheveled, and distressed third member of the crew barreled into the room. Blair and Farrah instinctively leaned toward each other, watching him. He shot a quick, frightened glance their way before casting his eyes wildly around the room in search of his accomplice.

"Yo, Cookie! Cookie!"

"What?" she screamed, sounding annoyed as she came flying out of the closet.

"I need all her money and her cell phone," he blurted out as he flicked another distraught glance at Blair and Farrah. "T told me to come up here and get her money and her cell phone."

"So get them then," Cookie said, rolling her eyes.

He stormed over to Blair and loomed over her. She grunted involuntarily and scrunched up her face at the smell.

"Where's your phone? And your money? I need all your money. All of it."

"There." Blair pointed her head in the direction of the Christian Dior red ostrich saddle bag on the nightstand. "In my purse, right next to the bed. Take whatever cash is in there."

He stalked over to the bag, but Cookie rushed across the room and snapped it up before he could get to it. She let out a low whistle as she surveyed it.

"Damn. This is nice." She turned it, examining it from different angles. She ran her hands along the stitching and the raised bumps across the front and back of the bag. She flipped it over, dumping everything onto the bed, pawing through the sparse contents. Blair's wallet, a champagne colored lip gloss, red lip pencil, powder compact, small tube of hand cream, some pens, and a small notebook. The guy shoved Cookie out of the way and snatched up Blair's wallet.

"I'm gonna tell!" Cookie yelled.

"Shut up," Dio said as he jerked open the wallet with trembling fingers. He slumped with relief as he went through the small stack of bills. "Five hundred dollars. That's good. That's good. Then whatever Ol' Boy had in his wallet." He looked at Farrah. "How much you got?"

"I don't know. Maybe about a hundred dollars."

"Okay, I'll go down there and get that. Plus the cars, that's good. That's real good."

"And the jewelry," Cookie added.

"Where's your phone?" he asked Blair.

Blair hesitated, thinking about her phone sitting on the kitchen counter. Maybe she could get to her phone, hit that button, save them all. "I'm not sure."

"We've got to find her phone. Can't leave that behind. Got to grab it on the way out."

"What you mean on the way out?" Cookie asked.

"I mean, now we can get up out of here."

"What you talking about?" the girl asked, her arms crossed. "We leaving?"

The guy shoved Blair's cash in his back pocket. "I told Tree that I got a bad feeling and that we ought to get up out of here while we can."

The girl tutted. "Well, if T said we ain't leavin' then we ain't leavin'."

"Did Theo put you up to this?" Farrah blurted out.

They both turned their heads toward them at the same time. Blair watched them. Both confused.

"Who?" they asked at the same time.

"Theo," Farrah plowed on. "Was this Theo's idea?"

Tree's voice came racing up the stairs, calling for his accomplices, until he was standing in the doorway, his arm attached to Malcolm's bicep.

"Daddy—"

"Oh my God." Blair gasped at the sight of Malcolm's bloody bottom lip and blackened fingertips glistening against bright red blisters on his right hand. "What the hell happened?"

"It's nothing, BJ Don't worry about it."

"What's going on in here?" Tree asked. "What you all doing?"

"Man, T, she got all kinds of jewelry in there—like a damn store up in here," Cookie said. "A whole safe—"

"I got the money, from her and Ol' Girl. She said she don't know where her phone is," the other minion said, sheepishly holding out his wares for his leader's inspection and approval.

Tree ignored him as he pressed his gun to Malcolm's temple. Blair's heart did a stampede across her chest. If Malcolm was afraid, he let his face stay as impassive as stone.

"I thought you said you didn't have no safe up in here, Malcolm."

Cookie rushed over, locking her hands around her boyfriend's forearm. "It's just jewelry, baby. There ain't no money. It's just a safe for jewelry." She reached into her pockets, pulling out a tangle of bracelets and necklaces. "See?"

Tree's eyes, big as saucers, locked onto the jewelry, as he shifted his feet. Blair shot a questioning glance at Malcolm, who only gave her a slight nod in return. Dio stood awkwardly to the side, his hands still clutching Blair's cash.

"That's good," Tree said. "Real good. Yeah. You done good, baby."

Cookie beamed as she shoved the jewelry back into her pockets. "Dio said we're leaving."

"Not yet." He looked at Malcolm again, a grin smeared across his face. "Me and Malcolm about to run a little errand."

"What? Where are you going?" Blair shot straight up in her chair, wriggling against the restraints. "Where are you taking my husband?"

"It's okay, BJ," Malcolm said, his voice steady. "We're just going to take a little trip to the bank."

"Daddy, no—"

"The bank?" Blair's head swiveled between her husband and Tree. "You're going to the bank?"

"I'm going to give them thirty thousand dollars. For their trouble." Malcolm's voice remained robotic and detached, as if divorcing himself from the proceedings was the only way he would *get* through the proceedings.

"Oh." Blair retreated, understanding, relief washing over her. Of course. Throw stacks of cash at the problem. Thirty thousand. They'd think they'd won the lottery. As usual, Malcolm had it all under control.

Malcolm nodded at Tree. "I need my car keys and wallet."

"Don't go with this guy, Daddy," Farrah said, glancing at Tree, who smiled and licked his lips.

"You want to go with me, huh?" Tree laughed at Farrah. "You want to give me a ride?"

"You're disgusting," Farrah spat as Blair hissed at her to shut up.

Malcolm stood in front of Farrah, blocking her from Tree's view. "It's all right, baby girl. We're gonna go and get this money then everything will be fine. Right?" He held out his good hand. "My keys?"

The guy snapped his gum as he continued to stare Malcolm down. Finally, he fished the requested items out of his pocket and handed them over.

"Did Theo put you up to this?" Farrah asked again, this time directing her query to Tree.

Tree turned, a look of amusement on his face. "Naw, baby, I don't know no Theo." He looked at Malcolm. "Time to bounce."

"We'll be back soon," Malcolm said to Blair as he calmly took the keys and wallet.

"Malcolm Gilbert," she called out.

"What?"

"Your lip. You should clean up your lip. The blood. So you don't look suspicious."

"That's a good idea, *Blair*," Tree said. "Let's clean up old Malcolm."

"Bathroom's this way," Malcolm said, advancing. Tree threw up his gun in his face.

"Yo, don't make no sudden moves. I might get all nervous and shoot you." Tree laughed.

Malcolm didn't say anything as he slowly walked in the direction of Blair's bathroom, Tree following close behind. Blair closed her eyes. They'd go to the bank, withdraw that money, come back here, give them a few cars. The girl had already picked out her jewelry. And Malcolm's Super Bowl rings.

That would do it. That would set them free.

Or maybe Farrah hit the panic button.

Which meant the police were on their way. Maybe they were surrounding the house right now.

Or maybe Malcolm could signal to the teller or the guard once they got there. They'd be caught.

Either way, it would be over.

Her eyes popped open. The anticipation of this nightmare coming to an end made it hard to sit still. Malcolm was walking back in the room, the trickle of blood gone, leaving behind a pulpy dot of red on his lower lip, easily explained away. He shoved his bad hand in his pants pocket.

"You in charge until I get back," Tree said to Dio. "You hear that, Cookie? D's in charge, so don't give him no problems. You sit in here and watch Wifey and Ol' Girl, make sure they don't try nothing. They do, you shoot 'em. Don't even hesitate."

Dio nodded while Cookie fumed. Without a word, Tree snatched Blair's cash from a trembling Dio and pocketed it. He took one last look around before pushing Malcolm out of the room.

MISSING

Lieutenant Dimitri Cora: Malcolm was to accept an award at a charity gala at the Spencer House Hotel downtown. There was a cocktail hour starting at six thirty, with the program starting at seven-thirty, and Malcolm scheduled to arrive at around seven.

Lieutenant Sharon Donahue: Theo Tillis was out right away. Was seen on CCTV at work all day that Saturday and we couldn't make any connections between him and the perps. Same thing with Farrah's new boyfriend, Eddie Nixon. No motive, no connections to the suspects, was with friends all day, so rock sold alibi.

Kimberly Fletcher: Malcolm called me on Saturday, which was kind of strange. Blair was supposed to come to my place at five thirty and she didn't show. I honestly thought that might have been why he was calling, to tell me she was sick or something.

Bridget Johnson: It was really weird my sister hadn't called me back all day. I wasn't worried necessarily. It was more, "Well, this isn't like Blair." Even when I called her, I think twice on Sunday and both calls right to voicemail, I wasn't freaking out, since that happens sometimes. However, I definitely felt ... uneasy.

Lieutenant Sharon Donahue: The chair of the event calls Malcolm around five forty-five to confirm that he still plans to arrive no later than seven. There's no answer and by seven fifteen, after several calls from Mr. Scali, they had no choice but to move forward with the event. Mr. Scali admits to being furious with Malcolm for, in his words, "Ditching him." He also noted it was highly unlike Malcolm and as he thought about it further, something about the situation didn't sit right with him. He continues calling and texting him throughout the evening but the calls go right to voicemail, the text messages go unanswered.

Kimberly Fletcher: He wanted to speak to my husband, Garvin, but wouldn't tell me why. And he wouldn't let me talk to Blair, either. I wish ... I just wish I'd realized they were in trouble.

Elena York: This is the point when things go from bad to worse.

12:45 P.M.

Malcolm hoped his sigh of relief wasn't audible as he slid his good hand into his pocket and closed his fingers around the small bunch of metal and plastic, mentally going over the keys on the ring: house keys, office keys, car key for the Mercedes that he'd attached to the ring that morning. Feeling those grooves of metal and hard plastic cases beneath his fingertips reassured him somehow, grounded him in a reality that he could return to once he woke up from this nightmare.

His captor's footsteps and breath were heavy behind him as he navigated his way down the staircase toward the kitchen. He didn't want to move too quickly, didn't want to appear too confident about this turn of events, lest he ignite Tree's rage. He ignored his throbbing fingers, resisting the urge to run to the freezer and stick his hand in the ice bucket. The thought of all that ice enveloping the heated tips of his fingers caused Malcolm's eyes to temporarily drift shut in imagined bliss. He glanced over at his captor as he pulled his keys out of his pocket and edged toward the door leading to the garage. He stopped.

You parked out front last night. The car is out front, in the driveway, not the garage. Remember?

"What? What you doing? What you trying to pull?" Tree asked as Malcolm whirled around and they collided.

"I forgot ... I parked out front. My car's in the driveway, not the garage."

Tree glared at him before stepping to the side and holding out his hands as if to say, "Lead the way."

Malcolm opened the front door, his heart skipping as it revealed a sunny day. A beautiful day to golf. Guilt washed over him. Was he really thinking about golf? He'd woken up today craving the links. Couldn't wait to get out of the house and away from Blair and her lunacy.

Except, if he was on that golf course now ... lining up his shot, bull-shitting with the guys ... instead of here, here with Blair, here with Farrah...

He would never have forgiven himself for not being here.

Tree shut the door, which locked behind him. His finger instinctively sought the alarm when he glanced at the red panic button.

Hit the button, the horn goes crazy. Except, nobody comes running out. We tune out car alarms, we tune out car alarms. They annoy the fuck out of us. Nobody pays attention, nobody pays attention. Or maybe somebody does come running out. What's all that noise? Hey, Malcolm, what's all that noise? Tree panics. Starts firing. The two upstairs panic, start firing. Bloodbath, bloodbath, bloodbath.

Malcolm ran his good hand over his face, his frustration bubbling over with nowhere to go.

The safe, the safe, the safe. Can I get to my other safe in the study? Maybe. Right now, though, focus on the better bet. And right now, the better bet is the bank. Get to the bank, get to the bank, get to the bank. Alert them. Stall, stall, stall. Cops would be here in a matter of minutes. They could take the three assholes out. Arrest them, shoot them, made no difference. The bank, the bank, the bank. Better bet.

Mind made up on his play, Malcolm deactivated the alarm to the Mercedes. He ran his tongue across the salty dot of blood on his bottom lip and let his eyes travel across the expanse of trees shrouding his house from the main street. In fact, he likely wouldn't be able to see any signs of life from his neighbors' houses once they reached the street. There would be no flutter of curtains, no growling lawn mowers—not that anybody mowed their own lawns in Highland Park. There wouldn't even be many cars moseying down the road. Not this quiet stretch. No one out to check the mailbox, give a friendly little wave to the neighbor across the street. Not even the lazy Saturday swish of a sprinkler. The entire street would be at its perpetual standstill, shielding them from the outside world and worse, each other. They all paid obscene amounts of money for the privilege of being left alone.

The silence screamed at him. Or maybe it was him screaming in his head, screaming for the street to wake up.

Malcolm put his hand on the driver's side door handle and Tree clamped his fingers across his wrist. His body tensed, ready to strike. He had to remind himself not to wrench his hand away or turn around and get in a few pops to the guy's nose.

Stay calm.

Instead, with cool and deliberate precision, he turned to Tree.

"Something wrong?"

"I think you should let me drive," he said.

Malcolm shook his head and chuckled. "I can't you let do that, man."

"What you mean, you can't let me do that? Thought you said you was gonna let me have whatever I wanted."

"I did say that. And I will."

"Well, I want to drive this car. In fact, I think this is the car I want."

"Listen, brother, people see you driving my car, that's gonna raise all kinds of questions. This is a small town where everybody knows everybody and bruh, let me tell you, a lot of people know who I am. They see you, they're gonna be asking themselves, 'Who is this guy? Why's he driving Malcolm Gilbert's car?' and that's gonna bring all kinds of suspicion. That what you want?"

Tree kept staring at him, furiously chewing the inside of his mouth.

"Is it?" Malcolm repeated.

"No."

"All right then. I'll drive."

Tree released Malcolm's wrist and flicked his head up. "All right. Cool. That's cool. Yeah. You drive."

Malcolm clicked his tongue against his teeth and proceeded to open the door.

Tree grabbed him again.

He drew up, his irritation swelling inside him like a balloon, *thisclose* to bursting. "What?"

"What's our cover story?"

"Our what?"

"You know, our cover story, for when we hit up the bank. So people don't get, like you said, suspicious."

Silent, incredulous laughter rippled through Malcolm. Was this dude for real? What, did he think they were partners in crime or something? Brothers? Two dudes just out to collect thirty thousand dollars from the bank on a random Saturday because, hey, why not?

Malcolm cleared his throat and tried to keep the mirth fastened down tight.

"Well, okay, if we need a cover story, then we could say you're the son of an old friend, in from out of town. Just showing you around for the weekend and I had to stop at the bank for a minute."

"Make me your nephew," Tree said. "That's more believable if I'm related to you. You know, that I would be hanging out with you."

"Yeah, sure, okay." The quiet laughter bubbled again. "We'll make you my nephew. My brother, Nate's, youngest son. If anybody asks."

"Yeah, that's good, that's good." Tree smiled. "That'll work."

Malcolm rolled his eyes as he got behind the wheel. Instinctively, he reached over to flip on the Sirius, changing his mind just as quickly. Keep Tree focused on him. Keep him talking.

The decision however was taken away from him when Tree jammed his hand against the power button, quickly changing from Malcolm's Classic Vinyl mainstay to a hip-hop and R&B station, jacking up the volume until the windows bounced with bass. The boy's head bopped in time to muddy, unintelligible lyrics that he was somehow able to mimic with precision.

Malcolm twisted his lips into a tight bow, understanding. This was the hostile throng, chanting derision, hurling taunts onto the field.

Just another Sunday at the stadium.

He pulled out onto the main road, his head swiveling slightly at the sight of the maroon van parked in the winding driveway to his house. His quick glance told him it was non-descript and clean. He strained to see a license plate out of the corner of his eye, to stuff some of the numbers, the letters, into his memory, but couldn't without drawing too much suspicion. For all anyone knew, he could have a worker at his house. A plumber. A roofer. Any laborer in the world, drawing zero suspicion. Did it belong to one of them? Did one of them work for a plumber, a roofer, or a laborer? His money was on Dio. He seemed capable of going to work every day, of putting in his time so he could collect his check. His gut told him Tree had serious problems holding down any kind of employment. A hot head. Trouble with authority. The kind of boy Daddy would refer to as trouble on legs. "That boy's just trouble on legs. Don't mess around with him."

So they had parked in the driveway.

Why?

Why hadn't they parked on the street and walked up to the front door?

And why his house? Why not the Wexlers across the street or the Robinsons next door?

Why them?

When I answered the door, he looked up at the doorframe. Like he was looking at the address.

Malcolm ran his tongue across the bloodied split of his lip before he cleared his throat and looked over at Tree, a stream of expletives dropping from the boy's mouth like coins from a slot machine as he rhymed along with the radio.

He could have been freaked out to realize he'd stumbled into Malcolm Gilbert's house.

Or he could have been checking . . .

To make sure he had the right house.

And the calling. Who does he keep calling? And the texting. Why does he keep texting? Who does he keep texting?

The air sailed out of Malcolm. They'd been targeted.

Not random.

Deliberate.

Why?

He glanced over at Tree again, his apprehension ratcheting up about ten notches.

Who are you?

"Who's this?" Malcolm asked, working to keep his cool. *Keep buddying up to him. Can I get him to drop some kind of hint?* "I kind of like it."

Tree scoffed. "Wouldn't be nothing you'd like. Wouldn't be nothin' you'd know about. They talkin' 'bout the streets, the life ... the *hard* life."

"My nephews, they like a lot of hip hop or whatever. Thought maybe I'd ask them about it next time I see them."

Tree looked out the window. Malcolm shifted in his seat as he hit his blinker to turn left.

"The Day," Tree finally said.

"Ah, okay, yeah, I have heard of him." Malcolm turned. "I'm sure my nephews know him."

Tree resumed singing—rapping—along. Out of the corner of his eye, Malcolm could see Tree giving him side eye. He shifted in his seat under the boy's menacing gawk, his anxiety over this whole disaster coiling inside of him like a taut metal spring. Malcolm took a deep breath, his eyes on the road.

Stay cool. See what you can find out.

"So your boy calls you Tree."

"Yeah. So?"

"'Cause you're so tall, right? What are you, about six six, six seven?"

"Six seven."

"Huh." Malcolm nodded as though this was the most fascinating thing in the world. "Tree. Yeah. That's cool."

"That's just what everybody called me when I was coming up."

"You play ball?"

"With my boys once in a while."

"What are you, shooting guard?"

"Yeah."

"I always wanted to play basketball." Malcolm lightly tapped the steering wheel. "My father said I had to play football."

Tree scoffed and shook his head.

"He played football," Malcolm continued. "So we all—me and my brothers—we all had to play football. We were a football family. Heard that every day of my life."

"You know I met you before."

Malcolm gripped the steering wheel with his left hand, turning his head to look at the guy. "What?"

Tree gnawed on his lip, and he suddenly shot his hand out to turn down the volume on the radio to an imperceptible muttering. Malcolm stole a glance. He was huddled against the window, staring at the palatial mansions zooming by, his elbow digging into his thigh, his fingers dancing over his bottom lip.

"It was a long time ago," he finally said, twisting around to look at Malcolm. "When I was a kid, like eight, nine, ten years old."

When he was a kid. Tree looked to be about mid-twenties, so what, fifteen, twenty years ago? Was *that* what this was about? Some imaginary slight from a million years ago?

"Where?"

"They had this assembly at my school. Out South. 'Come meet the big football star Malcolm Gilbert.'" Tree's voice curled around his name with derision. "You was talkin' 'bout 'work hard,' 'stay in school,' all that bullshit."

A rush of "the old days" flooded through Malcolm, his brain scanning the mishmash of schools, faces, gyms, and auditoriums, trying for some insane reason to pick Tree's childhood face out of the crowd.

"It's been a few years since I spoke at a school. When was this?"

"Shit, man, sometime in the two thousands. I don't know."

"That was a long time ago."

"After your speech or whatever, they let you throw the football to us. Pose for pictures. Get you to sign shit." Tree slouched in his seat and chuckled to himself. "I had you sign my Malcolm Gilbert number Forty Four jersey. Mama saved up for weeks to get me that jersey. Man, I idolized you. Had your magazine pictures taped to my wall, used to watch you on TV. Probably don't even remember going to my school, do you? Dash? Dash Elementary? South Side?"

"It sounds familiar," he said. A lie.

"Okay, okay, what you remember about the school?"

"I mean, I don't remember the details—"

"Aw, man, you don't remember. You probably did so many of those speeches—of course you don't remember. Sayin' the same damn thing every damn time." Tree shook his head. "Bet you forgot all about us little hood rats the minute you got in your big fancy car, went home to your big-ass mansion."

Malcolm flinched at the accurate accusation. He'd done so many of those stay in school tours, both while he was playing and after he retired, they became a blur of red brick, awkward, rambunctious kids with crusty trails of snot running out of their noses climbing all over him, and fawning teachers—the women and men alike drooling in his presence, for, mostly, different reasons.

The truth was, they had depressed him, these tours of duty through the decaying and crumbling public schools of a city that was maddeningly beautiful and ugly all at once. The poverty was suffocating. The distressing, hopeful looks from the kids. The naked, pleading adoration and desperation in their eyes. *Make it better for us, Malcolm Gilbert. Tell us we'll make it out of here. Tell us hope isn't lost. Give us something to cling to.*

He was but one person, one man. Personal responsibility and handouts had never been part of his DNA. Hard work. Bust your ass. That was who he was. That was the code he lived by, drilled into him from birth by the Admiral. "There's no handouts in this life, boy. Nobody's going to give you a damn thing. You want something, you go and grab it."

Malcolm shook his head, trying and failing as usual to wipe the gravel of the Admiral's voice from the hollows of his mind. Malcolm knew his message of study, work hard, and focus would land for only a fraction of those kids, if that many.

And he knew the rest would fall far short of their potential.

Still, after he retired, he was desperate to keep his mind, his hands, his time occupied. In those days, the silence hadn't been so welcome. In those days, the silence hung over him like a black hole, threatening to obliterate him, swallow him in one agonizing gulp. In those days, he hated the silence, the idle time, the idea of a blank spot on the calendar staring back at him. Be interviewed for a football documentary? Sure. Go to New York for a game? No problem. Give a speech at a luncheon? Steak was his preferred entrée, but he'd settle for chicken. Never fish. Speak at a school? Tell him when and where.

Malcolm kept his eyes trained on the red light in front of him. "So what did you do, Tree?"

"What you mean?"

"What kind of impact did it have on you? Did you hear any of what I said?"

"You wanna know what kind of impact you had on me?"

"Yeah."

"When it was my turn to get my jersey or whatever signed, I remember … I remember you said, 'And what's your name, son?' And … man, in that moment, I wished so bad that…"

"What?"

"That you was my dad."

Dad. *Father.* The boy wanted a father. He wanted Malcolm Gilbert to be his father.

"I never knew my pops. Not my real pops. That dude Moms married…" Tree shook his head, turning back to look out the car window. "He used to tell me all the time I wasn't worth nothing, that I should have never been born. You ever had anybody tell you they wish you was never born? No, of course, you wouldn't know nothing about that, because you Malcolm the Great. Malcolm the big football star. Everybody loves Malcolm. Like a damn TV show. Everybody Loves Malcolm."

Malcolm pursed his lips. "I'm sorry to hear that. Really. No boy should have to grow up without a father."

"Man, whatever."

"You've had it tough, Tree. I'm sorry. I really am."

"What you got to be sorry about? Huh? What the hell do you have to be sorry about? What, all that shit you was shoveling through the hood wasn't worth nothing?"

"I just meant I'm sorry to hear life has been so hard for you. I'm sorry things didn't work out for you the way you hoped."

Tree stared at Malcolm before erupting into maniacal laughter. "Yo. You sound like a damn greeting card. 'My condolences on your fucked up life.' What a bunch of bullshit." He was silent for a moment. "Bet you had a good daddy. Bet he didn't run away from you."

"No, no, there was no getting away from my father. He uh—" Malcolm chuckled and shook his head. "The Admiral was there for every game, every skinned knee, every lost tooth, every everything."

Tree scoffed. "Figures."

Malcolm didn't say anything as the bank loomed large in front of him. He pulled into the parking lot, took a spot directly in front of the door, and cut the engine.

"We're here," he said.

LOVE AND MARRIAGE

Lani Jacobs: Did they have a good marriage? Yeah. Yeah, I would say so. I never—the thing about ... you know they bickered a lot. I never saw them have a knockdown, drag-out fight or anything like that. No, they just picked at each other, but it wasn't serious. I mean, I didn't take it seriously. In fact at times, you could tune it out completely.

Mitch Gilbert: Did they have a good marriage? I mean, they had their ups and downs like any married couple. Blair ... look up pistol, in the dictionary, okay? Yeah. I mean (laughs), Malcolm would say she was a nutjob, but she was *his* nutjob.

Bridget Johnson: My sister had no idea how to cook when she got married—our mother didn't teach us that (laughs)—and she learned how to cook all of Malcolm's favorite foods. She went to every football game, every football event, even though she didn't know anything about football. And sure, Malcolm bought her jewelry, took her on trips, and all of that, but what she probably loved the most was that she could count on him. Always.

We had a screwed up childhood. I mean, really screwed up. We had no idea what a good relationship looked like, what a normal family looked like. We never knew our father—we don't even know if we had the same father or different fathers. My mother had a long string of men around, all losers. Anyway, Malcolm and my sister, they made it work.

Lieutenant Dimitri Cora: Everyone we talked to said overall, Malcolm and Blair had a good marriage. However, we couldn't rule anything out, so we had to really peel back that onion, see if there wasn't something their friends and family didn't know about.

Lieutenant Sharon Donahue: As it turns out, we did find something.

12:45 P.M.

"You heard Tree. *I'm* in charge," Dio said, jabbing the sharp point of his thumb against his chest. "That means you got to do what I say."

"That don't mean nothin' to me." Cookie rolled her eyes.

"Man, Cookie, come on—"

She stormed back into the closet, him following her, the two of them squabbling about who was in charge.

Blair closed her eyes and shook her head over the squabbling in the sandbox. Farrah scooted closer to her.

"There's only the two of them," she whispered. "We could try to make a run for it."

Blair looked over at the closet and shook her head rapidly. "No. Uh-uh. I don't think that's a good idea."

"What?" Farrah's voice went up a few octaves. She looked over her shoulder toward the closet. "No, really, Mom, I bet we could do it."

"No."

Farrah blanched. "Why not?"

"Because Daddy's got a plan and we should stick to it. Thirty thousand dol—seriously? These kids have never seen that much money." She leaned back and shook her head again. "No. Let's just wait for your father to get back then this will all be over."

"Since when do you listen to anything Daddy says?" Farrah said, frustration creeping into her voice.

"Farrah, just ... please. We're going to let your father handle this, all right?"

A cackle erupted from the closet and Cookie re-emerged, holding a pair of Blair's black Louboutins, an agitated Dio behind her.

"Damn, you got some big feet." She laughed. "Size nine? Yo, I think that's what men wear."

"Cookie—"

"Damn, Dio, would you leave me alone? Dang. Always bothering somebody." Cookie tossed the shoes over her shoulder. "I guess I won't be taking no shoes with me." She laughed again, another hearty guffaw at Blair's expense as she retreated to the closet once more. Dio followed her inside again, until she screamed at him that he was in charge, so act like it by watching them. Seconds later, Dio huffed out of the closet and plopped himself into a chair, stewing as he watched them.

As much as Blair didn't want it to, the insult about her feet stung. That had been one of Bibi's favorite targets. Her big, gangly feet.

Big Ugly Blair. Bibi's uninspiring, yet painful nickname for her eldest daughter.

Like all daughters, she'd grown up wanting to be like her mother. Specifically to be petite like Bibi, adding on that codicil to her seemingly futile prayers every night. Bridget had been the one to draw that lucky number seven. Blair's awkward limbs and size nine feet made her feel like a marionette next to the two little dolls in the house, all bones and sharp angles. To hear her mother and sister tell it, they had their own problems. Narrow size six feet necessitating difficulty in shoe shopping because regular shoes just billowed around their tiny little bones. Miniscule size two waists doomed to darling little dresses and cute little capri pants and snug little tops. Hell, they didn't even have to wear a bra half the time. There was also the unspoken contrast in their hues, Bibi and Bridget's light skin and light eyes casting a painful shadow over Blair's dark tint. Blair supposed she must have looked like her phantom father, whoever he was. Maybe another reason her mother had hated her so much. Of course, Blair had a long, curled-over list of reasons why she despised her mother.

The group is what finally infused Blair with confidence about her looks. Finally made her feel beautiful for the first time in her life. Stylists and wardrobe mistresses buzzing around her with glamorous gowns and gorgeous shoes and sparkly eye shadow, transforming Cinderella for the Ball. After "Keep Me" had hit so big, a magazine profile of the group had referred to her as "the stunning Blair Johnson." Stunning. Not gawky. Not ugly. Not ordinary. Not an "interesting face," which everyone knew was code for ugly. Stunning. As in lovely. Beautiful. Pretty. That's what the dictionary told her when she looked up the word. She didn't tell anyone, but she'd clipped that article and carried it in her wallet for years. Not because of vanity. Because of the acceptance.

The doorbell sounded from downstairs. Blair and Farrah gasped as Dio bolted up in his chair and Cookie ran out of the closet. They all four looked at each other, fear in their eyes.

Dio flew across the room, grabbing Blair's neck. "Who's that? Who's at the door?"

"I'm not psychic," Blair wheezed. "I have no idea."

The doorbell sounded again.

"What if it's the cops?" Cookie asked, hopping from foot to foot. "What if they got to the bank and they called the police and Tree got caught?"

"Mom—"

"That—" Dio loosened his grip on Blair's neck. "Did you set up my boy to get caught? Huh? You and Ol' Boy set us up?"

The doorbell chimed once more.

"Mom—"

"I don't know who it is, but if you don't let me answer the door, they won't go away. They might call the police."

"Oh my God. Mom—"

"Jesus Christ, what?" Blair snapped at Farrah, who grimaced.

"I forgot. Zoey. I told her to stop by."

"Zoey? Oh God." Blair pursed her lips and shook her head.

"Who?" Dio asked.

"One of my girlfriends, she—"

"Get up." Dio wrenched Blair out of the chair. She yelped as he ripped the tape from around her hands. "All right. You go down there. You go down there and get rid of whoever that is."

Farrah scooted closer to him. "It's my friend, I should be the one to go down there."

"I—wait, what would Tree do? What would he want me to do?" Dio muttered as his head swiveled between Farrah and Blair, panic slashing his face.

"Please. Let me talk to her. I can get her to go away faster and better than my mom can," Farrah said.

"No, no, no. I don't trust you. You might try to do something," Dio said. "No. Me and Ol' Girl going down there together."

"Mom—"

"It's all right, Farrah."

"And you say anything, you do anything, I will blow your fucking head off." Dio looked at Cookie. "Watch her."

Dio hustled Blair down the stairs and across the living room toward the front door, his fingers digging into her arm. He pulled out his gun and held it to her lower back.

"You get rid of whoever that is."

She exhaled before she opened the door.

Zoey smiled, the sun glinting off the copper ends of her shoulder-length locs.

"Mrs. Gilbert, hi, how are you?"

"What do you want, Zoey?"

She flinched and her chin trembled. "Oh. Um ... is Farrah here?"

Blair licked her lips, her eyes flicking to her left where Dio stood behind the door, out of Zoey's sight, the point of his gun digging into her spine.

"Farrah's at school. In Indiana."

"Um, okay, yeah, but we were texting last night that she'd be home and she asked me to come over around twelve-thirty. I can't make it tonight and I asked her to take my gift to the party." Zoey held up the iridescent light pink shopping bag from Rock N Rags to illustrate her point. "Phoebe's birthday party. Tonight?"

Blair bit her top lip. "Right. Yeah, she did." She snatched the bag from Zoey, who jumped back startled. "I'll give it to her."

"Okay, but um ... She is home, right? Didn't she drive in last night?"

Next to her, the agitation in Dio's breath inflated with each painful inhale and exhale. This was about thirty seconds from becoming a straight-up bloodbath. She had to get rid of her.

"Zoey, you've caught me on a bad day. There's just so much going on here today." She held up the shopping bag. "Thanks for stopping by."

"Is Farrah's phone broken?"

Blair swallowed, the barrel of the gun poking her side. "What?"

"Her phone. I—well first I texted her and she wasn't answering so I tried calling her a few times, you know, before I came over and it keeps going to voicemail—"

"It's a really bad time, Zoey," Blair said, pushing the door to close it. "I'm not kidding. I really can't talk to you right now, so you ... you've got to go."

"Oh, you must have some work going on today, because—" Zoey shook her head. "Anyway, okay, sorry, just let Farrah know—Well, I guess just tell her to text me, let me know if she still wants to go to Walker Brothers for Dutch Babies tomorrow before she drives back to school."

Blair slammed the door shut, the shopping bag slipping out of her trembling fingers and thudding to the floor. Maybe Zoey would tell someone, her mother, someone, that something weird was going on at the Gilbert house. Alert the authorities. Something.

"Good job," Dio said, still pushing the point of the gun into her spine. "Now get back upstairs."

She glanced back at the door, her slender hopes now pinned on a nineteen-year-old.

12:55 P.M.

"So you got our cover story?" Tree asked. He kept licking his lips and sniffing. Nerves. Drugs? Or maybe it was the thrill of getting close to the smell of thirty thousand dollars in cash. Of feeling the heft of it in his hands.

"Yeah, Tree, I got it," Malcolm muttered.

"You make one move. You do one thing, Im'a call my partner and my girl back at the house and tell them to blow Wifey and Ol' Girl's fucking brains out. You hear me?"

"Tree, I already told you, I don't want any trouble," Malcolm said, his hand resting on the car door. Tree nodded at him that it was okay to exit. Malcolm took a deep breath and got out, his eyes scanning the parking lot and street beyond for a police car, some sort of security.

There was none.

Resigned, he headed toward the heavy glass door of the bank and pulled on it.

Locked.

He yanked on the brass handle again, his stomach crashing to the bottom of his shoes. There were no lights on inside, no movement at all. His eyes flicked down to the transparent sticker bearing the bank's hours, his heart sinking even further.

Twelve thirty. Twelve fucking thirty.

"What's wrong?" Tree sniffed, his own eyes darting around them. "What's the problem?"

Malcolm sighed and shook his head a little. "Bank's closed."

"Closed? What you mean, closed?" Tree reached into his pocket for his phone, illuminating the screen. "You said they was open until one. It's not one."

"They are. They're supposed to—" Malcolm dragged his hand over his head, a forgotten, throwaway conversation with his assistant that they'd be closing one hour earlier starting in a few weeks, jamming into his brain. Why the hell hadn't Blair said something to him just now? She always kept on top of stuff like this. Appointments, hours, locations, names, dates, places. She knew his memory was full of holes, even on a good day.

Maybe she'd forgotten, too. The terror was scrambling all of their brains.

"Okay, look, I forgot. They changed their hours. I thought they closed at one. They've always closed at one—"

Tree kicked the trashcan, the sole of his shoe thundering against the metal slats. He hissed, "*fuckfuckfuckfuck*," before kicking the trashcan again. He paced and rubbed his palms across the top of his matted dreads, muttering.

"Tree. Tree!"

He ignored Malcolm, continuing to grouse to himself as he marched across the tiny patch of sidewalk, his agitation rolling off him in waves. Like a player stomping around on the field after the ref threw a flag on him.

"Look—"

He rushed back over to Malcolm, his index finger pointing down. "You promised me money, stacks of it, you said."

"And you'll get it."

"You playin' me? Huh? Huh?"

"Tree, do you—do you think I would have wasted your time, my time, coming all the way over here if I thought the bank would be closed? Huh? You think I would do that?"

"You trying to trick me. I know you are. Think you damn smarter than me—"

"Why would I try to play you? What am I gonna get out of that? And come on, man, you and I both know you're too smart for me to try and pull anything over on you."

Tree stopped short and drew up his shoulders. "That's right," he said, smugness threading his words. "And don't you forget it."

"I won't. I couldn't. I could tell the minute you got to my house that you were the brains."

Play him.

A slow smile curled around Tree's lips, Malcolm's words seeming to have the intended effect. "Man, those other two couldn't think their way out of a paper bag. I got to think of everything. Can't trust them to do nothing."

Malcolm nodded. *He's falling for it.* "I mean that's obvious. Real obvious. They don't seem too bright to me."

"Man, you ain't never lying about that."

"All right. Like I said, I know I'm dealing with a really smart man here. Someone I can talk to. Someone I can do some business with. And because of that, I'm being straight up with you. It was an honest mistake on my part, man. For real. Believe that."

Tree folded his arms across his chest. "So what you gonna do about it?"

"All right, I already told you, you can have whatever you want at the house. Whatever car, jewelry—"

"Man, I want cold hard cash sitting in my hands."

"Listen ... think about it this way. I give you a whole fistful of gold jewelry and you take it to the pawn shop and see at the pawn shop, they can melt that down, and that's how you get the cash. Because they do it by weight, right? And the price of gold is *hot* right now. Like real high. You could clean up, bruh. Clean. Up."

Tree's face seemed to quiver and droop as he thought of the possibilities. He sniffed. "Go on."

"Tree, you need to look at the big picture. You saw how happy your girl Cookie was, right? When she was showing you all that jewelry? She was like a kid in a candy store, right?"

"Yeah," Tree mumbled in acknowledgment.

"You know women. They love ice. Love it. Man, you let her keep all that hardware, she'll love you forever. Come on, now. You know I'm right."

Tree scoffed. "Maybe."

"All right, she got a birthday or something coming up?"

"She said something about next month."

Malcolm held up his palms in victory. "All right then. We just cut out the middle man. Direct to the consumer. Happy early birthday,

Cookie. You let her take whatever ice, whatever stones she wants. You clean up on the gold, split it with just you and your man, Dio, and *boom!*, everybody's happy. See? You see how this works? Plus the cars, plus the cash. Man, you gonna come out of this on high. I'm telling you."

Tree sighed. "All right, fine. I'll take the damn jewelry."

"Electronics. TVs, computers, iPad, whatever. And look. We're already at the bank, right? There's a drive through ATM right over there and I can withdraw five thousand from it right now."

"You say you can give me five thousand right now?"

Malcolm pivoted toward the ATM, ready to shove his card into the blinking green slot, when another, more urgent message flashed across the screen.

THIS ATM IS UNABLE TO DISPENSE CASH AT THIS TIME. WE APOLOGIZE FOR THE INCONVENIENCE.

He banged the side of the machine, his heart racing, his head moments from exploding.

"What's the problem, Mally Mal?" Tree asked from behind him.

He pursed his lips, frustration and oddly, fear, stopping him from turning around to face the boy. "ATM's out of service."

"You serious?"

"We can go to another ATM and take out some money and—Tree, listen to me—when we get back to the house, I'll write you a check, fifty thousand. You take it to any bank you want. They can call me to verify it."

Tree stopped short, opening his mouth to say something before turning his head slightly toward the bank. He pointed at the glass, tapping on the neat white lettering denoting the bank's hours.

"Says here they open at nine on Monday. I think you and me need to be here first thing Monday, right when they open the doors. Fifty thousand. Cash. No checks. No money orders. Cash. You feel me?"

Malcolm blinked, not sure he'd heard right. Had this punk just played him? Had this punk just announced that he and his crew would be making themselves at home at his house for the next day and a half while they waited for the bank to open?

He had. That son of a bitch had.

It was a rare thing for someone to outsmart Malcolm Gilbert. A very rare thing. He could count on one hand the number of times it had happened in his life. Less than one hand.

"I just offered to go to another ATM to take out some money. What, that's not good enough for you?"

Tree shuffled over to him. "You not in charge, Mally Mal. What I say, is how we do it. And I say, we gonna be back here first thing on Monday morning."

They stared each other down, both breathing heavily, both unable to take their eyes off the other. He had to think about Blair and Farrah. He had to play it cool until he could come up with something else.

He had to surrender. He closed his eyes, not believing what he was about to say.

"All right, Tree. First thing Monday morning. You and me. Right back here."

Tree exploded with laughter. Malcolm knew he was savoring his victory. Reveling in it. That was okay. He'd retreat to the tunnel for now and reemerge with a new plan for the second half. He just needed to think.

Tree looked Malcolm up and down. "Looks like you got yourself some company for the weekend."

12:55 P.M.

"Good job, Wifey. Glad I didn't have to take you out," Dio said as he yanked Blair up the stairs. She screwed her wrist around, yelping at the savagery of his fingers around her small bones. He yelled for Cookie as he forced Blair back to the master bedroom.

"Who was it?" Cookie asked as they plunked her back into her chair to tie her up again.

"Ol' Girl was right," Dio said as he re-taped Blair's wrists together, cocking his head toward Farrah. "It was her friend."

"Is Zoey okay?" Farrah asked Blair, her voice trembling.

"She's fine. Everything's fine," she said.

Cookie headed back into the closet as Dio folded his arms across his chest. "Tree'll be back soon then we can get up out of here."

"Can I have this?"

Cookie had emerged from the closet, the Barbie doll box in her hand. She shook it in Blair's direction. A momentary panic seized Blair.

The one thing she actually wanted to keep, the one sentimental item from those days that gave her any kind of warm and fuzzy sensation. Someone had thought a little black girl from the Bronx was worthy of becoming a doll. A beautiful, plastic, perfect doll, forever encased behind the glossy cellophane. Forever beautiful.

She stopped herself. Her life was worth more than a doll. Farrah's life was worth more than a doll. If that's what Cookie wanted, then Cookie could have it.

"Yeah, sure, fine, if you really want it."

The girl opened her mouth to say something when she was distracted by Tree's voice racing up the stairs in search of her and their other cohort. The hot pink box fell from her hands and landed with a clunk as she and Dio ran out to the hallway. Blair and Farrah glanced at each other before her daughter scooted over to the door, her ear cocked toward the living room.

"Farrah, get away from the door. Don't let them see—!"

"Shhh! I'm trying to hear what they're talking about."

Blair pursed her lips. "What are they saying?"

"Oh, God." Farrah whipped around to Blair.

"What? What did they say? What's wrong?"

"Something about the bank being closed and they're going to be here until Monday, that they have to stay here all weekend—"

"What? Are they joking? They can't do that." She craned her neck. "Where's your father? Can you see your father?"

Farrah peered around the doorjamb then shook her head. "The other two don't want to do it. They want to leave."

"What's happening now? What are they saying?"

Where was Malcolm?

Farrah leaned back against the wall and smiled. "Daddy just said he has another idea."

"What? What did he say?"

"He wants to call Garvin."

Blair closed her eyes, relief flooding over her once again, another pinprick of light to claw their way toward. Garvin. Of course. He'd come quickly, discreetly, help free them. She was convinced he kept a million dollars stuffed in each of his many mattresses, so laying his hands on thirty thousand would take mere minutes.

It would be over soon.

"The guy, Tree, or whatever his name is, he's pacing again," Farrah murmured. "Like he's trying to figure out what to do."

And then Blair heard it herself.

"All right. Call him."

1:17 P.M.

Garvin.

He should have thought of that from the jump, instead of messing with the bank. Monday Morning Quarterbacking.

The vein in his neck tightened and for a moment, he worried it would snap from the pressure. He held out his hand. No one but Blair would have seen the minor tremor. No one but Blair had seen the occasional massive quakes. No one but Blair knew just how tortured his days could be at times.

"I need my phone," he said.

Tree paced across the room, chewing on his bottom lip. Cookie and Dio watched him, a seeming mixture of fear and weariness twisting their faces.

"Okay," Tree said. "This how it's gonna go down. You gonna call the guy and ask him to bring fifty—sixty—no seventy thousand. That's it. Yeah. Tell him to bring seventy thousand."

"Okay." Malcolm nodded. "No problem."

"Yeah. Tell him to bring seventy thousand and put it in a—a suitcase. No, a gym bag. Yeah. Put it in a gym bag and bring it to the front door, ring the doorbell three times, and leave. Don't call no five-o, don't call no other buddies for back up, don't call nobody. Just come straight here, drop the G's, ring the doorbell three times, then bounce."

"Okay." Malcolm nodded again. "I got it."

"What's the guy's name?"

"Garvin. Garvin Fletcher."

Without a word, Tree pulled the phone from his pocket and commanded Malcolm to unlock it before snatching it back and pulling up Garvin's number himself, putting the ringing phone on speaker.

"You've reached—"

"Voicemail." He frowned as his heart tickled against his chest and Tree disconnected the phone. Malcolm's head flipped up. "Let me try again."

Tree snarled, but hit redial.

Voicemail again.

Malcolm shook his head and whispered to himself as he kneaded his forehead and asked Tree to keep hitting redial, the outgoing voice-mail message continuing to echo throughout the room.

"Man, what the hell?" Tree said as he threw the phone, sending it skittering across the marble before he rushed Malcolm, seizing the collar of his Polo. "You still trying to get me, aren't you? Still think you can outsmart me, don't you?"

Malcolm grabbed Tree by the wrists, ready to snap them. Like trained seals, Cookie and Dio immediately pointed their pistols at him. Malcolm let out a slow stream of air before he loosened his grip a little.

"Look, I don't know why he's not answering. He might be doing something where he can't pick up."

"I bet you that dude he's trying to call is five-o," Cookie said.

Malcolm glanced over at her, wanting to clamp his hand across the stupid girl's mouth to shut her up.

"Tree, I promise you, he's not. Far from it. Let me call him one more time and leave him a message, all right? He'll call me back. He will."

Tree didn't say anything, just continued staring at Malcolm. He unclenched his hands from Malcolm's collar.

"Just one more call," Malcolm said, holding up the index finger from his good hand. "He doesn't pick up, I'll leave him a message."

Tree let out a short burst of angry air. "One more call," he said, resuming his pacing. "Wasting my motherfuckin' time."

Malcolm took a shaky inhale as Dio retrieved the phone and handed it to Tree, who hit redial.

Voicemail.

"G, hey man, it's Mal. Trying to get you. Hit me back as soon as you get this. It's important."

He ended the call, the air sailing out of him, his shoulders deflating.

What now?

"I guess your boy ain't gonna get you out of this one." Tree shoved the phone back into his pocket.

Kim.

"Wait. Wait. Let me try his wife. Kim. She can track him down."

Steam seemed to push out of Tree's ears as he jerked backward, the infernal pacing that apparently soothed him seizing him once more.

They all watched him tramp around the room, muttering unintelligibly, another tic that appeared to quiet his frenzied train of thought. Cookie and Dio cut their eyes between Tree and Malcolm.

"All right." He came to a sudden stop. "Call and find out where her old man is."

Malcolm let out another breath.

Okay. Back in business.

"What's her name again?"

"Kim."

"Hmm. Kim." Tree kept his gaze pinned on him as he had Malcolm unlock the phone again before going in search of her number, his eyes razor-blade slits. "You better not call her nothing different, Kimberly or nothing like that. No trying to give her clues, nothing."

Malcolm nodded, his heart booming relentlessly against his chest. "Right."

"Saw that in a movie once," he said, chuckling as he looked over at Cookie and Dio. "See, you got to think about all the angles. Think ahead."

"You so smart, baby," Cookie cooed.

The phone trilled repeatedly.

"Hey, it's Kim, just—"

Take the phone. Leave her a message. Try to hit the panic button.

Malcolm grabbed the phone, turning his back on a fuming Tree as he stepped slightly away from a confused Cookie, who inched closer to him.

He only had a few seconds. If that.

"Hey, Kim, it's Malcolm." Cookie was next to him now, trying to get in front of him. He kept turning his back, dodging her. He caught a glimpse of Tree from the corner of his eye rushing toward him.

One second.

Stall, stall, stall.

He quickly pulled down his home screen, his eyes searching for the panic button, his back still turned as he continued to evade both Tree and Cookie, Dio still standing dumbly to the side, furiously scratching his forearm. "Kim, I was calling because I'm trying to catch up with Garvin. I need to talk to him. Now."

The button. Right there.

Got it.

He tapped the big red panic button, quickly, deftly, surreptitiously. The panic button would activate against the home alarm. The alarm company would call the police.

It would be over.

"Anyway, uh, like I said, trying to reach Garvin. It's important. Have him call me as soon as you get this."

He ended the call just as Tree came around to face him, menace smeared across his features, the gun, as always, pointed at him. "What the fuck you think you doing?" Tree asked, his voice low. Menacing.

"You want the money, Tree?"

The boy's jaw cranked beneath his skin, his lip curled into a snarl of frustration. He said nothing.

"Right. Then we do it my way," Malcolm said.

"You better be careful, Mally Mal," Tree finally said, his voice that same quiet, steady rumble. "Don't go thinking you running the show or nothing."

Another lightbulb exploded over Malcolm's head. A backup play if the other backups didn't work. "Hold on. I've got one more idea. My accountant. I'll call my accountant—"

Tree wrenched the phone out of Malcolm's bad hand, shoving it in his back pocket. "No. We ain't calling nobody else. I'm done with this shit. No more games." The agitated pacing resumed. "Got me out here fucking around with all this shit, wasting my damn time." Tree continued to mumble to himself, his stalking around the room growing more frantic with each step.

"Look, man, my accountant can have the money here—"

The gun came out again, pressing hard against his chest. Malcolm's hands went up, the blood booming in his ears.

"I said," Tree hissed, "I ain't fucking with nobody else no more. You feel me?"

"Hey, baby," Cookie said in a shaky voice.

"What?"

"I'm hungry."

Tree cocked his head, the gun still aimed at Malcolm. "Huh. Yeah. Matter of fact, I'm getting pretty hungry, too. What you got to eat in there, Mally Mal?"

"Whatever you want."

The prospect of food seemed to lift the boy out of his bad mood. Tree snapped his head in Dio's direction. "Yo. Go upstairs and get Wifey and Ol' Girl. Bring them down here to cook us up something."

Malcolm took a sharp inhale as he snuck a glance at his watch.

Garvin would call him back.

The police would come.

Everything would be fine.

1:30 P.M.

So now they wanted to be fed.

Blair had watched warily as Cookie and Dio had returned to untie her and Farrah, shoving them down the stairs toward the kitchen. Tree had his gun pointed at Malcolm. Blair and Farrah clutched each other and headed into the kitchen. Her eyes swept the counter looking for her phone.

Right there where she left it.

She tensed as she tried to calculate how fast she could get to it without any of them seeing her. It was a few feet away, if that.

She loosened her grip on Farrah and took a tentative step in the direction of the phone. She looked up to see Dio's eyes flick down at the counter before locking eyes with her. He shook his head before he walked calmly toward the phone and picked it up. She watched helplessly as he nudged Tree and handed it to him. Tree smiled and looked at it before dropping it to the floor and smashing it beneath his heel, causing them all to jump.

"Wow." Cookie's face lit up as she ran toward the glass refrigerator, designed as a walk-in unit, and flung the door open. "This is nice."

"Take whatever you want," Blair said in a dull voice. She didn't know how much longer she could keep this up, her nerves pulled tight, Farrah's queries about *why them* creeping back into her thoughts.

"What's in there?" Tree asked.

Before she could respond, he marched across the room and pushed her out of the way, taking his own inventory of the wicker baskets brimming with fresh fruits and vegetables, blocks of cheese, loaves of bread sealed inside stiff cellophane bags, and the neatly labeled acrylic containers of condiments and premade meals. He pawed through the baskets, yanking lids off containers, his distress growing with each discovery.

"Man, what the hell is this shit?" he yelled as he tossed the containers to the floor, food splattering against the tile, the hard plastic smacking against the floor like bombs detonating. He grabbed the carefully wrapped packages of meats and vegetables and slamming those to the floor, too.

"What do you mean, what is it?" Blair asked, perturbed. "What does it look like?"

"This ain't no motherfuckin' food, I'll tell you that. This ain't nothing but some damn vegetables." He looked at Malcolm. "Man, you eat this shit?"

Blair pressed her palms together and held them against her mouth. "Look, I can make you whatever you want."

"You trying to poison me or something?" Tree demanded, seizing Blair's arms.

Malcolm leapt across the room, but Dio was quicker. He pulled his gun and aimed it for Farrah's head, stopping Malcolm's advance.

"Don't do it," he said. "I'll take her out with one shot."

"Watch it, Tree," Malcolm said. "Don't do anything stupid."

"Please," Blair whispered. She could hear her barely contained composure ripping apart at the seams, her normally fiery temper nothing but embers. "Please. Whatever you want. I'll make you whatever you want."

Tree pushed Blair back, her hip bone banging against the island. She resisted rubbing it as she watched him pace again. He came to a dead stop before he whirled around, his gaze focused on Dio.

"I want you and Wifey to go to the grocery store." He resumed his pacing, as though it helped him to talk and think at the same time.

"Let me go to the store instead," Malcolm said. "My wife and daughter can stay here."

"I don't want you to go to the store. I want you to stay here. Keep my eye on you," Tree said.

"It's okay, Malcolm, really."

"BJ," Malcolm hissed, his head wobbling on his spine in disbelief. "Bla—"

"Malcolm, please," Blair whispered.

"Load that cart up with some real food. Get me some of them, uh frozen pizzas I like—"

"GeeGee's," Cookie said.

"Yeah, GeeGee's frozen pizzas, some chips, some grape soda, some donuts. You clean that bitch out." He flicked a glance over at Blair. "And get you whatever else you want."

Blair pursed her lips in an attempt to keep the terror clawing at her organs from slipping out.

"You staying here?" Dio asked as he lowered his gun away from Farrah's temple, and she breathed an audible sigh of relief.

"Me and Cookie gonna keep an eye on things. You text me when you get there, text me when you on the way back, you got it?"

"All right."

Tree shoved Blair toward his accomplice, who reached out to catch her, gripping her elbows. She pulled away from him, trying once again to stay calm.

"I need money," she whispered. "My credit card is in my wallet upstairs."

"Go upstairs with Wifey," Tree said.

Dio gripped Blair's arm, shoving her in the direction of the living room. Tree jumped in front of them, all three of them colliding.

"You don't try anything on my boy while you're gone. No trying to signal to nobody, no trying to get the cops. Anything happens to him, something's gonna happen to your girl and your old man. You got me?"

Blair nodded. "I understand."

He grinned, continuing to stare at her. Finally, he stepped aside to let them pass and she and Dio headed upstairs. Blair retrieved her keys and purse seconds before Dio clamped his hand around her arm and hustled her out into the hallway and toward the staircase, his fingers digging into her skin.

"We have to go through the kitchen," she said.

He shoved her in that direction, where Tree and Cookie were wrapping duct tape around Malcolm and Farrah's wrists. Blair shot Malcolm a beseeching look and he flashed her a tight, small smile in return. Her heart plunged at the sight of her daughter, the corners of her mouth drooping, tears staining her cheeks. She could only mouth, "love" to them both before Dio seized her arm and pushed down on the handle of the door, which refused to open for him.

"What the—" He repeatedly pushed down on the stubborn handle, his ire seeming to grow with each repetition.

"It's the—" Blair's hands flew to the electronic keypad affixed to the handle and she punched in the access code, the little green light granting them access. "It's a security measure, so no one can get into the house through the—"

Dio pushed her through the door, not caring to hear the rest of her explanation about the keypad. The door beeped softly as it slid shut. She fumbled with her keys as she tried to deactivate the alarm on her Range Rover and unlock it. Dio stood next to the passenger door, his eyes boring a hole into her.

"What's the problem?" he asked as he peered at her over the roof of the car.

"Nothing, nothing. I've got it, I've—" The reassuring click of the doors unlocking calmed her for a few seconds as she slid behind the wheel, trying not to flinch as he folded his long frame into the passenger seat beside her. Now confined inside this tiny, hushed space, her breath seemed to thunder against the plush interior. The rank smell of his body intensified. The jangle of the keys, the rustle of his jeans and t-shirt across the supple leather seat crashed against her ears.

She dropped her purse on the floor behind her and started the car. Malcolm had parked the Mercedes in the same spot, leaving her free to back out of her own space. As she pulled out of the long driveway, Blair's eyes jumped from house to house, straining past half-open curtains, searching for a front door magically opening, someone she could wave to, someone who would see this kid sitting next to her, wonder who he was, and think something just didn't seem right. Hell, she'd even settle for one of Felice's unwelcome drop-in's.

Would anyone's cameras be capturing this? Malcolm mentioning their own glitching cameras had irritated her. It wasn't that she didn't take it seriously. These things didn't bother her the way they did him. All these years living in Highland Park, they'd never even had so much as a newspaper stolen.

It wasn't a priority.

"Hey. Hey!" Dio yelled at Blair as he jerked the steering wheel toward him. She snapped to attention as she realized she'd almost hit the Wexlers' mailbox. She pressed her hand against her chest and took a few shallow breaths.

"Sorry," she said.

"You should keep your eyes on the road." He looked out the window.

Blair shifted in her seat, gripping the steering wheel while Dio drummed his fingertips against his kneecap and mouthed song lyrics to himself, despite no radio playing.

This couldn't be happening. Was she really driving her captor to the grocery store to feed the beasts at her house? Was she really acting like everything was fine? Was she really this casual? Like she was out for a Sunday drive. Like they weren't under siege. Like she was on some lovely excursion.

Like she wasn't sure she'd live to see tomorrow.

PHONE CALL
SATURDAY, APRIL 1, 2:00 P.M., CT

Tree: Man ... I been trying to reach you all day. Where the hell you at?

Look, all right, since you didn't call me and tell me what you wanted because of Malcolm and Ol' Girl being here, I had to change the plan. Had to change everything. And since you ain't call me back, you can't get mad about nothing.

(Silence) So, okay, I'm just letting you know, I'm gonna have to do things my way.

SEPARATE LIVES

Willie Dalton: Retirement is hard. You're desperate to fill the time. It's like a demon chasing you.

Bob Boswell: You see this all the time with pro athletes when they retire. On Friday, you know what your job is. Score touchdowns. Kick field goals. Run drills. Go to practice. Fly here. Fly there. And then on Monday, you literally have no idea what you're supposed to do all day. It hits you like the hard, cold brick that it is. That clock just keeps marching on. Those calendar pages keep turning. The boredom. The silence. That's what drags them down into the abyss. How are you going to fill that time? What are you going to do all day?

What are you going to do with the rest of your life?

Alex Martinez: Malcolm was one of those guys who had like twenty things lined up for when the end of his career came. Broadcasting, endorsements, speeches, business deals, appearances. The type of obligations that go along with being a former superstar football player and future Hall-of-Famer. He was always on the road, even in the off-season, always gone. He wasn't waiting around for the moss to start growing.

Bridget Johnson: Except the husband being gone all the time, not great for a marriage. It was hard on my sister. Brutal. Definitely not the happily-ever-after she had in mind.

Lani Jacobs: At first, Blair went everywhere with him. Every game, every event, every everything. Those professional athletes, you know they want you with them all the time. Your time is their time. For a while, she was up for it, wanted to be with him. But you can't keep that up forever. She'd spent all those years going all over the world with Captivate and I think she wanted a break and stay in one place. Put down roots. So, Malcolm bought her a house.

Bridget Johnson: He figured that would keep her occupied. Except my sister didn't have any idea how to decorate a house or run a household. No clue.

Lani Jacobs: So, now she's out here in Highland Park, by herself, no husband, no—all her friends were the football wives and they weren't around. Their husbands are still playing. The Captivate girls were busy doing their own thing. And she was miserable. Absolutely miserable. She didn't even know how to drive. Didn't even have a license!

Elena York: Blair wasn't a particularly ambitious person. She kind of stumbled into the whole singing career thing, but it wasn't something she'd dreamed about her whole life or anything. She really became a success with Captivate by accident, not because she wanted it necessarily, but because it fell in her lap.

Isabelle Ryan: Blair was task-oriented. Give her a job to do and she would give it her all. So, while she wasn't a go-getter or all that proactive, she was an incredibly hard worker, which is why she did so well with the singing group. Learn these dance steps, put on this costume, sing this song and boom, she's going to hit it out of the park. But once she didn't have anyone to tell her what to do or where to go, she floundered.

Elena York: For most people, this would be a real opportunity to cultivate all of the interests you never had time to pursue, but quite simply, Blair didn't have that kind of drive, didn't have those passions.

Lani Jacobs: She'd go grocery shopping practically every day because she thought that's what she was supposed to do, even though she had no idea how to cook anything. She'd wander around the mall all day but never buy anything. She'd jog to the city early in the morning and then walk home—a four-and-a-half-hour walk—because it killed time.

Bridget Johnson: The worst part about that time, though? The women. Malcolm was such a player when my sister met him. I mean, he had the *worst* reputation. Don't get me wrong—I love Malcolm, but he was a dog. There'd always been tabloid stories about him, but after they got married, they escalated. Like through the roof. He was having an affair with this one, spotted coming out of a club with that one. Paternity suits. Women coming up to my sister on the street or at a restaurant, ringing the doorbell, holding babies they claimed belonged to Malcolm. Sending my sister pictures and letters—panties, used condoms, you name it. Going on talk shows, selling stories, accusing him of all kinds of stuff. It was relentless.

Ricky Gilbert, Malcolm's Brother: Yeah, my brother ... he could be messy back in the day. But once he and Blair got together? That all stopped. Cold. It was all noise. No truth to any of it whatsoever.

Lani Jacobs: Well, he was gone all that time, so that didn't help matters. All she could do was imagine the worst. The most dangerous thing in the world is a woman with an overly active imagination and all the time in the world.

Bridget Johnson: I told her to divorce him. To me, it just wasn't worth all the drama.

Skye Stafford: Because so much about this case was so strange, one of the angles police pursued was the possibility the family had been targeted by a long-lost illegitimate child of Malcolm's out for revenge, or orchestrated by a past spurned lover.

Elena York: There was one woman in particular, Laurie Sanders, who was especially vocal in the media about what she claimed was a long-term affair with Malcolm. She'd bombard the couple with e-mails, phone calls—send her panties in the mail to Blair, stuff like that. Eventually, they had to take out a restraining order against her.

Bridget Johnson: All of this took a devastating toll on my sister. And so ... she lashed out.

Isabelle Ryan: Why do women have affairs? A variety of reasons, but in Blair's case, it was a mix of boredom, neglect, and rage. A potent combination.

Lani Jacobs: Sure, I think that's why she did it. To send him a message.

Bridget Johnson: She saw a flyer at the grocery store one day about cooking classes. That's how it started. A cooking class.

1:45 P.M.

Blair snuck a quick glance at her passenger—her jailer—wondering if she should try to get him talking, work him in some way to get him on her side, play him against the ringleader.

She didn't have a clue how to do that, though. She couldn't even wrack her brain for some book or movie she'd seen for a reference. She avoided those types of movies like a fungus. She didn't like scary movies of any kind. No car chases, no running through the dark woods to elude a knife-wielding maniac. No mind-bending psychological thriller with a twist at the end. No blood. Nothing that would invoke tossing and turning at night. Nothing that would wake her from a fevered sleep, sending her scurrying around the house in search of locked doors and intact window panes. Nothing she'd have to watch through splayed fingers, crouched in the corner, the thumping of her heart only slightly less audible than the foreboding music or piercing screams on the screen.

Instead, she reveled in bubbly romantic comedies. Frothy confections with gentle, hokey laughs and sunny, storybook endings. She'd probably seen every Hallmark movie ever made at least ten times. As a kid, she'd save her little pennies for the movies every Saturday and watch whatever comedy was on the bill, the sillier the better. Anything to make her laugh, anything to make her feel good. Anything to escape that apartment.

Those kinds of movies agitated Farrah. "Schmaltz," she called them. "God, Mom, are you watching that drippy dippy crap again? Where's the schmaltz police?" she would say, rolling her eyes and groaning. "How can you stand it?"

Blair would always laugh at Farrah saying something like "schmaltz." The privilege of growing up in Highland Park. You didn't hear words like that in the Bronx. Not the crumbling corner of the Bronx she'd grown up on, anyway. And yet, Blair would laugh, embarrassed, charmed by her daughter, proclaiming how cute she thought her fluffy little movies were, despite their cheesiness. The corny cheesiness was exactly what she loved. Then they would dissolve into giggles and Blair would pull her daughter down on the couch to force her to watch, though Farrah's squirming and cynicism would soon send her bolting from the room in search of something comforting on her iPhone. A true crime podcast. One of Sondra Ellis's grim and gritty documentaries. Old episodes of *Girls*. *Insecure*. Nirvana's *Nevermind*, a discovery her freshman year of high school that ignited what Farrah laughingly referred to as her angsty-black-teen-trapped-in-white-suburbia years.

Tears ballooned inside Blair at the thought of her daughter. In an instant, she appeared like a mirage in front of her. She'd never tell anyone this, but she was so glad Farrah looked like her. The dewy dark bronze cheeks, often flushed with excitement, blooming with health, happiness, and love. So unlike the façade of her own adolescence—the perpetually growling stomach and worn clothes patched together with stolen masking tape and safety pins. The girl's glittering, wide-set eyes, one light brown, one hazel. The rubber band limbs and spuds for breasts. The long, lush blue-black ringlets, typically tumbling out of a fraying ponytail holder. The high swell of her bottom, the dimple of her chin and playful curve of her thin lips stretched into a megawatt smile, marred only by the crooked front tooth stubbornly hugging its straight mate. The one ear studded with a row of hoops, the other adorned with a single silver stick earring.

And her laughter. Farrah's laughter. Light and infectious. Blair so desperately wanted to hear those sparkling notes again.

Which meant she had to try.

Blair cleared her throat to catch Dio's attention. He didn't budge.

"So, how old are you?" she asked.

He gave her a lazy glance. "Twenty-three. Be twenty-four next month."

Blair grabbed the pendant of her necklace and rubbed it. "Any special plans for your birthday?"

Dio laughed, a heyna-like cackle that made her flinch. "Do I have special plans for my birthday?" he asked, imitating her. "What?"

"Look, I just meant—"

"What, you mean, like a party or something?"

"I guess—yeah. A party."

"There ain't gonna be no candles on a cake. Nobody singing me 'Happy Birthday.' Nobody bringing me no presents—nothing." He sniffed and looked back out the window. "It's just another day."

They sank back into silence. The turn for the grocery store was at the next light. There was another store a few miles away and she wondered if she should go there instead. He wouldn't know the difference. Of course, if she went to her regular store, maybe someone would recognize her, think it was strange she was back the next day—and with someone she'd never been in with before. Her grocery schedule was like clockwork. Malcolm had never been to the store with her. He wouldn't know the first thing about grocery shopping. Farrah would come with her sometimes when she was home. Mostly, it was just her. Always her. Someone had to see something. Notice something was wrong.

The choice was clear. They would go to this grocery store and she would have to hope she was able to signal to someone or someone would be alert to the oddity of this young man grocery shopping with her and not on her regular day.

Decision made, Blair pulled into the lot, bustling with people, cars, and carts, and parked near the front. This was the very reason she hated going on Saturdays. Then again, the odds of running into someone she knew shot to the top of the charts. A neighbor. An acquaintance.

Someone.

She slung her purse over her shoulder, holding it close, scanning for eyes, lips, strands of hair, someone familiar. Dio walked in step with her, hands shoved into his pockets, he, too looking around.

The doors slid open and Blair grabbed a cart. She glanced over her shoulder at Dio. His mouth had dropped into an 'O,' his head rotating around at the sights, lights, and sounds.

"Damn." He let out a low whistle. "This like Disneyland or something. This where you buy your food?"

"Yeah." Blair shrugged, her head swiveling slowly, scanning, still coming up empty. "It's nothing special. Just a regular old grocery store."

"This ain't like no grocery store I've ever seen."

She didn't answer, still distracted by the hunt for a familiar face.

"We got a corner store and a gas station a little further up," he continued, either not realizing she hasn't responded, or not caring. "That's where we buy our groceries. Every few months, Mama gets on the bus—two buses actually—to go to the big grocery store, which ain't even nowhere near as nice as this. Ain't no five minute drive, neither. Two hours there and back. She got to save up a little extra, 'cause it's expensive as hell and all of us got to go with her to help carry the bags and—" He shook his head again. "This? This is something else."

Blair chewed on her bottom lip as she steered the cart toward the bakery section. "That's how it was with me, too."

"What do you mean?"

"I'm from the Bronx."

"Get the hell out of here—you—you from New York? Miss Mansion? Miss Highland Park? The Bronx? Boogie down Bronx?"

"South Bronx." She felt her feet slide onto solid ground, wondering why she hadn't thought to make this connection before. Probably because she liked to forget. "Mott Haven."

"What's that, Mott Haven?"

"The PJ's. Projects. You know."

"The projects? You? You grew up in the projects? The hood?"

"Until I was eighteen."

"Man, I would have never, *ever* guessed that about you, miss. Not in about a million and a half years. I thought you was gonna tell me you grew up in some mansion or something."

"Oh no. Not me. No, my husband grew up in a mansion in Malibu. Right on the ocean."

"Damn." He cocked his head toward her. "But for real, you really from the Bronx?"

"Like I said, born and raised." Blair paused, amused that her accent, the one that had smoothed out from traveling the world and twenty years surrounded by Midwestern twang, had crept in during this little exchange. Like knew like.

Maybe if he knew she was like him, she could use it to her advantage.

"It was just my mom and my sister. I never knew my father. I don't know if me and Bridget even have the same father. Ma wouldn't ever tell us. Anyway, she raised us on her own. If you could call it that. Sometimes, it's like she was the kid. It was the three of us in that little one-bedroom apartment. Well, us and the roaches—"

"You ain't never lyin' about that, miss." He chuckled. "Roaches."

"Ma had the bedroom and Bridget—that's my sister—me and Bridget, we shared a pullout in the living room until I was eighteen. But yeah, we used to get our groceries at the bodega."

"Bo who? Bodega? What's that?"

"It's like the corner store. You know you go for like your milk, your bread, your cereal, your cigarettes. Your groceries. Bodega."

Dio rubbed the back of his head. "Oh. I ain't ever heard of no bodega."

"It's a New York thing." Blair looked around, her frustration rising in tandem with her fear, yet proud of herself for not showing it. Maybe there was hope for her after all. "I can remember the first time I was ever in a grocery store like this. I thought it was like Candyland or something. It didn't smell like incense or—"

He erupted into laughter, holding his hand over his mouth, tagging Blair on the shoulder like they were old buddies. "Right? Right? Man, the corner store stays smelling like incense. Worst damn thing you ever smelled."

She pursed her lips to keep from gagging as another whiff of his BO sailed past her, the irony clearly lost on him. "Oh, I know, I know. It's nasty, huh?" Blair looked down, scoffing to herself. "Yeah, you come into a regular grocery store and it's clean. Smells nice, right? All the food is fresh. You know nothing's moldy or black or whatever. And there's a lot of it, you know? You don't have to choose from just three kinds of cereal. There's thirty."

"Man, I wouldn't know what to do with thirty kinds of cereal."

Blair twisted her wedding ring around. "We can go. To the cereal aisle, I mean. Whatever you like. Whatever you want."

His face lit up. "Anything? Anything at all?"

"Sure." Blair swung the cart in the direction of the cereal aisle where a clerk was stocking the shelves.

"Hi," the genial young man said, smiling. His nametag instructed her to call him Urv. "Need help finding anything today?"

Blair opened her mouth, desperate to tell him that yes, she needed a SWAT team at her house. To say, "Yes, Urv, I need you to tackle this kid to the ground and hold him there while I escape." Dio gaped at the clerk, unaccustomed, it seemed, to common courtesy from a stranger. He flicked his eyes toward Blair, as if he knew what she was thinking.

"Naw, naw, man, we good," Dio said.

Blair chewed on her bottom lip, watching helplessly as the clerk smiled and turned his back on them to resume stocking cereal. Should she try to make a commotion and send an avalanche of cereal boxes to the floor and in the confusion, get word to the clerk she was in trouble? There likely wouldn't be enough time. Should she try to make a run for it? That wouldn't work either. He'd call those two back at the house before she ever ditched the cart.

She still had no choice. She had to play cool, play along, play her part.

"You wasn't lying about this cereal, though." Dio stood thunderstruck in front of the shelves brimming with multicolored boxes.

His awe quickly dissipated, swapped out for frenzy as he scooped up every sugary, chocolaty, artificially colored brand of breakfast candy in his eyesight: loops, balls, flakes, crunches, crackles, jacks, and clusters, dumping them gleefully into the basket.

The beast was unleashed. Having dipped his toe in, Dio was going for it. He sprinted through the store, the fingers of one hand firmly locked around the handle of the cart, the fingers of the other gripping her wrist as he dragged Blair behind him. She was surprised at how adept he was at maneuvering around shoppers with essentially one hand, bounding down aisles in search of everything he'd ever wanted but had always been denied. Cans of potato chips, TV dinners, crinkly plastic containers of bakery cookies, rivers of pop. Blair was dizzy from being jerked all over the store, the excited puppy dog inquiries if he could really get *this*, get *that* too. All the while she looked. Looked at the busy Saturday shoppers. Looked for a face that knew her. Looked for a face to be puzzled.

Something. Someone.

Dio placed four barrels of ice cream on top of the bulge of food inside the cart and stood back, satisfied with his handiwork.

"Man, we gonna be eatin' good tonight." He motioned to the cart. "Come on. Push it to the front."

Blair was silent as she pushed against the cart, skimming the lines and more importantly, the cashiers. These men and women—they knew her. She was here all the time. They didn't know Dio. One of them had to—

Wait.

That one.

The chubby woman with the bubble of orange hair, cherry red lipstick creeping over the edge of her full lips, the mole on her chin, three stubbly hairs sprouting from the middle. She'd just seen Blair yesterday morning. They talked. What was her name? She knew Blair. Always mentioned her by name. "Good morning, Mrs. Gilbert. How are you today? And how's your daughter? Oh, she's such a beautiful girl. I hope she's getting on well in college."

She was the one.

Blair steered her cart toward the woman's line, despite it being the longest. Dio tugged on her arm and pointed to another, shorter line.

"Not this one. Over here, where there's no line."

Before Blair could come up with an excuse as to why they couldn't do that, three other shoppers with teeming carts joined the line. She exhaled.

"We should stay in this one. You know, every time you switch lines, it stops moving."

He didn't say anything, just shoved his palms underneath his armpits and went still.

Blair's heart beat faster as they inched closer to the cashier. Dio grabbed a divider and began to throw groceries onto the conveyer belt. Blair half-heartedly helped him as she tried to make eye contact with the woman. *Come on, come on, come on.* Figure this out. She knew the types of groceries Blair bought—had commented on it countless times, inquiring about what organic, sugar-free, all-natural thing she was buying now, engaging her in conversation about the difference between steel cut oats and instant, almond flour versus wheat, whether it really was okay to use butter and not margarine. Blair unloading a cart of junk food would have to trigger a question, raise a red flag of some kind. She had to think it was odd, out of place.

Had to ask her about it. She was standing here with a weird kid in cheap, ripped-up clothes.

Pay attention. Notice something is wrong.

Which one of these is not like the other?

The customer in front of them loaded their bags into their cart and departed. Blair was now standing in front of the cashier. She licked her lips and smiled at the nametag.

"Irene. Hi. How are you today?" She'd never referred to the woman by name before. This would have to activate something.

"Oh, I'm doing all right." Irene smiled weakly as she grasped a bag of potato chips, the purple acrylic nails click-clacking against the scanner, her gaudy, green-tinged gold rings squelched by fleshy fingers. "Today's not my normal day and I'm not used to working on Saturdays. I don't care for it. Too busy."

"Right, right. You mentioned yesterday you normally don't work weekends. How come you're here today?"

"Oh, someone called off sick and they couldn't find anyone else to work, so I drew the short straw." She sighed. "At least it's a half shift, so that's something."

Blair watched Dio watch Irene scan the items, an odd intensity burning in his eyes, a smile tugging at the corner of his lips. She dragged her still-shaking fingers across her forehead, trying to catch the woman's eye.

Notice something is wrong, Irene.

"I remember you saying to me yesterday that you'll be having Sunday dinner with your family tomorrow. Are you cooking?"

"Hmm? Oh, no, I don't cook. God forbid anybody but my sister cook. Not that she's any good at it. Carries on like she's Julia Child or something."

"That's funny. Julia Child." Blair stole another glance at Dio, still entranced by the mountains of food sliding past him. She turned back toward Irene, leaning in a little. "It's so different in here on a Saturday. Since I usually come in on Friday. Yesterday."

"Uh huh." Irene frowned as she picked up a lumpy bag of frozen French fries and scanned them a few times, the price not registering. "Do you remember how much these were?"

"No, no I don't, but I could—"

"Oh, don't worry about it. I'll just charge you two-ninety-nine." Irene winked as she keyed in the price and swiped the bag across the scanner, ice crystals flying into the air. "Our little secret."

"That's very nice of you, Irene," Blair said. "I've always thought you were a really nice person. Every time I come to shop here, you've always been so nice to me, Irene."

Irene stopped scanning and looked up at Blair, a wide smile on her face. "Well, that is so nice of you to say, Mrs. Gilbert. You've just made my day."

Blair was about to say something else when a manager came over to inform Irene this was her last customer and to take her break. Blair's chest tightened and her heart somersaulted anew. She was running out of time. This might be her last chance to make a move of some kind. Any kind.

She opened her purse, digging around frantically, shooting Irene an embarrassed look. "Can't seem to find my wallet," she murmured. "I may have to run out to the car, see if it fell under the seat. Gosh. I hope I didn't leave it at home."

Blair flinched when Dio plunged his hand into her purse, extracting the slender Coach wallet she'd tried to push to the bottom. Without a word, he pressed it into her hand.

Defeated, Blair could only smile half-heartedly as she pulled it out and handed Irene her credit card. There was no chance the card would be declined. No chance she'd have to try a number of cards before one took. No calls to the credit card company to straighten out a misunderstanding. No chance for any other delays.

"Don't worry about it. Purses are black holes sometimes, aren't they?" Irene said.

Blair kneaded her forehead. "Yes. A big black hole."

The clerk bagging the groceries loaded the last of the sturdy brown paper bags into the cart. "Ma'am, would you like some help outside?"

"Naw, man, we got it. We cool," Dio said, stepping between Blair and the clerk. He motioned for her to take the cart and she obeyed. She glanced over her shoulder at Irene in one last vain effort.

All for nothing.

"Have a good day, Mrs. Gilbert," Irene called out as she departed her post and another cashier took over.

I expected better, Irene.

As they pushed the grocery cart through the parking lot toward the car, tears sprang to Blair's eyes and she blinked furiously to keep them from sliding down her cheeks, the fading sounds of the grocery store behind her making her heart sink.

THINGS FALL APART

Irene Tucker, Grocery Store Clerk: I didn't understand why she kept talking about "yesterday." Of course I remembered she had been in the day before, but I (sobs), I wasn't paying attention. Yes, I thought she was acting strange and it was weird that she was with someone—she came in with her daughter sometimes, but that was it. I —I just didn't understand what she was trying to tell me ... I will never forgive myself. Never.

Lieutenant Sharon Donahue: The family has panic buttons on their phones that's connected to their home security system, which would alert the security company to call the police. Farrah pressed hers, Malcolm managed to hit his. Unbeknownst to them, though, one of the panels in the system was malfunctioning, so no signal was ever sent.

Lieutenant Dimitri Cora: Surveillance footage outside the bank shows Malcolm Gilbert with a young man just before one p.m. About an hour or so later, Blair Gilbert is at the grocery store alongside another young man shopping.

Isabelle Ryan: Can you imagine grocery shopping in the middle of this nightmare? Unbelievable.

Zoey Patton, Friend of Farrah Gilbert: There was definitely a bizarre vibe happening at the house. The way Mrs. Gilbert was acting. Then there was that van parked out front, no logo or anything on the side. She said there was a lot going on, so I thought maybe there were workers at the house and that's why she was being so rude because she was dealing with that. (Shakes head). She was trying to get me out of there to keep me safe.

Lieutenant Sharon Donahue: So, now we've got Farrah Gilbert who's supposed to be at a party downtown with her friends, Blair who's missed a hair appointment, Malcolm who's missed a golf game, Blair and Malcolm both MIA from a charity event. CCTV footage of Malcolm, CCTV footage of Blair. Unanswered texts and phone calls. A series of strange phone calls. All of it painted an incredibly disturbing picture of a family in trouble.

Lieutenant Dimitri Cora: With cases like this, the trail either goes cold almost instantly and stays cold or it unravels real fast.

This case? It unraveled real fast.

5:45 P.M.

The walls vibrated with the thumping bass of a movie—something they'd found on one of the streaming services. A cinematic blight stuffed with fiery car crashes, booming gunshots, and indecipherable hip-hop screeching from the surround sound speakers every fifteen to thirty seconds. Their ashy feet lolled on the massive black leather ottoman. Gangly, foreign limbs reclined on the matching couch. Tree and Dio were higher than kites, having found Malcolm's stash during another search of the house for a safe with more money. Cookie curiously had abstained from the Grade A Kush, though she must have had a contact high. God knows Blair felt like she did. Maybe Malcolm would get one.

Blair's eyes jumped between Tree and Dio, skipped over to Cookie and back again, watching as they guffawed and screamed at the movie-theater screen built into the wall, jumping out of their seats to cheer the sneering, gun-toting, quip-spouting hero every time he blew holes into some well-deserving baddie's chest. Her skin itched as she looked around at the disaster of the room and worse, as images of her kitchen, stacked high with dishes, smeared with splatters, drips, and crumbs, floated through her head. The theater room was a morass of crusty plates smeared with pizza sauce, rubbery cheese, stalks of crust and crumbs, crumbs, crumbs everywhere. Empty bottles of pop. Crinkled wrappers smudged with sticky frosting. The remnants of her phone still scattered across the kitchen floor.

She'd come home to find Tree in his boxers, about to go for a swim. An excited Dio had stripped down to a pair of dingy white boxers to join him. Blair cringed at the thought of that kid in her pool, images of brown scum floating on top of the water flashing across her eyes. There wasn't enough chlorine in the world. But the biggest sin of all, was Fat Cookie, as she now decided to call her, parading around in one of Blair's bathing suits, rolls of flesh looking for escape through every possible opening. Blair took smug satisfaction that whenever Fat Cookie got where she was going (Prison? Yes, prison. This girl was headed to prison), she wouldn't be wearing any of Blair's bathing suits or dresses.

Okay, maybe she wasn't fat. She was short, though. Compact. Chubby. Perhaps that was the word. The girl was on the chubby side. Thick. A droopy stomach, chunky thighs, and high, round butt. She didn't have Blair's long lines.

Blair knew she was being bitchy and nasty by concentrating on this girl's weight, but she really didn't care. Being a bitchy and nasty grudgeholder was how she got by in life.

And so, after shoving the bags of food into the refrigerator and throwing the tubs of ice cream into the freezer, this terrible trio herded the family into the pool area, marveling at the skylight, the glass wall that disappeared into the ground below at the touch of a button. They stretched duct tape around Blair's wrists and put each Gilbert on opposing sides of the pool, before cannon balling into the water. Over and over, they plummeted, dunked, and belly-flopped into the pool, splashing mountainous waves of water at each other, playing Marco Polo an asinine number of times. All of this was in between Cookie and Tree sequestering themselves in one corner of the pool and making out while Dio pretended not to look.

After an hour, they remembered their supposed hunger and demanded Blair cook for them. She managed to sneak a few handfuls of Cheetos and two tiny squares of pizza to her daughter. Blair herself wasn't hungry. Even if she could eat, she wouldn't eat this garbage. Malcolm refused the hot dog she tried to give him. Apparently, he couldn't stomach anything either.

As she prepared the food, she tried not to look over her shoulder at the key ring holder fastened to the wall next to the garage door, the keys to all the cars hanging there like forbidden fruit. Tree had confiscated her purse and keys as soon as she walked in the door. Her phone was dust, obviously. None of them had seemed to notice the row of keys. If they could at least get into the garage with a set of keys, they'd be golden. The door would lock behind them, trapping the gang in the house. They wouldn't be able to get out of the front door either, since the handle wouldn't recognize any of their fingerprints. It didn't surprise her that Dio hadn't noticed that when she opened the door earlier for Zoey. They'd have to kick out a window to escape, which would take time and by then, the Gilberts would be long gone.

She pushed escape to the edge of her mind, letting it dangle there until she could figure out the best way to get it back on firm ground. In the meantime, she, Farrah, and Malcolm became a makeshift kitchen staff, forming an assembly line of sorts to satiate the bottomless pits of their captors' stomachs. Farrah shoveled frozen pizzas and TV dinners in and out of the two ovens in the kitchen, while Blair cooked. Cookie demanded Blair make her homemade French fries, thinly sliced, skins peeled, and double cheeseburgers with potato chips, pretzels, and Cheetos smashed between the stacks of bread and meat. Just so she could watch Blair do it while she pointed and laughed maniacally. Getting off on the power of her false empire in this odd space between absurdity and terror.

She could see Malcolm drooping, meaning the fog had descended, so she gave him the mindless, menial task of repeatedly filling glasses with ice and pop and cramming huge glass bowls with buttered microwave popcorn, sour cream and onion potato chips, and pretzels. Unbelievably, after inhaling the mounds of food, they wanted ice cream. Ice cream sundaes, to be exact. Rocky Road, strawberry, chocolate chip. Topped with whipped cream, chocolate sauce, and cherries. Blair couldn't scoop it into the bowls fast enough before like petulant, vicious children, their tongues, hands, loud voices, empty bowls, and licked-clean spoons commanded more, more, more.

Now, the six of them sat in the movie theater in the basement. Three people bound and gagged with electrical tape, wide-eyed, and petrified. Three people sprawled across the U-shaped black leather couch, two of them higher than high, watching a movie without a care in the world. Occasionally, Cookie nibbled on the bits of popcorn from the bottom of one of the glass bowls.

The Gilberts were lined up against the wall at the far end of the room. The vein in Malcolm's neck bulged fat as a welt. Farrah stared glassy-eyed at the movie, her head resting lightly on the wall behind her. Blair alternated between letting her eyes drift closed and rolling her head around in a vain effort to relieve the cricks settling into her neck joints. Their tormentors laughed at the movie, almost as if they forgot that a few feet away sat a family tied up and terrified.

Between the noise, the stench, and the fear, a monstrous headache simmered in Blair's temples. All she wanted was some aspirin, a cup of tea, the comfort of her soft white sheets scented in lavender, her down pillows, the shades drawn and these monsters to be on their way.

A car exploded on screen. The hero escaped, unscathed, to his sexpot girlfriend's immense relief.

And from somewhere deep in one of their pockets, a phone rang.

SECRETS AND LIES

Zane Ingram: I was teaching a cooking class for a little extra money—I was a part-time waiter and line cook, looking for a sous chef position and Blair was a student. When she started, she was a disaster. Her chicken would always be raw in the center and black on the outside. She would forget to defrost things, leave bones in fish. She couldn't get anything right.

I had no idea who she was, who she was married to—that she even *was* married. Not until later. She didn't wear a wedding ring. I found her mishaps in the kitchen funny. She did a lot of extra work outside of class and slowly, she got better. In fact, she got really good. We'd go for coffee after class, and she'd pick my brain about different techniques or recipe ideas she had. She was beautiful, of course, and charming. A little on the odd side, but people say that about me, so it was like finding a kindred spirit. This went on for a few weeks and you could feel the chemistry, that heat. Next thing you know, we're back at my crappy studio apartment.

I can honestly say, I fell in love with Blair. I thought we had a future together. She really encouraged my dreams and that I just had to keep trying to make a go of it in the restaurant business. (Smiles). I named my first restaurant after her. Bella. That's what I used to call her. Bella Blair.

And then one day, she just disappeared. This was back before cell phones, email. I finally got a phone number from the school and called her, but her husband answered. I was too shocked to say anything and hung up. I was devastated.

Bridget Johnson: I think Farrah might have been about seven when Blair told me Malcolm wasn't her father. Farrah ... When she was a kid, she was a klutz. Blair was pretty graceful and Malcolm of course, being an athlete, was light on his feet. We were at the park one day and Farrah was playing with some of the other kids and she tripped and fell like she always did. I made some offhand comment about wondering why she was always falling all over everything. And very quietly, Blair said it probably came from her father. I mean, I just stared at her, my jaw hanging open. And she told me that she'd had this affair with some guy she met at her cooking class and got pregnant.

Mitch Gilbert: Well, she had to tell him when she got pregnant, because Malcolm was sterile.

Nate Gilbert: That's what made all those paternity suits such a joke.

Skye Stafford: This was a bombshell when it came out during the investigation. A total game changer. People wondered, did Malcolm know? And what about the biological father? What's his possible role in all of this?

Terry Gilbert: My brother definitely wanted kids and they'd talked about adoption as one option. He didn't see it going down like this.

Nate Gilbert: He was devastated when she told him. A gut punch. He walked out on her. Told her the marriage was over.

Bridget Johnson: He wasn't there when Farrah was born. I think he arranged to be out of town for a game or something. It was all super convenient. I think the media at the time said he was stuck somewhere, "Desperately trying to get back for the birth of his daughter."

Mitch Gilbert: He visited Blair and Farrah at the hospital. I think the curiosity was too strong and the minute he saw her, he fell in love with that little girl.

Ricky Gilbert: I mean, my brother didn't want it *this* way, but he made the decision that Farrah was his daughter. End of story.

Zane Ingram, Farrah's Biological Father: About three years after the last time I saw Blair, I get a call from a lawyer informing me I have a daughter and it was highly suggested I sign away my parental rights for some crazy amount of money.

Bridget Johnson: Malcolm made the commitment to be that little girl's father. She may not have been his biologically and she may not have gotten here the way he wanted, but she was here and he loved her.

Zane Ingram: I didn't want the money. I mean, would millions of dollars have solved a lot of problems for me at that time? Yeah, of course. But truthfully, I wasn't in any position to raise a kid. I could barely take care of myself. I didn't take the money. My only condition was that I get to meet my daughter and that Blair talk to me, tell me what happened.

Bridget Johnson: After Zane signed away his parental rights, Malcolm officially adopted Farrah. His name was already on the birth certificate. He just wanted to be sure no one could ever take Farrah away from him.

Zane Ingram: Blair agreed to meet me at a park with the little girl —Farrah. She was beautiful. Looked just like her mother, something I'm sure Blair was relieved about. She apologized for how she handled everything, how she'd panicked when she found out she was pregnant and how she wanted to save her marriage. The only reason our affair wasn't a mistake was because of the baby. She told me she thought that's probably why we met—so I could give her this gift. We parted on good terms. I gave Farrah a teddy bear. I signed the termination papers the next day.

That was the last time I saw her or Blair. I'd Google them on occasion, that kind of thing. They seemed like a happy little family.

Elena York: Of course, Farrah's biological father became a suspect right away.

Lieutenant Dimitri Cora: We also had to consider that *Malcolm* was behind the whole thing, that this was some incredible ruse on his part and he was the one pulling the strings. All to get back at Blair.

5:45 P.M.

Everyone snapped to attention.

It was his phone. His ringtone. The current NFL theme song.

Garvin. For the love of God, please be Garvin.

Three sets of eyes popped wide and stared at each other, as though no one was sure what to do. Cookie was the first to make a move by pausing the movie, the only sound in the room now the pleading phone.

"Answer the phone, baby," Cookie said. "Or at least see who it is."

Tree shook his head vigorously seemingly to get his bearings from the double whammy of food and pot, and extracted the phone from his pocket, the ringing now amplified. Malcolm grunted, his voice muffled as he wriggled against his restraints and banged against the wall, trying to indicate to Tree to let him answer his damn phone.

Tree looked at the screen. "Who's *Phil?*"

Malcolm's shoulders wilted. In the next instant, his heart jolted. Phil Scali. Calling about tonight.

Who else would call him about tonight? Vince Adams? Jake Blardon? Lance Karr? All three men and their wives were supposed to be sitting at his table. He could hear the voicemail messages looping through his head, gentle bewilderment growing into panic morphing into irritation, settling into resignation. Malcolm had disappointed them. Malcolm hadn't kept his word. Since when? He'd never missed a dinner, a speech—hell, the opening of an envelope. If someone asked him to be there, he was there.

What about text messages? Had anyone been texting him? Probably. In fact, there were likely a trove of texts from Guy, Kip, and Don about today's golf game. Would somebody drop by, wondering what had happened? Or would they just chalk it up to him being a jerk? Never mind the fact that he hadn't missed a game in the seven years they'd been playing.

Malcolm never missed anything.

Who would miss him?

The police, the police. Where were the police? He'd hit the panic button ages ago. Where were the police? Something was wrong, something was wrong. The cameras. The cameras on the security system had been glitching. Was the whole system glitching? Damn it, damn it, damn it.

Now those other guys might not suspect anything ... but Phil ... *Phil.* He would keep calling. That guy. Persistent motherfucker. Had been since their days at UCLA. Wasn't the fastest guy, or the strongest, but he could *hit.* Like a Mack truck on speed. And when he wanted something, he was like a bulldog.

Come on, Phil. Keep dialing, man. Keep calling. Sound the damn alarm. Figure out that something's going on. Send the cavalry.

The phone stopped ringing and Tree stuffed it back in his pocket before motioning to Cookie. "Cut the movie back on."

"Maybe he should call Ol' Boy again," Dio said as he sat up and looked over at Tree with puppy dog eyes. "You know. About the money."

Tree seemed to mull this over. Without warning, he whipped his arm out and delivered a thunderous slap against Dio's ear. He yelped like a wounded dog and scurried away in anticipation of another blow. Out of the corner of his eye, Malcolm saw Blair and Farrah flinch. "I decide when *Malcolm* gets to make any phone calls. You got me?"

Dio opened his mouth to protest before letting it drop shut.

"Yeah, T," he mumbled. "I got you."

Dio continued to cower against the couch cushions, sniffing repeatedly. Malcolm thought he saw the glisten of a tear gliding down his cheek.

Except that boy's pain was of no consequence to him right now. He had, as his father would always say, bigger fish to fry.

The phone rang again.

Once again, everyone snapped up, all eyes on each other.

Tree looked at the phone.

"Think this might be Ol' Girl," he said. He paused the movie again and signaled to Dio to rip the tape from Malcolm's mouth. "Only thing you ask her is where her old man is at. That's it. You feel me?"

Malcolm didn't say anything, as he waited for Tree to hold the phone near his chin.

"Kim—"

"Hey, Malc—"

"I need to speak to Garvin—"

"Oh, he had to fly to Hong Kong at the last minute. Some emergency with an investor. His flight took off around noon."

Malcolm's heart toppled off the rollercoaster and smashed to the ground below as his eyes sank closed and he shook his head a little bit.

"Okay. But he's going to call you, right? Like later today or tonight? Like while he's waiting for his connection?"

"Hmm? Oh, no, this is a nonstop flight, so I won't hear from him until sometime late tomorrow night. You know it's fifteen hours."

Malcolm glanced at the trio. Tree fumed. Cookie looked annoyed. Dio trembled. "Okay, Kim, just—when you do talk to him, have him call me right away. Doesn't matter what time it is. As soon as he can."

"Malcolm, what on earth is going on?"

Tree motioned for him to wrap it up. "I have to go, Kim. Just—you need to have Garvin call me the first minute he can. It's important. I can't stress that enough."

"Wait. Is Blair on her way? I keep calling and it's going straight to voicemail—"

Tree abruptly ended the call and turned the phone off before he threw it down on the couch next to him.

"Since Ol' Boy's not coming through for you, Mally Mal, you won't be needing your phone this evening," he said as he resumed the movie.

Before he could answer, Dio slapped a fresh piece of duct tape across his mouth. Malcolm scowled, his frustrated sigh trapped against the sticky goo of adhesive. He dropped his head back against the wall and stared at the ceiling.

CLUES

Elena York: The house was just a trove of DNA. Fingerprints, hair, blood, fibers—clothing, even—spoons, forks, glasses, you name it, it was all over that house.

Anita Sanchez, the Gilberts' Housekeeper: I work for the Gilberts for ten, eleven years. Sometimes, I wonder why Mrs. Blair hire me (Laughs). She keep a very, very clean house. I think she clean before I get there (Laughs). But, Mrs. Blair, Mr. Malcolm, so nice. So, so nice. Mr. Malcolm, he always laughing and joking—he always say, "Good morning Anita-nita." "What's the good news today, Anita-nita?" (Laughs). And Mrs. Blair, sometimes she say, "Oh, don't worry about cleaning today, it's such a beautiful day. Let's sit on the beach, have a cup of coffee, watch the water." But she still pay me for full day. Very nice, very generous, very beautiful couple.

Skye Stafford: On Monday morning, the Gilbert's housekeeper, Anita Sanchez, came to the house at eight a.m. as she always did. The first thing she noticed was it was an absolute disaster, not at all how Blair Gilbert kept her kitchen. The second thing she noticed was the smell.

Anita Sanchez: I walk in, through the back, in the kitchen and the house is very, very dirty. Filthy. Like pig. Dishes stacked in the sink, food everywhere. The floor, it is very sticky. And the smell, oh my gosh, it smell terrible. I think I drop my keys, my purse, when I see this mess. I almost pass out. I couldn't believe it.

Elena York: At this point, Anita starts to call out for Blair Gilbert, kind of inching her way out of the kitchen into the rest of the house, because she doesn't know what's going on. Is there someone else in the house? Is she in danger?

Anita Sanchez: I start calling out, "Mrs. Blair, Mrs. Blair are you here? Are you here?" And nothing. She doesn't answer me. Now, I am a little scared, because I don't know what is going on, what am I going to find.

Skye Stafford: It was a pretty massive crime scene—it's a huge house, lots of rooms, lots of square footage. It took a while to process the scene and the DNA—it's not like on TV and the movies where you get the DNA back after the commercial break. Investigators knew it was going to take some time.

Lieutenant Dimitri Cora: Forensic evidence really told a story with this case. There were fingerprints all over the doorknobs, light switches, remote controls, silverware, plates, cups, and glasses. There were strands of hair on pillows, the couches. They ran through all of Malcolm Gilbert's medicinal marijuana, leaving DNA on the blunts. I mean everywhere you looked, there was DNA. It was like Christmas.

Elena York: In the meantime, a gift was dropped in investigators' laps.

Farrah decided she should try to make a run for it.

Clearly she hadn't made contact with the panic button after all. The cops wouldn't be coming.

There was a window in the bathroom upstairs, next to the kitchen. It was a small window, but she was tiny. She could probably wriggle through it.

Farrah did a mental scan of the neighbors houses. The Crandalls across the street, the Robinsons next door, the Wexlers on the other side. Her mom told her the Crandalls travelled a lot now that they were both retired. In fact, she had mentioned they were in some couples' travel club, where they went somewhere faraway and exotic every other month for weeks. So they probably weren't at home.

The Robinsons. They would probably be around. Even though it was Saturday night, they were older than her parents—like way older—so a quiet night at home was likely all they had going on. Dinner at four, followed by a night of Mr. Robinson dozing off and on in front of the

TV while Mrs. Robinson read a book or played solitaire or called a friend or their daughter or something.

The Wexlers. They could go either way. Mr. Wexler was a lawyer. Mrs. Wexler—Dr. Wexler—a plastic surgeon, so between working all the time and galas and dinners and stuff, they might not be home. Of course, they also had a lot of parties, so they *might* be home—and with a bunch of people around to boot.

The Robinsons were probably the best bet. They were the most likely to be home. And Mr. Robinson loved her dad—not that the other neighbors didn't—everyone loved her dad. The old man had told her over and over from the time she was five that her father was a national treasure. She overheard him say to another neighbor once that Malcolm was probably disappointed he didn't get a son to carry on the legacy and what a shame it was the Malcolm Gilbert football prowess would stop with him. Like that meant anything. You didn't see either of Michael Jordan's sons—or his daughter for that matter—breaking any basketball records. At least that was what Grandma Gilbert would always mumble when she'd read those stories or heard some announcer mention it in some offhand, poor-pitiful-Malcolm Gilbert way. Besides, she had like eight boy cousins who all played football, so nothing was dying. The Gilbert football dynasty would carry on. Mrs. Robinson, on the other hand, in her sing-song voice, would always want to know if she would grow up to be a singer like her mommy or a cheerleader for a football team. It used to bother Farrah until she learned to shrug it off. Two harmless old people with nothing better to do than say stupid shit followed by even stupider questions.

Either way, Mr. Robinson would love the idea that *he'd* been the one to save the Gilberts. Running to the Robinsons maybe wasn't the best idea, but it was the best she had.

Farrah banged her foot against the floor and grunted, squirming around as much as she could to get their captors' attention. The heads of both her parents whipped toward her, alarm stamped across what little she could see of their faces in the darkening room with all that tape over them—wide eyes, furrowed brows, heaving chests.

Tree ran his tongue along his bottom lip as he looked at her. Like she was meat or something. God, he was gross. He told Cookie to pause the movie before he flicked his chin toward Farrah.

"What you need, baby?"

Cookie shot him a confused look before narrowing her eyes at Farrah. She tried to avoid looking at her, focusing on Tree instead, since he was supposed to be the one in charge.

She moaned and whimpered, continuing to wiggle around. Tree stood up and walked over, standing over her with that same stupid grin on his face.

"T—" Cookie started.

"Shut up," he said, never looking in her direction. He bent down until he was eye level with her. He puckered up his lips in a mock kiss before laughing. Next to her, her mother's breath seemed to explode in a frenzy, and her father, sitting next to her mother, tried shifting closer to her, as though he might be able to reach across and stop Tree.

"Something I can do for you, baby?" he asked Farrah.

She bobbed her head in the direction of her crotch and banged her foot on the floor again, continuing to groan.

He reached up to her face and Farrah flinched, wanting to yank herself out of his touch. He laughed before falling silent, his gaze boring into her with an unsettling combination of desire and contempt. She hoped the disgust she felt wasn't evident as he cupped her cheek with his hand, running the cracked, dirty pads of his fingers across her cheekbone.

"Damn, you got soft skin," he murmured as he continued stroking her cheek. "I ain't never felt nothing so soft in my life."

Cookie flew across the room, her claws digging into Tree's shoulder. Shock flashed across his face and he turned around, grabbing her flailing arms.

"What are you doing?" she screamed. "Why you have to do that? Why?"

"Yo—get off me! Stop! Stop it!"

The two tussled for a few moments. Farrah's breath was heavy in her chest and the pounding in her heart was all she could feel and hear. She tried to stay still, afraid any movement on her part would either indicate interest, or telegraph her fear. She didn't see either one having a good outcome for her.

Tree got the upper hand, straddling Cookie before he slapped her a few times as she screeched and cried. Finally, he stood up and she rolled onto her side, cradling her cheek in her palm. Tree wiped his forehead with the back of his hand as he struggled to his feet.

"Stop all that noise and go somewhere," he said.

Cookie didn't say anything, crawling back in the direction of the couch, rocking back and forth and whimpering.

Her father grunted again and banged his own foot to get Tree's attention. Tree reached over and slapped Blair before he pointed a finger at Malcolm. Farrah's heart leapt and tears sprang to her eyes. She could see her father's shoulders tighten and the veins in his neck pop like massive clusters of blisters as he attempted to lunge toward Tree, stymied by his restraints.

"Shut up." He pointed a finger in Malcolm's face. "Stop all that noise. Me and Ol' Girl—what's your name?"

Farrah stared at him dumbly. Confusion flashed across his features for just a second before the leering returned. He let his hand slither across her face once more. Without warning, he ripped the tape from her mouth and she screamed, her skin burning. She clamped her mouth shut, determined to keep the tears in.

Determined not to let him see he terrified her.

"What's your name?" he repeated.

"Farrah," she said quietly.

"That's real pretty."

"Thank you."

"Sound like a fairy. Like a little fairy angel. You an angel, girl?"

"I'm just a girl," she said. "Nobody special."

"Oh, you're special. Yeah. 'Cause you real sweet and soft, just like an angel. I'm gonna call you that. My little Farrah Angel. You like that?"

"It's very nice, thank you," she said. Her throat burned, her mouth glue. Fear choked the words.

"Good job, Mommy and Daddy," he said to Malcolm and Blair as he clapped. "You all done real good, making this ... fine-ass girl." He looked her up and down one more time. "And then gave her a pretty name."

"Tree—" Cookie tried again as Malcolm and Blair grunted.

"I told you to shut up," he said, never looking in his girlfriend's direction, only focused on Farrah. "I'm trying to have a conversation. Now ... what did you want, little Farrah Angel?"

"I have to use the bathroom," she whispered. She cleared her throat and tried again, forcing more bravado into her voice than she felt. "I need to use the bathroom. Like really bad."

"What would you do if I made you hold it?" he asked, a grin spreading across his face. "You shit all over yourself? Pee your pants?"

"Please?"

"You let me watch?" he whispered. "Huh? You let me watch you go?"

She hoped he couldn't see the revulsion on her face. "I don't think I can."

He laughed, like it was the funniest thing he'd heard all day. Farrah gulped.

"Hmmm ... you probably right. I wouldn't want to make you nervous or nothing. Besides, that's kind of nasty, and I ain't no freak," he said, his voice still low, his gaze still on her. She could swear his hands were twitching, itching perhaps to touch her again.

"Can you help me stand up?" she asked, turning so her bound hands were out toward him. "Please?"

He didn't say anything for a moment before reaching out to pull Farrah to her feet, making a point to yank her harder than he needed to so she would fall into his arms. He snaked a hand around her waist, holding her to him until they were doing a bit of a dance. Farrah went stiff.

"I'm sorry. I don't know how much longer I can hold it."

He released her, begrudgingly, it seemed. He ran his thumb across his lower lip as he continued to survey her, his eyes traveling up and down her body several times in the space of a few minutes.

"That's all right, baby girl. We'll dance later. Malcolm, you ought to take a lesson from your little girl. See how polite she is? How she don't talk back? How she asks nicely for things? You should teach your daddy some damn manners. He don't know nothing about respect."

A shudder rumbled deep inside Farrah. She felt dirty. "I learned everything I know from both my parents. My father included."

Tree scoffed. "Take Ol' Girl to the bathroom," he said over his shoulder to Cookie. "Watch her every move—"

"You want me to watch her pee?" she asked, incredulous.

"Stand outside the door, all right?"

"Can you?" Farrah held up her hands to their captor again. "My hands? Please?"

He sniffed. "Cookie'll do it for you. Won't you, Cookie?"

Cookie struggled to her feet before slouching over to Farrah. Once she was standing next to her, her energy seemed to return and she seized Farrah's arm, digging her fingernails into her flesh. Farrah sucked in her breath and tried to twist away, but the girl held on.

"Hey!" Tree shouted. "You better be nice to her. Shit ... maybe you can learn some manners from her, too."

Cookie loosened her grip only slightly as Farrah turned toward the stairs as Tree restarted the movie.

"Which way?" Cookie asked.

"There's a bathroom on the first floor. Guest bath. Right off the kitchen."

She hoped her voice didn't betray her. There was a bathroom down here in the basement, tucked into a guest bedroom that they also didn't know about.

Except there was no window in that bathroom.

"Don't try nothing." Cookie sneered as she shoved Farrah in the direction of the stairs. She stole a glance at her parents, hoping to send them a signal, to let them know she was going to try. Cookie hustled her up the stairs before she could.

The two girls stumbled upstairs and Farrah flinched at the sight of the kitchen. It was like staring at a stranger's kitchen, all that crap everywhere. In fact, nothing about it felt like her house anymore.

And maybe not ever again.

"It's that one right there." Farrah pointed her hands in the direction of the bathroom door.

Without a word, Cookie tugged and yanked at the tape to try to unwind her hands. After several tries, Farrah reluctantly pointed to the knife block on the counter, hoping she wasn't about to make a colossal mistake.

"There's a pair of kitchen scissors in there. You could use those," she said.

Cookie snorted but obeyed and grabbed the scissors from the knife block, liberating Farrah's hands with one cut. Relief and release coursed through her. It felt so good not to have tape or a belt digging into her wrists, slicing into her skin with each rub, each movement. To be able to roll her arms around and to liberate the stiff joints.

Just as Farrah turned to rush into the bathroom, Cookie grabbed her, the sharp steel of the scissors hovering above Farrah's face. She wilted.

"Bitch, I thought you got the message earlier about staying away from T."

"I—what? No, no."

"I will cut you to the white meat you try and step to him."

Farrah swallowed, the glint from the scissors seeming to blind her. "I promise you, I'm not interested in him. At all."

Cookie snapped her gum, moving the scissors closer to Farrah's cheek. "You like girls or something?"

She stifled a laugh. If you could resist Tree's charms, it had to be because you were gay. What else could it be? Not that he was trash. Disgusting trash.

Cookie trailed the point of the scissors down the length of Farrah's cheekbone, the cold metal like ice against her skin. She stopped breathing, afraid that one move, one *half* quiver, would send those scissors plunging into her flesh. Blood squirting everywhere, pain igniting across her body, her nerve endings on fire.

"I asked you a question, little girl. I said, '"You like girls?"'"

"No." Farrah shook her head, flinching as the point of the scissors dented her cheek. "I have a boyfriend."

A lump rose in her throat at the thought of Eddie. She'd told him she'd call him this afternoon. Had he tried calling her? She had no idea what Dio had done with her phone after he took it this morning.

Cookie's breath bloomed out in front of her in a cloud of pepperoni pizza and strawberry ice cream. She retracted the scissors, a snarl on her face as she threw them on the counter and sniffed.

"Well if you going, go," she said, waving toward the bathroom.

Farrah edged away, afraid to take her eyes off Cookie, afraid if she turned, those scissors would find their way dead center into her back.

She rushed into the bathroom, opening the door just a fraction, not wanting Cookie to see the tiny sliver of light from the window, or glimpse the curtain. She slammed the door shut, locking it behind her.

Farrah surveyed the window. It was higher up on the wall than she remembered. And smaller. A little box of a window letting in a tiny ray of rapidly fading daylight. There was a possibility she would get stuck.

There was also the possibility she would slither through and make the short drop to the grass below with no problem.

She flung the lid of the toilet up, making sure it clanked against the tank, just in case Cookie could hear it. Her mother hated the toilet lid to be left up. She flipped on the fan, cocking her ear toward the door to ensure the girl wouldn't try to come barreling into the room, shattering her ruse. Quietly, she set the lid of the toilet back down and stepped onto it. Her foot wobbled a little on the shiny porcelain top and she reached for the latch on the window and tugged.

Stuck.

"Come on, come on, come on," Farrah chanted to herself as she pulled on it again, throwing her weight into it. The metal pinched her fingers and her joints cracked. Her foot slipped and she yelped as she held on to the ledge of the window to keep from toppling to the marble floor below.

Farrah took a deep breath and closed her eyes, mumbling inspirational mantras to herself about how she could do it and she wouldn't know if she could do it if she didn't try.

Daddy would be proud.

She attacked the latch again, grunting to herself as she played push/pull with the stubborn metal.

The hushed room exploded with Cookie's pounding. Farrah's foot almost slipped again as she gripped the ledge to keep upright.

"Hey! What the fuck you doin' in there? Hurry up!" Cookie's muffled screams were accompanied by even more furious hammering. The door rattled with the girl's fury and Farrah was certain it would fly off the hinges.

"I'm not done!" Farrah yelled. "Just give me a minute."

The jack hammering ceased and Farrah waited a second before turning back to the window latch. She pushed at it again, the tips of her fingers burning, threatening to snap off under the pressure. She squealed to herself when she felt some give, imploring the lock to go a little further. She pressed again. This time, the latch turned with a soft pop.

Farrah clamped her hand across her mouth to keep from squealing with happiness. She looked at the door before hooking her hands underneath the slender ridge of metal and tried to pull it up softly.

It didn't budge.

Farrah wiped sweat from her palms across the back of her boxer shorts and flexed her fingers. She took a deep breath and pushed again. With one big whoosh, the window snapped up and smacked the top before Farrah could stop it.

"Hey. Hey!" Cookie pummeled the door again. "What the fuck you doing in there?"

Farrah's head whipped toward the door. Would she run downstairs for Tree to come and blast the door open or would she try to do it herself?

Farrah jumped to the floor, flushing the toilet as she did. She swept the soap dispenser down with one swoop of her hand before turning on the faucet.

"I knocked something over. I'm washing my hands," Farrah called out.

"You got to come out right now!" Cookie screamed as she rattled the doorknob.

"Shit." Farrah bounded back up onto the toilet and pushed against the screen, her fingers scratching against the mesh as she tried to pop it out of the window. She punched against it, bending the flimsy net in half, and pushed it out. It landed with a soft *thunk* on the lush grass below.

Cookie had stopped pounding and rattling and was now throwing herself against the door, screaming her head off. Farrah hoisted herself up, her arms trembling as she poked her head outside, relishing for just a moment, the clean air, the warm evening wind. She grunted as she shimmied her way through the window, like a worm wiggling its way through the wormhole. The top of her thigh caught on the jagged handle of the window, digging into the soft flesh, tearing it open, marking time until it became a long, ugly scar to add to her collection of scratches, burns, and other ill-healed scrapes.

The ramming against the door had stopped, which likely meant Cookie had run downstairs for backup. Farrah looked down at the ground, took a deep breath and jumped. The grass tickled her bare ankles and the snap of crickets filled the evening air. She ignored the throbbing in her thigh and the stinging of her left foot from the minor impact of the fall, but almost instantly, she was up and running in the direction of the Robinsons' house, relieved when she could see the warm glow of a light emanating from the house. Just a few hundred feet.

She glanced over her shoulder to see the scrawny Dio easily slithering through the bathroom window. Lines of sweat trailed down her face as she whipped her head back around. The Robinsons' house was so close.

Behind her, his footsteps slapped against the grass, his breathing heavy. He was gaining on her.

Farrah opened her mouth to scream.

Just not fast enough.

Before she could force the sound out, the shout for help, his body collided with hers and he tackled her to the ground, stuffing his fist into her mouth.

She writhed beneath him, uselessly shrieking into his dirty, balled-up paw, saliva vibrating in her throat, her vocal chords scraped raw. Her arms and legs thrashed as she tried to brace her body to stay on the ground. Her eyes darted around her, searching the grass in vain, grasping for hope there was a stick or rock she could use as a weapon. The other wish was someone would have heard or seen something, which she knew was impossible. The price you paid for a tranquil little life in the suburbs was no prying eyes around when you actually wanted them.

Dio yanked Farrah up like a weed, dragging her back toward the house, her limbs flailing helplessly against him, one hand clamped across her mouth. She could see Cookie and Tree through the kitchen window, scurrying around for something to shatter the glass, unable to open the electronic lock on the door.

He pressed Farrah against the doorjamb and pointed to the handle.

"Open it," he said.

Farrah hesitated, her mind racing to come up with another escape plan.

He cocked his gun and pointed it at her cheek. "Open it!" he screamed.

With trembling fingers, Farrah quickly punched in the code and pushed against the upright metal lever. Immediately, Tree jerked her from Dio's grasp.

"What the fuck you think you, doin', huh?" he shouted, his eyes red with rage, spit flying from his mouth.

From downstairs, the screen still pounded with movie explosions, the bass thumping beneath her feet. Someone—Cookie probably—smacked the side of her head, causing her neck to snap sideways.

"Take your hands off me." Farrah squirmed, tears flooding her eyes. She continued to wriggle and flail, pushing her hands against the concrete of Tree's forearm around her waist.

"You trying to run away? Huh? You think you can get away from me?" he asked, grabbing her face. His finger slipped into her mouth and she bit down as hard as she could, certain her teeth would snap off.

He howled. She bit harder, ferocity surging through her until her mouth filled with the salty, unmistakable spice of blood.

"Got-dang!" He dropped her as he pulled his hand back, waving it around in the air before examining the wound. Cookie flew to his side, cooing over his injury.

Farrah whipped around to find Dio, on top of her as always. She faked right, then left and ran for the front door. Once again, he was too fast for her, clinching her around the waist. This time, he didn't bother trying to muffle her screams as he dragged her back to the kitchen.

Tree yanked her hair, pulling her head back. She trembled as his hot, wet breath misted against her cheek.

"You gonna pay for that, little girl," he said. "You gonna pay."

Before she knew it, she spit at him. The frothy white blob landed just to the left of his nose, most of the mass sliding down to his chin.

"Beat her ass, Tree. Beat her 'til she can't see straight," Cookie said.

After he wiped the spit with the back of his hand, Tree slapped her. Hard. For a moment everything went black before stars danced across the backs of her eyelids. The blows came over and over again. Farrah screamed, Tree cursed, and Cookie cheered. She didn't know what Dio was doing.

"Stop, please," Farrah panted, her arms useless against the rain of slaps against her face. "I'm sorry. I'm sorry I tried to run." She sobbed. Every part of her face stung with pain.

"Yeah, you about to be sorry. I'm about to show Mommy and Daddy what I do to bad little girls," Tree hissed, finally stopping his assault. He grabbed her arm and lugged her downstairs. Her face continued to burn and all she could do was whimper and continue to try and put the brakes on his forward momentum.

Her mother and father, their eyes wide, terrified, their restrained limbs kicking and writhing as they no doubt imagined the worst. Tree flung Farrah around to face her parents, their distressed, muffled grunts crowding against her ears. It was hard to discern tears from sweat on their faces.

"Take a real good look at your baby girl, Malcolm ... *Blair*. A real good look," he said. His fingers dug into her arm, breaking the skin. He withdrew his gun and pressed it to her temple, causing her to inhale sharply. Her parents shrieked, each attempting to wriggle closer to her.

"Please, please, I'm sorry, I'm sorry." Farrah gasped, sniveling now. "Please don't kill me."

He jostled her, and they swayed back and forth, the gun's cold metal barrel moving up and down and side to side against the throbbing vein of her head. She closed her eyes, tears and snot streaming down her face as she shrieked and begged for mercy. His staccato intake of breath matched her own.

This was the end.

"You know what?" Tree asked, seemingly more to himself than anyone else. Farrah's tears stopped, the breath she'd been holding released, only a little. "I bet I can come up with a real good way to teach this little girl a lesson. What you think, boo?"

"Yo, I bet you could put this bitch in her place quick. For real, though," Cookie snarled at Farrah.

"Mmm-mmm." He leaned closer, his face inches from hers. "It's like I keep telling your daddy. It's about respect. You disrespected me. Lied to me. Told me you needed to go to the little girls' room. Then you try and sneak outta here. Run away. Then you bite me. Naw. Naw. We can't go out like that. You gonna have to learn a lesson."

"Okay, Tree, I was wrong and I'm sorry—"

"Shut up!"

Farrah obeyed and fell silent, her chest heaving, silent tears continuing to fall. Her parents own ragged breaths raged behind her.

"Yo, Dio," Tree said. "Bring me that bowl."

"This one?" Dio asked, gesturing to the heavy glass bowl which had housed buttery microwave popcorn just a few hours earlier. All that remained now were shiny kernel husks and bottom-of-the-bag bits of popcorn.

"Yeah. That one."

Her eyes grew wide as she shook her head, attempting to run, knowing it was useless.

Dio dutifully brought the bowl over to his leader, who promptly turned it over, littering the floor with popcorn remnants. He pressed his palm against the inside bottom, gently bopping it up and down, as though he were testing its heft, getting a feel for it in his hand. He gripped Farrah's arm and twirled the bowl around the tips of his splayed fingers, like he was spinning a basketball.

Farrah heard her parents muffled screams behind her. Her own screams stopped dead in her throat.

In the second before it happened, she understood what Tree was about to do to her.

BIG BREAK

Lieutenant Dimitri Cora: Three, maybe four days later, we're still processing the scene and a woman walks into the station saying she has information vital to the case.

Lieutenant Sharon Donahue: Blair Gilbert was not known for being flashy, or over-the-top. Very low-key in her normal, everyday appearance. She wore hardly any makeup and very minimal jewelry.

Lani Jacobs: Well, she looked like a hobo most of the time (Laughs). I mean she had the labels and the jewelry and all of that, but she pretty much ran around in yoga pants and flip-flops. I mean, to look at her, you'd never know she had money.

Lieutenant Sharon Donahue: Except for this one piece.

Bridget Johnson: At some point, I'm not sure when, Malcolm designed this necklace for her. Absolutely stunning. My sister cherished this necklace. It was definitely the kind of thing that made you say, "I wish I had a necklace like that."

Lani Jacobs: Oh, it was a beautiful piece. Spectacular. When I think of Blair, I think of that necklace. She wore it all the time, never took it off.

Isabelle Ryan: It was a series of three infinity diamond circles, interconnected and stacked on top of each other. Each circle was engraved with their names, Farrah's date of birth, and Malcolm and Blair's wedding anniversary.

Lieutenant Sharon Donahue: This was a very distinctive piece, very one of a kind, very original. There was no way you could mistake it for something else or belonging to someone else. Everyone who knew Blair said this necklace was her signature piece of jewelry.

Lieutenant Dimitri Cora: This woman, she has the necklace.

Lieutenant Sharon Donahue: And then we had a name.

7:59 P.M.

Before she met Malcolm, Blair had never seen a football game. Not in person, not on TV. Monday Night Football did not dominate the grainy little black and white in their family of three girls. There'd been Friday night games during junior high and high school that she could have attended but never did. Hanging around football players was more Bridget's thing than hers. The first time Malcolm brought her to a game, she was straight up shocked. She had no idea of the brutality involved. Every time Malcolm was tackled by the opposing team, whenever he was wrestled to the ground, flung to the gridiron, pummeled like one of those tackling dummies, something broke inside of her, like the snap of raw spaghetti.

She took every hit with him.

As Tree slammed the heavy glass bowl into Farrah's face, watching her fall back without benefit of thrashing limbs, bent knees, without a scream or a noise, just straight down like one of those weighted clowns people used for punching—except she didn't pop back up, ready for more—something cracked inside of Blair.

Blair took the hit with her daughter.

The room erupted. Farrah lay on the ground, clutching her mouth with both hands, hysteria streaming from her lips, her face swathed in blood. She and Malcolm screamed as much as their gags allowed, knocking against the floor, desperately inching closer to their sobbing, writhing daughter. Cookie let out a stunned, "damn," before exploding into loud, wild laughter, hooting, hollering, jumping up and down, and pointing. Dio dropped to the ground, his face a mask of dumbfounded disbelief and shock, rocking back and forth, grasping his elbows with the opposite hand.

Tree just stood there, clutching the bowl, staring. The bowl slipped from his grip, thudding to the carpet. He shook his hand around, as though he were the one in agony. Blair's body vibrated with fury as she listened to him howl about his hand. She clenched her fists, twisting her wrists around, hoping to weaken and break the tape so she could claw his eyes out.

"Baby, I can't believe you did that," Cookie crowed. "Boom! Cold-cocked that bitch!"

"Damn!" Tree squeezed his hand several times and shook his head. "That hurt like a motherfucker."

"You okay, baby?" Cookie asked him.

Tree didn't answer her, but instead came over to stand in front of Blair. Farrah continued to lie on the floor, curled into a fetal ball, her shoulders shaking with silent tears. Malcolm knocked back against the wall, shaking his head and moaning. Blair looked up at this monster, hoping he could see the rage etched into her face.

"I'm gonna need you to fix me up, Wifey."

She shook her head, frantically pointing it toward Farrah.

He cupped Blair's face with his good hand and slammed her head against the wall behind her. She screeched as pain exploded across her head, the duct tape wet with tears and sweat. Stars danced across her eyes. She blinked several times to try to get her bearings.

"You wanna be next?" he asked. She could only cry. He snorted. "I thought so. You need to fix up my hand. It feels all messed up now."

She whimpered again, tapping her foot against the floor in Farrah's direction. Exasperated, he ripped the tape from her mouth. She grasped at the air, taking huge swallows. She bent over coughing and heaving.

"Fix up my hand, Wifey," he repeated.

"My daughter first," she said, wheezing.

"I said—"

"I heard you! I heard you the first five fucking times! Now, either I help my daughter or nobody gets help. Got it?"

He gripped her arm. "What did you say to me, Wifey? Huh? You talking back to me? Is that what you're doing?" He pulled out his gun and pointed it at her nose. "Say it again, *Blair*. Say it one more time."

She felt herself blanch, her breath now coming in smaller gasps. She looked at Malcolm from the corner of her eye. He shook his head slightly. She took a shaky inhale.

"I will fix your hand, but you have to let me take care of my daughter first." A fresh wave of tears burned behind her eyes. She willed them to stay put. "Please."

The claws of his fingers relaxed a little and he put his gun back in his waistband. "Well, since you asked so nice, Wifey, you can take Ol' Girl upstairs and fix her up. Fix her up, then you fix me up. Real nice."

"My husband, too."

Tree blinked. "What about him?"

"His hand. From earlier."

"Don't push your luck, Wifey. You lucky I'm letting you fix up Ol' Girl."

Outrage bubbled to the surface, clawing and scratching to get out and fight. She glanced at Farrah. Malcolm was tough. Farrah wasn't.

Numb, she stuck out her bound hands toward Tree. His eyes never leaving hers, he tugged at the corners of her restraints and the sound of ripping tape filled the room. Her heart galloped as her hands sprang free and she groaned as she rubbed at the gooey grooves of her wrists. She crawled over to Farrah and gently lifted her weeping baby into her arms. She rocked her for a moment, murmuring sweet nothing's into the girl's ear, her body shuddering with the uncontrollable sobs of pain and despair.

"Come on, baby, let me look at you. Let me see," Blair said, cupping Farrah's face in her hands. She winced at the shiny red streaks. The jagged, broken edge of one tooth. The black, pulpy gap where the other tooth should have been. A bulbous purple lip split in two, blood trickling from the crack. Blair swallowed hard and kissed her daughter's cheek.

"I'm going to take you upstairs, baby, okay? We're going upstairs and I'll take care of you. Just like I always have. Right?" A spurt of tears escaped her eyes. "Like when you had chicken pox. When you had bronchitis. When—remember, that time you fell off your bike and you scraped so much skin off your knees, you thought you would need new knees? Remember that?"

Blair's reminisces elicited a short, somber chuckle followed by a grimace.

"I remember," Farrah whispered, already lisping from the missing tooth.

"Mommy took care of you then, and she's going to take care of you now."

Without a word, Blair lifted Farrah up to stand and snaked her arms around the girl, who slumped against her. She ignored Tree, walking past him toward the staircase. She could hear him commanding Dio to help him hoist up Malcolm, as he wanted to keep an eye on him. Cookie sniffed repeatedly behind her and she wondered if the girl would try to shove or trip them as they all made their way upstairs.

The girl did neither, shuffling behind them as Blair practically carried Farrah first up to the ground level then to her bedroom. Tree and Dio sat Malcolm down on the same chair Blair had been in earlier, while Cookie gripped her arm, stopping her from advancing toward the bathroom. Tree leapt on top of the bed, bouncing up and down a few times, before sweeping the mass of decorative white, gray, and sea glass green pillows populating the top half of the bed to the floor, and reclined against the white padded leather headboard. He lay spread-eagle against the California King and did snow angels, laughing the entire time, the pain of his hand seemingly forgotten.

"You ever seen a bed this big, baby?" he asked Cookie.

"Naw, baby," she said. "I ain't never seen a bed this big."

He propped himself up on his elbows as he looked around the two-room suite. "Maybe I'll buy us a big bed like this when we get our money. Huh? What you think about that?"

"That sounds good, baby."

Cookie pushed Blair and Farrah into the bathroom. She heard Tree ask where the remote for the TV was and seconds later, sound packed the room.

Blair sat Farrah down on the toilet, then with quivering fingers tilted her daughter's wobbly face up to get a closer look at the damage. Mostly swelling. Blood everywhere. She had no way of knowing if her nose was broken, though given the balloon of it, it was a safe guess. A thin crimson trickle ran down her thigh courtesy of a deep scratch. The most severe visible injury was to the teeth. Save the crooked one, now gone forever, Farrah had been blessed with beautiful teeth. Ivory white, no cavities, or pesky wisdom teeth. She'd call Dr. Sueler on Monday to make an appointment for an emergency temporary until—

Monday. That was so far away. A good thirty or so hours from now.

Cookie perched herself on the far end of the counter as Blair pulled the giant brown bottle of hydrogen peroxide and the first aid kit down from the medicine cabinet. She grabbed a handful of cotton balls from her clear Plexiglas canister on the counter and opened the kit, moving the fat rolls of gauze to the side in search of the instant ice pack.

Her hands brushed across the scissors at the bottom.

Scissors.

She'd forgotten there were scissors in the first aid kit.

Blair glanced over at Cookie, who was picking at her nails, not paying attention. Blair pressed her lips into a thin line as she eased her hand into the kit, letting her fingers close around the hard plastic of the scissors.

Cookie was still looking down.

In one quick swoop, Blair grabbed the scissors and hid them behind her, quickly tucking them in the waistband of her workout pants. She adjusted the hem of her top to conceal them, before reaching back into the kit to retrieve the instant ice pack.

Cookie looked up briefly and flashed a bored look in their direction before letting her eyes drop once more to the infinitely more interesting show being put on by her cuticles.

This was good. The spandex would keep them snug against her back. No chance of them falling from a baggy waistband and clattering to the floor or poking a hole through pants pockets.

She'd just have to find the right time to use them.

Blair doused a cotton ball with peroxide and dabbed at Farrah's split lip. Her daughter winced and took a few deep, shuddering breaths.

"I'm sorry, baby. I'm so sorry," Blair whispered as she continued to dot Farrah's mouth and lips with peroxide.

"It's okay, Mom."

Cookie banged the back of her foot against the cabinets below, her eyes back on mother and daughter. She whistled softly between her teeth before lapsing into humming. Blair snuck a look at her. What she wouldn't give right now, right this instant, to jam those scissors anywhere into that girl's body.

"Yo, you almost done?" Cookie asked.

Blair turned on the faucet and ran a washcloth under the warm water. "Almost."

Cookie fell silent again and Blair gently wiped away the blood trailing from Farrah's nose and coating her cheeks. She finally turned her attention to the blood on Farrah's thigh, the long rip in the skin bubbling white when Blair dabbed it with peroxide.

"You got any more kids?" Cookie asked.

"No."

"Just Ol' Girl, huh?" Cookie resumed kicking the cabinet with the back of her shoe.

"Would you stop that?" Blair snapped.

"Bitch, I'll do whatever the hell I want to." However, she complied and looked at Farrah. "You remind me of my sister."

Farrah didn't respond, letting an equally silent Blair continue tending to her wounds.

"My sister try to act like she better than everybody, talking all proper."

"You shouldn't be mad because your sister wants to better herself," Blair murmured.

"You don't know nothing about her, so shut your damn mouth!" Cookie yelled before falling quiet again, her gaze drifting back to Farrah. "Anyway. All I know is, I ain't never going to be like my moms or my sister. I'm going to have a whole different life from them."

Blair looked away, uncomfortable, not really wanting to know anything about this troubled girl's home life. Not caring. She probably should have compassion for these monsters. They didn't come from the factory this way. She'd grown up with kids like these, poor kids scratching for every scrap of anything. She'd *been* that kid. The spawn of mothers, too addicted, too self-absorbed, too tired from working three jobs to care. Fathers either passed out drunk, high, or never around to begin with. Even if Blair was so inclined to empathize, because she knew, she *knew*—just like Cookie, she could have very easily been Bonnie to someone else's Clyde—it was out of her hands. Cookie was not her problem to fix.

She knew all about trying to fix problems.

That was how she thought of her mother. A problem to fix. Maybe if she could fix Bibi, wipe away all her troubles, she'd be happy. She'd act like a mother. The kind of mother she'd tried to be to Farrah. The way Bibi would hound her for money back when she first got into

Captivate. All hours of the day and night. Incessant phone calls, telegrams. Every time, Blair told herself *this time would be the time.* Her mother would be grateful.

The gratitude never came though. It only got worse after she and Malcolm got married. Charge accounts at stores, credit cards. A car and driver at her disposal. A penthouse apartment in Manhattan. If Blair was an ATM, Malcolm was the Fed.

And still, Blair waited for the gratitude.

Then the lung cancer diagnosis came. Blair insisted on moving her into the house, Bridget following not long after. Yes, Bibi was awful. Yes, leaving the woman to fend for herself against a savage illness was her first instinct. In spite of how revolting Bibi was, she was her mother. That's all Blair could say. She was her mother.

All of them in the house together. The longest two years of Blair's life. She lost count of how many times Malcolm walked out. She couldn't blame him. Hell, she wanted to beg him to take her with him. How their marriage didn't implode beneath the weight of her affair, her family, Farrah, could only be described as a miracle. He didn't realize when he took the vow of "for worse," Blair would endlessly put it to the test.

"I'll get you something to help you sleep," Blair said to Farrah, as she snapped back to her current nightmare. She applied two fat Band-Aids to Farrah's thigh before she repacked the first aid kit and put it back into the medicine cabinet. She crossed over toward the door to Malcolm's bathroom, causing Cookie to jump up, her hands reaching for her weapon in her waistband.

"Bitch, I will put a damn hole in your face—"

Blair stopped and held her hands up. "I'm—I just want to get a sleeping pill for my daughter, out of my husband's medicine cabinet in his bathroom."

Their eyes remained locked until Cookie lowered the gun a few inches, her face still in awe.

"All right," she said. "But don't try nothing."

Blair edged toward the door and headed straight for the medicine cabinet, searching for the big bottle of sleeping pills, plucking it out and opening it. She dumped a pill into her hand then bit it in half, depositing the leftover chunk back into the bottle.

"That's nasty." Cookie grimaced from the doorway. "What you do that for?"

"She doesn't need more than a half."

"No, I mean, why did you put that back into the bottle after you had your mouth all over it?"

"I do it for my husband all the time. It's fine." Blair handed the jagged half pill to Farrah, who bent over the sink, wincing, as she took a gulp of water from the faucet.

"Come on." Cookie grabbed Blair's arm. "Tree's turn."

"Let go of me." Blair wrenched out of Cookie's grasp. "I'm going to put my daughter to bed and I'm going to stay with her until she falls asleep."

"You supposed to take care of T—"

"I will take care of my daughter first." Blair paused. "And then, I'm going to take care of Tree."

THE SUSPECTS

Isabelle Ryan: Terrell Winters emigrated to the United States from Jamaica when he was three years old with his seventeen-year-old mother, Marilyn. For a few months, the two lived with relatives in Kansas City before eventually settling on the South Side of Chicago. It's fair to say he had a horrific childhood.

Skye Stafford: Terrell's biological father died when he was about six months old. His mother came to America for a fresh start and she hoped—better opportunities for her and her son.

Elena York: Terrell's mother remarried and had six more children. His stepfather regularly beat her, beat the children and, by all accounts, Terrell received the brunt of his rage. His mother tried to be a buffer, but she was terrified and so dependent on her husband, she wasn't able to do anything to protect Terrell or any of the children from his wrath.

Isabelle Ryan: Beatings with electrical cords, kicked, punched, a broken leg, broken wrist, burns ... these were all a part of Terrell's daily existence.

Skye Stafford: Terrell dropped out of school when he was fourteen and by the time he was sixteen, he'd been in and out of juvie multiple times: possession, intent, weapons charges, robberies. He hadn't yet graduated to murder, but it was only a matter of time.

Elena York: When he was nineteen, he was sentenced to seven years in prison for a series of car-jackings, assault charges, and burglaries. So, this already hardened young man goes into jail with rapists and murderers. There was just no good path for him.

Yvonne Pilley, Terrell Winters' Neighbor: Even with all the evil in that house, Terrell, for a long time, was a nice little boy. He could be charming, even. He would always say hello to me, ask me how I was doing. Had the biggest smile. And he would give me the most amazing pictures. He could draw anything—buildings, people, trees, birds, whatever. He loved to draw the skyline. I still have every picture he drew for me. I tried to let him come over and watch TV, give him a little something to eat, but his father, or I guess it was his stepfather, he put a stop to that. It was almost like he didn't want anyone showing that boy any bit of kindness.

Isabelle Ryan: In between his criminal activities, Terrell stayed incredibly busy fathering children by multiple women. By the time he was twenty, he was the father of seven children by six women. By all accounts, Terrell was a deadbeat dad, spending little to no time with any of his kids.

Skye Stafford: Terrell met Courtney Miller, nicknamed Cookie, at an under-twenty-one club downtown. She was seventeen and he was twenty-eight. Again, nothing good could possibly come from this.

Elena York: Seventeen year-old Courtney Miller, nicknamed Cookie, was born into a middle class family in Chicago's Bronzeville neighborhood. Her mother, Margaret, was an elementary school teacher and her father, William, owned a very popular haberdashery in the neighborhood. Courtney was an honor student, she volunteered at the local community center. Very nice, very bright, very smart young lady.

Elva Haines, Courtney Miller's Neighbor: Courtney was the sweetest, smartest little girl. Always with her nose in a book. Always. I would see her walking home from the library down the street four or five times a week with a stack of books in her hands.

Skye Stafford: Courtney's parents did everything "right"— provided a stable, loving home, took Courtney and her sister on vacations every summer. She wasn't spoiled with wealth by any means, but she had a very nice, very comfortable life.

Crystal Miller, Courtney Miller's Sister: I honestly don't know what happened to my sister. She was on the straight and narrow her whole life. Never gave my parents any trouble (Sighs). I guess Terrell happened.

Skye Stafford: The attraction was instant. Terrell represented the bad boy for Courtney, a way for her to break out of her good girl persona. And of course, her parents were horrified, which probably sweetened the deal all the more for Courtney.

Isabelle Ryan: It was like a switch flipped in Courtney. Gone was the sweet, smart, dutiful all-American, straight-A student who volunteered at the library on the weekends, played the piano, and taught tumbling to little girls at the community center. Literally, overnight, she starts lying to her parents, smoking pot, drinking, and staying out all night. Stealing money from them so she could shower Terrell with gifts, float him money whenever he asked for it, which was often. She let him borrow her car on numerous occasions, which he racked up a number of parking tickets on. Her parents took the car away, grounded her, forbade her from seeing him. They even tried to have Terrell arrested for statutory rape, but were unable to make the charges stick as they had no direct evidence. Cookie was fascinated by his dangerous lifestyle and in fact, saw them as some sort of power couple, an epic, us-against-the-world love affair. His being a bad boy, her parents' vehement disapproval ... all of this just heightened his appeal in her eyes.

Elena York: And then her parents' worst nightmare comes to bear. Courtney becomes pregnant with Terrell's eighth child. Her parents plan to send her out of state to Louisiana to live with her grandmother, and try again to have him arrested. Before they can, Courtney runs away and moves in with Terrell and three other guys, in, what was essentially a flophouse. One of the guys who doesn't live there, but is around quite frequently is Lenard "Dio" McKinney.

Skye Stafford: Lenard McKinney was the oldest of three children, born and raised on the South Side. His mother, Rosemary, worked overnights in a nursing home, and a part-time job as a custodian, so very similar to Terrell he very rarely saw her. This left him to look after his brother and sister the best he could. This also left him free to run the streets and fall in with the wrong people.

Isabelle Ryan: Another issue that Dio had to grapple with was his father's sexuality. His father was gay and though he'd only seen him a handful of times in his life, the last of which was when he was around fourteen, fifteen years old, this was an incredible source of embarrassment to him. Everyone in the neighborhood knew about his father. His entire family gossiped about it. It didn't help that his mother was incredibly denigrating toward his father, blaming him for her lot in life and displaying general bitterness toward homosexuality, which rubbed off on Lenard.

As a result, he carried a *huge* chip on his shoulder about his own sexuality and was known to be incredibly taunting toward members of the LGBTQ community. It sickened him.

Elena York: Dio was not exactly the sharpest tool in the shed. Like Terrell, he'd been in and out of trouble most of his very short life, though his transgressions were limited to misdemeanors: shoplifting, trespassing, disorderly conduct, some marijuana charges. He also had a borderline IQ and was very susceptible to going along with the crowd as it were, making him the perfect pigeon for Terrell.

Yvonne Pilley: I didn't know Lenard as well as Terrell. More like I knew of him. He seemed nice, though yes, there were rumors or comments that he was a little slow in the head. But like I said, from what I saw, always nice. Always looking after his brother and sister, walking them to school every morning and bringing them back in the afternoon. From what I seen (shrugs), he seemed like a nice boy.

8:25 P.M.

Malcolm watched Tree massage his hand as he lolled on the bed, mesmerized by whatever movie he was now watching. Even from across the room, he could see the knuckles rising like dough. Cookie lay sprawled next to him. Dio was rooted to the floor, curled into himself, staring at the TV, though Malcolm doubted he absorbed much of what was flashing on the screen.

His bladder wasn't bothering him, but he wouldn't have minded walking around to relieve the cramps invading his joints. A bucket of ice for his hand would have been welcome.

He wouldn't have minded punching that punk Tree right in the mouth for what he'd done to Farrah. For all of this.

He wouldn't have minded getting more than just that contact high of Kush.

Malcolm lit up a few mornings a week, depending on how many cobwebs were hanging over his brain from the night before. He'd felt fine today. He probably wouldn't tomorrow.

It was funny. He'd been such a straight arrow his whole life when it came to drugs. No roids, no dust. Creams, pills. Sure, he liked his drinks, but he wasn't trying to have his whole career go up his nose in a cloud of powder.

Then the headaches started about five years ago. Like a sledge-hammer to his temples. Couldn't get out of bed some days, it was so bad. His lifelong mental sharpness began to fade. He became forget-ful. He'd always been a talker, but there were times he couldn't put any kind of brake on his brain. He'd chalked it up to getting older, the natural order of things.

The mood swings had done it, though. Blair's were bad enough. There couldn't be two of them in that house undulating back and forth like pendulums. They'd kill each other.

Malcolm didn't want to admit what he knew was likely the cause. The dirty "C" word.

And indeed concussion was the diagnosis.

He was lucky. Unlike so many of his former teammates and rivals, he could afford the doctors and neurological treatments he needed to keep him functioning. They recommended crosswords and jigsaw puzzles to keep his brain busy. His brother, Mitch, told him to get on the blunt. After all, it was medicinal, and he could afford the best of the best. He'd resisted for a long time. The Admiral wouldn't go for his prized QB dipping into the herb and even after all these years and everything he'd accomplished, there was still that part of him that couldn't stand the thought of disappointing his father.

Malcolm crossed and uncrossed his legs before splaying them out in front of him. He moaned at the relief of his limbs finally lying in a long straight line, at the explosions in his joints as they were released from the stiffness and forced immobility. He could've done cart-wheels, it felt so good.

Blair came out of the bathroom, her arms still around Farrah, her eyes vacant as she fought sleep. His daughter's mouth was slightly ajar and Malcolm gasped to himself at the sight of her decimated teeth. The swollen, misshapen face. Blair stroked the girl's hair. His hand involuntarily curled into a ball. She gently laid the girl down on the couch, propping throw pillows under her head and draping her with the gray afghan hanging across the back.

"All right, Wifey, you done. You gotta fix me up now," Tree said, sitting up, swinging his legs over the side of the bed.

"As soon as she falls asleep," Blair murmured as she looked down at a drowsy Farrah. "In the meantime, let my husband use the bathroom."

Tree was quiet for a moment before cocking his head toward his minions and pointing in the direction of the bathroom. Cookie and Dio untied Malcolm and ripped the tape from his mouth before shoving him in the direction of the bathroom. Within seconds, Tree flew across the room, the menacing endpoint of his gun pressed to Blair's temple. She didn't gasp, barely even flinched. She chewed on her bottom lip and closed her eyes. His own heart stopped.

"Don't try nothing," he said.

"Don't worry," Malcolm said. "We're cool." Tree narrowed his eyes as Malcolm shut the door of his bathroom. He dropped his head into his hands. The fingers of his right hand still throbbed with heat from this morning. He let his shoulders hunch around his ears.

He stayed in that position for a few seconds, loud, heavy bursts of his breath filling the bathroom. Finally, he raised the lid of the toilet, caught off guard as his bladder pressed against him in response to the clanging porcelain.

Malcolm turned on the faucet, sticking his hot, blistered hand under the stream of cold water, groaning from the relief. After nearly a minute, he gingerly washed his hands, then looked up at the medicine cabinet.

The medicine cabinet.

He pulled the corner of the pristine white wood, ready to yank it off its hinges, before thinking better of it and easing it open instead.

The big, beautiful bottle of sleeping pills stared back at him.

He grabbed it, opening it with shaking fingers. He tapped out a handful of salmon pink ovals, a few of them broken in half, Blair's comical attempt to control his dosage. She didn't know that most nights, he waited until she was snoring softly before sneaking back into the bathroom to down three more halves with water. That it never occurred to her to lock the pills up, that she never counted them, was funny to him.

He lifted the edge of his shoe to the countertop and quickly shoved about half of the pills into one sock, the rest into his other sock. He hopped around a few times to force the pills down the length of his foot and make sure he could walk comfortably without drawing too much suspicion. Why he was bothering with the pretense, he didn't know. After all, he was a busted old football player. None of them walked right anymore.

"Hey. Hey!" Tree's fist exploded against the door. "What the fuck you doin' in there? I'm a blow up Wifey you don't come out now. Right now."

Malcolm shut off the faucet and yanked the door open. Tree fell inside and Malcolm had to sidestep to avoid a collision. Tree looked around, crazed eyes darting around the room searching for some sign that Malcolm had tried to escape, had tried to pull one over on him.

"All yours."

Tree made a big show of straightening up and tucking the hem of his dress shirt far down into his pants. "Come on, Wifey. Get in here. Fix me up."

Malcolm could see the scene had shifted only slightly. Dio was still hanging off the corner of the bed, eyes trained on the TV. Farrah snoring softly on the couch. Cookie had taken her man's place, her gun pointed at Blair, who sat on the couch at Farrah's bound feet.

Tree stalked out of the bathroom over to Blair, sticking his hand in her face. "What you think, Wifey? You think you can take care of me?"

She recoiled as if he'd stuck a mound of rotting meat and vegetables in her face for inspection. "I think you need some ice for the swelling. We have to go to the kitchen."

"What about that thing you used on Ol' Girl?" Cookie piped up. "That ice pack thing or whatever?"

"It's only good for one use. It won't work now."

"Damn, you got us going all up and down this house—basement, kitchen, bathroom, back to the kitchen—"

"Do you want my help or not?" Blair asked.

"Cookie, go downstairs, bring some ice up for my hand."

"What about Ol' Boy?" she asked.

Blair winced as Tree wound his fingers through the ends of her ponytail. "Wifey and me will be just fine, ain't that right? Mally Mal knows if he tries anything that Wifey'll take the hit."

Neither Blair nor Malcolm responded and Cookie huffed out of the room toward the kitchen. Tree nodded at Malcolm. "Sit in that chair."

"Let him stay here, let him watch our daughter," Blair said.

Tree didn't say anything but kept the gun on Blair as she stood up and motioned for Malcolm to take her place watching over Farrah. He eased down onto the couch, flexing his feet against the pills in his socks.

"We're good, man," he said to Tree. "I'm not gonna try anything."

TURNABOUT

Isabelle Ryan: Terrell Winters' mother, Marilyn, was the one to turn him in.

Elena York: According to Marilyn, although he didn't live there anymore, Terrell would sometimes come by the house whenever his stepfather was out of town. He came over late that Monday morning and she immediately knew something was wrong. He was jittery, limping. He had a black eye and swollen mouth. He stayed glued to the TV, constantly checking his phone.

Skye Stafford: She watched him over the next few days and he became more and more erratic. She grew fearful about him being there and asked him to leave, but he refused. She realized he was hiding out.

Lieutenant Dimitri Cora: Marilyn Winters didn't trust her son, was certain he'd brought drugs into the house, which is why she decided to search his room while he was in the shower. She found Blair Gilbert's necklace. She sent him on an errand to get him out of the house so she could escape to the police station.

Skye Stafford: The police knew they had to move fast and catch him by surprise. Marilyn told Terrell she had to work and would be home late, but in reality, she was with police the whole time. They waited until the dead of night, when she knew he was likely to be asleep in front of the television. And that's where police found him.

Elena York: Marilyn took a huge risk. So much could have gone wrong. But as she told police, she had no other choice but to turn her son in.

Isabelle Ryan: And now it was time for police to find out what happened.

10:30 P.M.

"Do you think they're asleep?"

"Maybe. Hard to tell."

"Do you think they can hear us?" Blair whispered.

He craned his neck a little. "I don't think so. Still, we should keep our voices down, just in case."

Blair glanced over at Farrah, still asleep. The TV droned with yet another loud movie. A surprise rainstorm with the occasional crack of thunder raged outside the window. One of the three, she wasn't sure which, was snoring softly. She could see the outline of Tree and Cookie's bodies snuggled up against each other on her bed. Dio was curled up on the bench at the foot of the bed. He'd been lying that way, perfectly quiet, not even a twitch, for the past twenty minutes, leading her to believe that he too was passed out cold. It was the quietest they'd been since they'd gotten there.

After she'd tended to Terrell with ice, peroxide, and gauze he didn't really need, the gang of three had re-tied Blair and Malcolm's hands and feet back together, though they'd left them gagless. They settled back into watching movies, endlessly fascinated with the number of channels and streaming services available to them. Blair and Malcolm shot furtive glances at each other every few minutes until one by one, each of their captors drifted off to sleep. She and Malcolm sat on the floor, their backs against the sofa.

"You're sure they're asleep?" she asked again.

"Blair, unless I go over there and look, I don't know for sure. I'm just guessing."

"Okay, okay." She bit her lip and took another glance at the bed. "I think they're asleep."

"Thank God," he muttered.

"Malcolm." She turned so that her back was to him.

"What?"

"My pants," she whispered. "The scissors from the first aid kit. They're in my pants."

Malcolm groaned softly in appreciation as he maneuvered himself around to get his hands closer to her. He groped across her waistband until the fingers of his good hand gripped the scissor handles. She held her breath as she felt him fumble around, relieved at the *snap!* of the tape giving way and liberating her wrists. She took the scissors from him and cut the tape around her ankles, quickly snipping the tape around his hands and feet. They glanced at a sleeping Farrah and Blair mimed to Malcolm to carry her. He bent down to hoist her over his shoulder, while Blair slid her hand over the girl's mouth to stifle any screams if she woke up.

Cookie rolled over, mumbling to herself, her soft snoring temporarily halted.

They froze, watching and waiting to see if she would wake up and see them. Within seconds, her snoring resumed. Blair swallowed and motioned to Malcolm to head for the door.

They crept quietly out into the hallway, Blair keeping her palm over Farrah's mouth, while looking over her shoulder every few seconds, her ears on high alert for befuddled screams when Tree, Cookie, and Dio realized the Gilberts were gone.

They moved quietly, slowly down the staircase, their footsteps whispering across the floor. The TV grew more muffled the further away they got from the bedroom.

Halfway down the stairs.

Four steps.

Three steps.

One.

They reached the bottom. Farrah continued to sleep. Blair gripped Malcolm's forearm as they hurried in the direction of the kitchen. Once they reached it, Blair ran over to the key ring holder and slid off the spare key for her car, while Malcolm maneuvered Farrah a few times so he could punch the keypad next to the door leading to the garage.

It beeped and lit up green. Blair and Malcolm smiled at each other.

And that was when Cookie woke up.

INTERROGATION
SUSPECT #1, TERRELL WINTERS

Note: DC is Lieutenant Dimitri Cora; SD is Lieutenant Sharon Donahue; TW is Terrell Winters

DC: State your full name for me, please.

TW: Don't you know it already?

DC: Pretend like I don't.

TW: Terrell Robert Winters.

SD: Terrell, do you know Malcolm Gilbert?

TW: Shit, everybody know him.

SD: I didn't ask about everybody, I asked if you know him.

TW: I mean, I don't know him personally, but I know who he is.

SD: How do you know him?

TW: What you mean, how do I know him? He a damn football player. Won a whole bunch of Super Bowls.

DC: But you don't know him personally?

TW: No, I don't know him personally. What the hell kind of question is that?

DC: Where were you Saturday, April 1, around twelve-fifty-five in the afternoon?

TW: Hell, I don't know, man. I was around.

SD: (Throws down surveillance photo of Terrell and Malcolm, points to timestamp). What's the date on that?

TW: (Doesn't look). I don't have my glasses.

SD: Do you recognize the two people in the photo?

TW: I told you, I don't have my glasses.

SD: Look harder.

TW: It's too blurry, man. I can't see that.

DC: (Throws down plastic evidence bag with Malcolm Gilbert's phone, retrieved from a dumpster). What about that? You recognize that?

TW: Should I?

DC: It's got your fingerprints all over it.

TW: I don't know what to tell you man but that ain't my phone. I think you trying to set me up.

SD: Do you know Farrah Gilbert?

TW: Who?

SD: What about Blair Gilbert?

TW: Man, I ain't got no idea what you talking about—

SD: (Throws evidence bag with Blair Gilbert's necklace on the table). What was Blair Gilbert's necklace doing in your house, Terrell?

TW: I ain't never seen that before. Ya'll must have planted that shit.

DC: Your mother gave it to us. Found it in your room. Did she plant it?

TW: (Long pause). Man, that bitch ain't worth shit.

DC: All right, Terrell, let's stop wasting time. We know you were in the Gilbert's house from Saturday at eleven a.m. until approximately six thirty on Monday morning. Your fingerprints are all over that necklace. Your fingerprints are all over the house, your DNA is all over that house, and you left your clothes there, so believe me when I tell you, you're not walking out of here today, so you might as well start talking.

TW: (Silent for several minutes). Shit.

DC: I'm waiting, Terrell.

TW: (Sighs).What you want to know?

TIP OF THE ICEBERG

Detective Andrea Chang, Highland Park Police Department, Phone Analyst: All of us, each one of us, our phone calls and text messages tell a story about our lives. We tend to text and call the same people. The same people tend to text and call us. And there's usually a pattern to those texts and calls.

Blair had a very predictable call and text pattern. She pretty much talked and texted with the same people: Malcolm, Farrah, her sister, Bridget, in Long Island City, her neighbor, Lani Jacobs, her friend Kimberly Fletcher, her hair dresser. Of course, there was some disruption to that pattern on occasion, depending upon different circumstances that may have arisen, but by and large, Blair Gilbert had an incredibly predictable calling and texting pattern.

Malcolm's calling and texting pattern, I would say, was predictable chaos. While Blair's pattern was exceedingly reliable, Malcolm had both a highly predictable pattern and a wildly *unpredictable* pattern. His wife, daughter, golfing friends, his brothers, parents, business associates, they were all a part of his regular pattern. However, new people popped up in Malcolm's life all the time: new business associates, new friends, friends or associates he hadn't talked to in years. Still, the calls and texts followed a pattern, as erratic as it may have been.

Any kind of interruption to an established phone pattern is usually an indication something is about to happen, some event is about to occur.

Lieutenant Dimitri Cora: A crucial part of the investigation was to put together a timeline of the family's movements during the last twenty-four hours before the invasion. A lot of times, those actions immediately preceding the event will reveal a clue.

Lieutenant Sharon Donahue: Farrah Gilbert had one class on Friday morning at ten. She and her roommate met for lunch at eleven thirty at the student union before returning to their on-campus apartment. Throughout the afternoon, Farrah was texting with friends about her plans for the weekend. She got in her car to drive home to Highland Park about five thirty. She stopped for gas in West Lafayette, Indiana at seven forty-five. She was on the phone with her new boyfriend, Eddie Nixon, for about an hour during that drive from Bloomington. Her cell phone was pinging off towers all along I-55, up the Edens, all the way until late Friday night when she arrived in Highland Park at approximately ten fifteen, stopping at a nearby Taco Bell before heading home. Her phone went silent around midnight and didn't go off again until Saturday morning.

Elena York: On Friday morning, the Gilberts' housekeeper, Anita Sanchez, came to the house at her usual time of eight. Shortly afterward, around eight thirty, Blair Gilbert went to her regular Pilates class in nearby Glencoe. Afterwards, she picked up a coffee, went home to shower and change clothes, before heading out to run some errands, returning home at approximately four p.m.

Lieutenant Dimitri Cora: Malcolm Gilbert left his house on Friday morning at nine thirty and headed to his offices in the Loop.

He arrived at approximately ten thirty and spent the morning answering emails and returning phone calls. At twelve thirty, he left his office for a lunch appointment on Michigan Avenue, returning around two thirty, leaving for the day at three p.m. Every Friday afternoon, he took his car to his favorite car wash in Highland Park. He got there around four thirty, left around five fifteen to head home. He and Blair left the house at six thirty to have dinner with Cap Gleason and his wife, got home at ten, shortly before Farrah's arrival.

Lieutenant Sharon Donahue: For the most part, there was nothing that stood out about the family's activities.

Lieutenant Dimitri Cora: Except, that Friday morning, we found something unusual in Blair Gilbert's movements.

10:45 P.M.

Cookie was screaming. Bloody murder screaming. Cookie must have woken up and seen they were gone and was now sounding the goddamned alarm and that meant they were seconds from running downstairs and catching them. Stopping them.

Blair cursed to herself as she ran into the garage and unlocked her car, Malcolm following behind, Farrah still in his arms. He stopped to hoist her up.

The voices were growing louder. Closer. They were probably only seconds away.

She opened the back door so they could slide Farrah inside.

She glanced up.

The kitchen door was standing wide open.

"Malcolm, the door. The door! Shut the fucking door!"

He grunted, putting Farrah down on the steps, before reaching up to slam the door shut.

Tree's foot blocked him.

Malcolm leapt up the steps and pulled at the door. Tree's arm shot out from the crack between the doorjamb and door like a branch, clawing at air, trying to make contact with Malcolm. Farrah's body sagged down the length of the steps, as Malcolm tried to avoid stepping on her. Behind him, Blair could hear Cookie and Dio screaming. Her eye fell on a shovel propped up in the corner. She grabbed it and bounded up the steps, raising the shovel over her shoulder and slamming it against Tree's hand. He screamed and retracted his arm a little. She hit him again while Malcolm kept pushing against the door. Over and over, she smashed the shovel into the dogged appendage, which kept flailing but refused to yield.

She grunted and brought the point of the shovel down on Tree's foot, like the proverbial sword into stone. He howled and fell backward. Farrah slid down the steps and Malcolm reached down with his burnt hand to grab her, groaning as he did so.

The handle of one of the wooden spoons from her kitchen drawer jutted out from the door crack. Malcolm threw his free hand against the door, but it was too late. In that second, Dio and Cookie jumped over an ailing Tree and pushed the door open. Cookie fumbled for her gun in her waistband, clumsily whipping it out. Blair swung the shovel against the girl's hand, sending the gun skating across the garage, while Malcolm punched Dio square in the jaw.

Dio stumbled, then charged for Malcolm. Both men tumbled over the banister, smacking against the floor below. Cookie bolted for Blair, who landed a blow against her shoulder with the shovel. Cookie yelped and charged for her again, this time grabbing the handle of the shovel, pushing Blair back.

Below her, Malcolm and Dio were easing their way back to their feet. Malcolm got there first and managed to land another blow to Dio's cheek. The younger man staggered to his feet and reared back with a shaky fist.

The garage exploded with a single gunshot.

Everyone froze.

Tree dragged himself through the door with one hand, his other hand pointing the gun toward the ceiling of the garage. He lurched to his feet, heaving, his face twisted with pain and rage.

"Everybody back in the house," he said, his voice low and controlled. "Everybody get in the house or the next bullet I fire from this gun—" he shook the gun at Blair "—is gonna go right between your eyes."

She gripped the shovel, swaying a little. Sweat raced down her back. She could hear Malcolm's ragged breath behind her.

"In the house!" Tree shouted.

Blair reluctantly dropped the shovel, the clang of it reverberating across the garage. Frustration and defeat flooded through her like a tidal wave. Her head plummeted to her chest as Cookie, having retrieved her gun, put it to Blair's spine and pushed her back into the house.

What were the chances someone heard that single gunshot, would call the police?

Not with a thunderstorm roaring outside.

Tree fell against the kitchen island, grimacing. Blair had to hide the smile of satisfaction she felt at his agony. Dio had his gun on Malcolm, who was carrying a surprisingly still-sleeping Farrah in his arms. Dio shut the door behind him, which beeped, taking any hope of freedom.

Tree sniffed and pointed his gun at Malcolm. "Put her down right there."

Malcolm reared up as though he were going to challenge Tree. Instead, with some effort, he bent down and gently propped Farrah against the kitchen island.

Blair made a motion to join Farrah, but Cookie yanked her ponytail, snapping her back.

Tree attempted to pace but was stymied by his mangled foot. He had to settle for leaning against the kitchen island, his head in his hands, his breathing still broken and heavy. Cookie kept her grip tight around Blair's arms. Dio's gaze flipped between Malcolm, Farrah on the floor, and a grimacing Tree.

"So," Tree finally spoke, looking up. "Thought ya'll was gonna get out of this, huh? Thought you were going to pull one over on me, didn't you?"

Nobody said anything. Blair looked at the floor, fighting back tears, while Malcolm stood stock still, staring straight ahead.

Tree pushed himself off the counter and hobbled over to Malcolm, his bad foot hissing against the floor as he dragged it behind him. The two were toe-to-toe.

"What kind of punishment should I give you for that shit, Mally Mal? What do you think I should do?"

Blair strained against Cookie, while Malcolm pursed his lips, his eyes locked with Tree's.

"How bad do you want that money on Monday, Tree?"

"What?"

"I said ... how *bad* do you want that money on Monday morning?"

"Oh, I want it real bad, Mally Mal. Real bad."

"Then I don't think you're going to do anything to me or to my family. That's what I think you're gonna do. Not a goddamned thing."

Tree landed a blow to Malcolm's stomach with the butt of his gun, causing him to double over. Blair writhed against Cookie, managing to get one arm free, but the girl retaliated by putting her in a choke-hold and wedging her gun to Blair's temple.

Malcolm coughed, his hands on his knees, his head hanging down. Tree bent down until they were eye-level.

"Say that again."

Malcolm straightened up. "Tree ... you and I need to reach an understanding here."

"What?" He sprang back, offended. "An understanding?"

"You make things bad for me and my wife and daughter, the worse it's going to be for you? You feel me?"

Tree laughed. A hearty, belly-shaking, tear-inducing laugh. He wiped a tear away before he stopped and looked Malcolm square in the eye.

"You about to find out how much worse things can get."

INTERROGATION
SUSPECT #1, TERRELL WINTERS, CONTINUED

Note: DC is Lieutenant Dimitri Cora; SD is Lieutenant Sharon Donahue; TW is Terrell Winters

DC: Why the Gilberts?

TW: What?

DC: Come on, Terrell. Why the Gilberts? Why them? Why their house?

TW: It's complicated.

DC: Simplify it for us.

TW: It wasn't supposed to be the family. It was just supposed to be her.

SD: Her who?

TW: Wifey. Blair. Somebody hired me to show up, kidnap her and take her out.

SD: Who?

TW: I—shit. I don't know, all right. I have no idea.

DC: You have no idea who hired you to kidnap Blair Gilbert?

TW: No, I—look, this what happened, all right? One of my boys called me, said he had a job for me, said it was gonna pay a lot. He said he couldn't do it on the day the person wanted it done, otherwise, he would've done it himself—

SD: What's this guy's name?

TW: Trip. I mean, Traymond. Anyway, he says he got this job and tells me to call this number, but says I have to do it on one of those burner phones. And he was out after that—

DC: So you called this number that Traymond gave you.

TW: Yeah.

SD: When was this?

TW: February.

DC: And what happened when you called this number?

TW: So, I call this number and first we're just you know talking. Not about anything really, just talking. (Chuckles). Almost like we was on a date or something.

SD: Was this a man or a woman you were talking to?

TW: A man.

DC: What did this man sound like? Did he have an accent or any phrases that he used, any particular speech pattern?

TW: Naw. Just a regular sounding dude.

DC: So this man told you he wanted you to kidnap Blair Gilbert. Did he say why?

TW: Just said I had to be there on Saturday morning by a certain time.

SD: So what happened when you got to the house on Saturday morning?

TW: Man, she was supposed to answer the door. Her husband was supposed to be gone, so she was gonna be there by herself. I was supposed to wear a suit and a tie, act like I was looking for some street, you know, like I was lost or something. I was supposed to ask if I could use her phone. Then we was supposed to force her into the van and take her to this warehouse out South, and you know, tie her up, buy a lighter and burn her fingers with it, or whatever for a little while. Then we was supposed to kill her on Sunday night, be back in touch Monday morning.

DC: For how much?

TW: Was supposed to be ten thousand. Ten thousand to kidnap her, take her out.

SD: When were you supposed to get paid?

TW: Two thousand up front. The rest when it was over.

SD: And did you get paid?

TW: Picked it up from a locker at Union Station a few days ago, no problems. Was supposed to get the second payment the same way next week.

SD: So, you said Blair Gilbert was supposed to open the door and you were supposed to kidnap her, but the plan changed.

TW: Hell, yeah, the plan changed. Was pulling up just as some old ass lady with a shopping bag walked out. Had to wait for her to leave—

SD: After that.

TW: Man, I'm getting to that. Anyway, first thing that happened, damn Malcolm opened the door. He wasn't supposed to be nowhere near that house. Was supposed to be long gone. Playing golf or some shit. Then the damn daughter came downstairs.

DC: So Malcolm was there, Farrah was there—

TW: Yeah! They *wasn't supposed to be there.* You feel me?

DC: So what did you do?

TW: (Scoffs) Man, I'm not gonna lie, it threw me. All of it threw me. Made me all kinds of mad. And nervous, too. So I'm trying to think, trying to figure out what to do. And then Malcolm starts offering me all this shit—take my cars, take my watch, take my wife's jewelry. My Super Bowl rings. And I'm thinking, okay, okay, I can take this thing over here, I can take that thing over there. Then he says, he's got ten G's in the house, another two on him. But, I'm like, there's got to be more paper in this house.

DC: Okay.

TW: So, I start looking for paper. Searched everywhere.

DC: Then what?

TW: So then Mally Mal says to me, we go to the bank and I'll give you thirty G's. That's twenty more than I was gonna get for poppin' Wifey. Hell, yeah, I was gonna take that shit.

SD: So you and Malcolm go to the bank.

TW: Damn bank was closed. All I could do was wait. I was like, yo, hang out at the crib until Monday, bank opens up, *boom!* Grab the cash, everything else, and split.

SD: Did you reach out to your contact to let them know about the plan changing?

TW: Man, I tried calling and texting him all weekend. Couldn't get a hold of him. I just had to figure it out. I didn't have a choice.

DC: So what about the rest of the original plan? Were you supposed to leave a ransom note, make a call, what?

TW: All he said was kidnap Ol' Girl and then send him pictures of her after I iced her, you know to prove I'd done it or whatever. Didn't say nothing about no note or call.

SD: What happened then?

TW: (Sighs). Everything went wrong, that's what.

11:00 P.M.

"Whatever you're thinking about doing, Tree, don't," Malcolm said.

Blair swung her head between Malcolm and Tree, her breath suspended in her chest, her limbs heavy with fear and exhaustion.

What now?

"Put Ol' Mally Mal in a chair and strap him in real good. Real tight," Tree instructed Dio. He paused, rubbing his bottom lip with his thumb. "And tape his eyes shut, too. Real tight. I don't want him to be able to see even a crack of light. Nothing. Don't forget his mouth. Be sure he can hear. Don't put no tape over his ears. You got me?"

Dio nodded before dragging a kitchen table chair over to the island and shoving Malcolm into it. Blair flinched along with Malcolm at the screech of duct tape as Dio unwound the long strips from the roll, over and over. Tree's weight sagged against the kitchen island the entire time as he watched, grinning and nodding.

"Don't do something you can't take back, Tree," Malcolm said as Dio hovered over him, intent on carrying out his mission.

"'Don't do something you can't take back.'" Tree laughed at his mimicry. "Let me tell you something, bruh, I don't regret nothing. Only a sucker regrets things, and I ain't no sucker."

"Tree, please—" Blair whispered.

"You know what, Wifey? You talk too damn much. Does that—does that drive Mally Mal crazy? Huh? Does it make him want to straight up sock you in the mouth?"

"Shut up," Malcolm said.

"You tellin' *me* to shut up?" he scoffed. "No, what you need to be doing is you need to be telling Wifey to shut the hell up. I don't see how you stand it. My woman talked as much as your woman, man, I'd want to shoot myself." He looked down at his gun and burst out laughing. "Maybe I'll just put you out of your misery and do it for you." Blair's heart leapt as he pointed the gun at Malcolm and mouthed, "Pow!"

Dio held up the cardboard oval, stripped of all its tape before he placed it on the kitchen table and stood back expectantly, waiting for his next set of marching orders. Tears poked Blair's eyes at the sight of her strapping husband, his bulk cocooned in silver, including strips across his eyes and mouth.

Tree nudged Farrah with his toe.

She didn't stir.

He kicked her. Blair flinched.

Still nothing.

"Get some ice water," Tree said to Dio. "A big bucket of it."

Dio hesitated before jogging over to the refrigerator and pulling out the ice drawer, brimming with fresh cubes. He filled it with cold water then came to stand over Farrah. He waited.

"Come on, bruh. You know what to do. Wake that bitch up."

Cookie held a crying Blair back as Dio tipped the tray over, water and ice cascading down, pelting Farrah on the face. Her eyes popped open and she screamed. Malcolm's muffled howl was almost as loud as Blair's as she continued her useless push/pull against Cookie, tears stabbing her eyes, her own screams burning in her throat as she watched her daughter flail. A still-bound Farrah flopped against the floor, disoriented, the shock of the icy wake-up, bewilderment over being in the kitchen, and the tape binding her wrists, all stamped across her face.

"Mom?"

"It's okay, baby, it's okay. Mama's here."

Farrah sobbed when she saw Malcolm, for all intents and purposes, blind and mute, taped to a chair. On instinct, Blair attempted to bend down to help her daughter to her feet, but as usual, Cookie was there to stop her.

Dio stood in uncomfortable silence as Tree and Cookie cackled and pointed at Farrah's distress. Her tears.

Tree stopped laughing and sniffed as he pushed against the table to hoist himself up to a standing position.

"Untie her. We about to take a little trip."

The hairs prickled along Blair's neck. "What are you doing?" she asked. "Where are you taking her?"

"Oh, we ain't going far. Just to the living room," he said as he watched Dio cut Farrah's restraints with her kitchen scissors, then jerk her to her feet.

Blair took a shallow breath. Maybe they weren't going to do anything except tie them up and leave them in the living room.

Except why leave Malcolm in the kitchen?

Because something bad was going to happen in the living room.

"Mom?" Farrah lisped and sputtered, which brought a fresh round of tears for them both.

Tree motioned for Cookie and Dio to take them into the living room. She tried again to reach for Farrah, managing to break one arm free and grasp her daughter's wrist.

"Why do you want us to go in the living room?" Blair rasped.

For once, Tree didn't have a snappy comeback, just repeated his command to his minions to take them into the living room. Cookie pushed Blair, while Dio shoved Farrah, the ringleader following close behind, grunting with each limp he took. The cold barrel of Cookie's gun in her back was the only thing propelling Blair into that living room. Tree directed his crew to make Blair and Farrah sit on the couch where they huddled together. Tree eased himself down into the white overstuffed chair opposite them and steepled his fingers together as he stared at them through the slits of his eyes.

"You know Ol' Mally Mal is right about one thing. I do want that money on Monday. Now, he don't know this yet, but for all my aggravation, for all this shit I've had to put up with today—getting bit, my hand, my foot's all messed up—the price has gone up to a hundred thousand. You hear that, Mally Mal?" he yelled in the direction of the kitchen. "I want one hundred thousand dollars on Monday."

"My husband already told you he'll pay you whatever you want," Blair said. "That he'd give you whatever you want."

"Whatever I want…" Tree shifted his gaze to a trembling Farrah, huddled against Blair, who gripped her to her as tightly as she could.

"Look, you'll get your money, I swear—"

Tree leapt across the room in one surprisingly fluid motion and slapped Blair, who screamed.

"As I was saying before I was so rudely interrupted," he said, flopping back against the chair. "I do want that money and believe me, as much as I want to bust Mally Mal in the face, bust him till the white meat shows, I can't do that. That'll attract too much suspicion. No, I got to have him stepping into that bank looking right."

"And I know my husband appreciates that—"

"I don't give a fuck what he appreciates." Tree shifted in his seat and propped his bad foot up on the coffee table, his eyes rolling back at the apparent relief. "So, since I can't beat that bitch like I want to, I got to find another way to show Mally Mal just how disappointed I am in him for disrespecting me."

Blair went cold.

"What are you going to do?" she whispered.

He stood up, shaky on his good foot, and reached across the table. He snatched Farrah's arm, pulling her toward him.

"No." Blair tugged on Farrah's other arm and grabbed at her waist. A literal tug of war. Farrah pulled back toward Blair, her muffled whimpers growing into thunderous sobs as she shook her head repeatedly.

"Leave me alone. Leave me alone!" Farrah screamed.

"Hold that bitch!" Tree yelled at Cookie as he continued to wrestle with Blair.

"What you about to do?" Cookie asked. Blair could hear the fear, the uncertainty vibrating in the girl's question.

"I'm gonna show Mally Mal that you don't fuck with me." Tree grunted, trying to wrest control of Farrah away from Blair.

She threw herself against Farrah, hoping to knock her to the ground, and by extension, Tree.

It worked as all three fell down, Blair scrambling to pull Farrah up, to use her own body as a shield. Tree screamed at Dio and Cookie to restrain Blair. Although she couldn't see them, from the sounds of their leader's increasingly agitated demands, they didn't seem to want to follow his orders.

Blair grasped Farrah and pulled her up in one swift move before shoving her behind her. Farrah quivered against her back.

She held out her palm toward Tree, who struggled to stand.

"Leave my daughter alone. Whatever it is you're planning to do, just please—she's a child, she has her whole life ahead of her. Whatever you're going to do, do it to me instead. Please."

"Oh, Wifey, don't you worry ... you gonna get yours, too. Know that."

Blair's heart rammed against her chest. Her words stuck in her throat, her mouth gaping.

"Please. Tree. Please—I'm begging you."

He was on his feet. In one swift motion, he wrenched a hysterical Farrah from behind Blair's back, who leapt toward them.

"Grab her. Grab her!" he yelled at Dio and Cookie.

Dio was the first to snap out of his malaise, hooking his hands around Blair's elbows, jerking her upward. She flailed against him, shrieking. Farrah writhed and twisted around in an attempt to unscrew herself from Tree's grasp.

"What you about to do?" Cookie asked again, her voice shaky. Quiet.

Blair whipped her head in the girl's direction. "Cookie, please," she pleaded. "Please, don't let him do this. Don't let him do anything to my daughter. For God's sake. You can stop this. You can—"

Cookie looked helplessly from Blair to her boyfriend and to Farrah. She pursed her lips, her eyes cast down as she shuffled over to grab one of Blair's arms from Dio. Tears exploded against Blair's eyes, the dread and terror welling inside of her.

Tree grinned and pushed a wailing Farrah to the floor, straddling her. She squirmed and kicked and beat her fists against him. His belt buckle clanked against his hand as he unzipped his pants and revealed himself. Both Dio and Cookie looked away while Blair continued her useless struggle to save her daughter from the monster.

"Damn, I been wanting to do this all day," he whispered as he lowered himself to the ground.

PART 2

SUNDAY, APRIL 2
HIGHLAND PARK, ILLINOIS
THE RESIDENCE
OF
MALCOLM AND BLAIR GILBERT

6:45 A.M.

Blair jerked awake, her head swerving, eyes blinking, breath racing, the natural on-waking instinct to stretch her arms and legs, roll over and kiss Malcolm good morning on the cheek, curbed by mounds of tape locking her hands, waist, and feet to her dining room chair, her mouth stuffed with a kitchen towel. Last night's thunderstorm was gone. Sunlight streamed in through the picture window, warming her neck and face. Birds chirped on the other side of the glass.

Farrah was asleep in the chair next to her, her chin tucked into her chest, her mouth similarly corked with a towel, soft snores somehow floating from the swollen, broken fragments of nose. Blair breathed a sigh of relief before panic surged through her at not seeing Malcolm. She whipped her head to the other side, the crick in her neck protesting, to see that unsurprisingly, he was wide awake, watching her. He was still bound to the chair, but the tape had been removed from his eyes. She gave him a questioning glance. He pointed his head in the direction of the living room.

All three captors were sprawled across the furniture: Tree splayed on the chaise lounge, strings of drool falling out of his open mouth.

Cookie was in the fetal position on the settee, one of the couch cushions wedged beneath her head. Dio was on the couch on his stomach, one hand resting on the floor below, the other flung across his back.

She wrinkled her nose at the rancid smell. Not just Dio, but something else—

Her. She'd vomited on herself after ... Blair squeezed her eyes shut against the memory of his skin slicing into hers like a razor, of his crudeness, his stench.

Of him raping her.

The torture of it flooded back like the horror movies she so desperately avoided. After assaulting Farrah, Tree demanded Dio take his turn with Blair, since she, in his words, still looked good for an old bitch. Taunting Dio for being unable to get it up, mocking him about his father, an indignity Blair couldn't decipher, before finally declaring he'd show him how it was done. Cookie's stony silence as she watched the revolting scene of a daughter and her mother being raped, and doing absolutely nothing to stop it. Malcolm's muffled screams from the kitchen, not seeing the scene, but hearing every grunt, every sob. Blair's heart broke at the sound of Malcolm helplessly hopping up and down, scooting his chair forward in stuttering stops and starts in a futile attempt to get to them. Dio hunched in a corner, crying quietly, as he too, banished himself to the sidelines, complicit.

But it was watching Tree violate Farrah ... that was really what triggered her sickness. Watching that animal desecrate her ... it had roiled her stomach acids, had strangled something deep inside of her. She'd move past this, would find a way to squash it down and never think of it again.

But her little girl ... her little girl would never be the same.

Her gaze fell on Malcolm once more.

I'm sorry.

A tear slid down her cheek and she shook her head.

It's not your fault.

A primal yawn thundered from the living room. Blair froze. Tree was up and moving around. She shot Malcolm another look.

What now?

He wiggled the blisters of his fingers in her direction, an attempt at soothing.

Stay calm.

She watched Tree work his way around the living room, slapping Dio awake, shaking Cookie. Slowly, they all stretched to life, rolling cricks from necks, picking crust from eyes as their heads swiveled slowly around the room to reacquaint themselves with their current sleeping quarters.

Tree limped into the dining room, scratching his bare chest with one hand, rubbing sleep from his eyes with the other. Dio and Cookie followed dutifully behind. He sniffed under his arms, his face scrunching up at the smell.

"Whew! Damn, I stink." He laughed. "I need a shower. Or maybe I'll have me a little morning swim before breakfast. Isn't that what rich people do? Get in a *swim* before breakfast?"

Dio hung back in the entryway, eyes cast downward, Cookie looking equally sheepish as she glanced at Blair and a still-sleeping Farrah.

"What you think, Wifey? After I get me a little swim and a shower, you make me some breakfast? Huh? Huh?"

Blair stared at him through her own half-awake lids, tears simmering beneath the surface.

Don't show him. Don't give him the satisfaction.

She blinked, relieved no teardrops snaked down her cheek. Tree laughed out loud as he shed everything but his dingy boxers, leaving the clothes on the floor where they lay, commanding his soldiers to stay behind and keep an eye on them. Dio dropped to the floor, his knees pressed to his chin, staring at the Gilberts, though Blair didn't think he really saw them.

Cookie looked as though she wanted to protest but decided against it. Instead, she slumped down in a chair, never making eye contact with Blair.

And she cried.

GREEN-EYED MONSTER

Dreena Harrison Grace: Bridget's Captivate audition. What a disaster that was.

Gwen Majors: Did you ever see the movie *Fame*? You know Leroy —the dancer? So Leroy goes along with his friend, like as a favor, 'cause she asked him to, to her audition for the school. And she's terrible. I mean, homegirl's got no business in a leotard and tights, right? But Leroy just blows everyone away with his moves. He winds up getting a spot and she doesn't and she just goes off, "F*** you, this was my thing, not his, blah, blah." I mean that is almost verbatim what happened at that Captivate audition with Bridget and Blair.

Dreena Harrison Grace: Blair tagged along because her sister asked her to. Then, Bridget was so nervous, she couldn't get out a note, like nothing at all, so she asked Blair to sing with her, some little song their mother used to sing to them or something. Anyway, Bridget opens up her mouth and it's a disaster—can't sing, can't dance. It was like what gets the hook at the Apollo.

Anyway, Slick, our producer, stops the audition like not even midway through, says thank you, and for them to wait outside. Slick and Skinny have their heads together for like five minutes, then they send out their assistant to grab Blair, and the three of us sing together for the first time. They asked us to sing "Lovergirl" by Teena Marie.

Gwen Majors: They had us sing something by Janet Jackson. I'm pretty sure it was "When I Think of You." I think. Anyway, Blair was kind of surprised and kept asking if they were sure they wanted her to sing some more and what about Bridget, blah, blah, blah. Skinny and Slick were like, no, no, no, we want to hear what you three—meaning me, Dreena and Blair—sound like together.

Dreena Harrison Grace: We did it on the fly and it sounded like we'd been singing together for years. It was that good.

Gwen Majors: Slick sends Blair out, and he and Skinny put their heads together again—and you know for whatever reason they asked me and Dreena for our opinion, which, let me tell you, was the first and last time that happened (Laughs). And we're like "she's the girl" and they agreed.

Dreena Harrison Grace: They send their assistant out again to tell Blair she's in and you could hear Bridget go *off*. Nuclear-grade meltdown—"F*** you" and "F*** this" and "What do you mean she's in? What about me? What about me?" I couldn't hear what Blair was saying, but I'm sure she was upset. I mean you'd have to be.

Gwen Majors: Slick and Skinny had to physically walk Bridget out of the building. It was like she was possessed or something, the way she was screaming.

Dreena Harrison Grace: We had to start rehearsals the next day and to be honest, I didn't think Blair was going to show up. You know loyalty to her sister or whatever. Months later, she let it slip one night after a show that after all of that with Bridget, she wasn't going to join the group, but her mother made her.

Kiki Downs: The official story in the press packets and all their interviews was that Blair tagged along with a friend to the audition as moral support and wound up being chosen for the group. No one ever said it was her sister. It wasn't a lie so much as omitting certain details.

I only met Bridget once, when she was supposedly Blair's assistant and she came with the group to an in-studio interview we were doing. Bridget threw a fit because she got told where to stand off-camera during the interview, because she kept getting in the shot. *She didn't like where she was being told to stand,* so she had a meltdown. Throwing things, spit in our floor director's face, screaming like some kind of—I don't even know what. Blair was mortified and you know, as a result, Bridget was banned from our New York studios. I mean, listen, we were used to diva behavior or whatever, but from the stars so, you know, you kind of have to put up with it. But from an assistant? No way.

Gwen told me about the botched audition years later and I was of course, shocked. I don't know if Blair told her to keep quiet about it or if Bridget just decided on her own not to say anything—or maybe it was the mother—but she never made a peep about it. In the end, she was probably too embarrassed. So, she kept her mouth shut all those years.

Apparently, though, Bridget never forgot.

9:15 A.M.

The scent of soap, her soap, wafted under her nose, waking her all over again. Original Musk. She'd just bought four bottles last week. Her eyes drifted open to find Tree tucking one of Malcolm's Polos into a pair of his pants as he staggered into the dining room. He looked ridiculous, like a little boy playing dress-up in his father's closet. The clothes billowed around his string bean frame and he'd looped one of Malcolm's belts around him twice to keep the pants from sagging to the ground.

"Whew! Damn, I feel good. Damn! I see why rich people like to get in a swim before breakfast and yo, that shower, that shower was no joke." He looked down at Dio. "You ain't never seen a shower like this. Five showerheads, all coming at you at once and steam. Man. I won't be able to take a regular shower again."

Neither Dio nor Cookie answered him, shame still smeared across each of their faces.

"Hope you don't mind, Mally Mal, but I borrowed a little something out of your closet. Now that I'm all fresh and clean." He laughed as he eased himself down into a chair. "Yo. Wifey. I'm hungry. Fix me some breakfast."

Blair inhaled, staring at him. Tree reached over and tapped his girl-friend on the shoulder. "Untie Wifey so she can fix me something to eat."

Silently, Cookie rose from her seat and plodded over to Blair. She unwound the tape from her wrists and chest, still unable to look at her. Once Blair's limbs were free, she groaned from the release. Everything hurt. Her back, her neck, her knees—her ears even—every nerve ending, joint, and muscle prickled with pain. Cookie plucked the gag from her mouth and threw it on the counter.

"I need to use the bathroom," Blair said, her voice dry and gravelly.

"Well, you ain't going to use the one over there."

"I'll use my own bathroom. And my husband's going to use it, too."

"Whatever." Tree propped his feet on a chair in front of him. "Go up there with her, Cookie."

Cookie pressed her lips together and let out a short burst of air, as though she wanted to defy him, like she wanted to lash out at him for all of this destruction. Instead, she grabbed Blair's arm and the two of them went upstairs. Blair rubbed her wrists and continued to roll her head around, hoping to dislodge the obstinate crick in her neck.

Her bed was a mess, still rumpled from Tree and Cookie lounging on it yesterday. Yesterday. Had that only been yesterday? The remnants of the torn tape from their ill-fated escape attempt and the scissors used to aid the flight, lay forlorn against the rug. Her fingers itched to snatch them up, stab that girl in the chest, and flee.

Blair went to close the bathroom door when Cookie slammed her hand against it.

"I have to watch you."

She fixed her eyes on the girl. "Like you watched last night?"

Cookie looked away, another round of tears shimmering in her eyes. "He was just mad. Because ya'll tried to escape."

Blair pulled her pants down and plopped down on the toilet, already stripped of dignity, no longer caring.

"Have you ever heard of karma, Cookie?"

The girl folded her arms across her chest, looking away.

"I'll take that as a yes," Blair said, flushing the toilet and washing her hands. "We all have choices in life and last night, you made a choice. Trust me, Cookie, or whatever the hell your name is, the choice you made last night—all of this—is going to jump up and bite you in the ass one day." She wiped her hands on a towel. "I just hope to God I'm alive to see it."

The girl's tears fell faster. Blair let her gaze drift over the girl's shoulder. How fast could she get across the room to those scissors?

"What's going on up there?" Tree's voice boomed from downstairs. Cookie jumped like she'd been reprimanded by her master. She wiped away her tears and grabbed Blair's wrist, yanking her down the stairs, where Tree stood, his hands on his hips and scowling.

"What's going on up there?" he repeated.

"You said you wanted breakfast, Tree." Blair wrenched her arm from Cookie's grip and walked past him, her voice a monotone. "Then you should let me do that."

His mangled foot whispered across the tile behind her and he struggled to keep up with her as she headed to the dining room. Malcolm and Farrah were still tied to their chairs. Farrah was awake. Her face puffy. Lips swollen. Eyes dead and wild all at once.

"Hey, Wifey, I want eggs and bacon."

WHAT YOU DON'T KNOW   257

"Untie my daughter. And let my husband use the bathroom."

Tree scoffed, but complied, untying Farrah and Malcolm, who hunched over his knees, letting out a soft groan.

"Go. Use the bathroom," she said.

"I'm fine, Blair," he said, his voice raspy with exhaustion.

"Are you sure?"

"Yeah, I—" He glanced at their captors. "I want to keep an eye on things."

She slipped her arm around her daughter's waist and hugged her. "How are you holding up, baby?" she whispered.

"I'm okay, Mom." The lisp was still jarring. The muffled, pinched voice. Foreign. Horrifying.

Blair bit her lip to hold in the tears, unable to respond.

They all shuffled into the kitchen like zombies, easing themselves down into chairs. Her heart sank at the sight of her kitchen, her just-yesterday, beautiful, glittering, showroom-new kitchen, buried beneath this graveyard of crusty pans, dried-on, caked-on pots, and greasy dishes. The kitchen had become a metaphor for this nightmare. Saturday, a shiny, beautiful life. Today, soiled and unrecognizable.

Blair beelined for the sink and turned on the water, mentally scrubbing the pots, loading the dishwasher, wiping down the counters. Those thoughts, those inconsequential thoughts about inconsequential things, were all she could focus on to keep her tears at bay.

"You supposed to be cooking me breakfast, Wifey."

"I'm washing the dishes."

Tree popped out of his chair and hobbled over to her, proverbial steam pushing out of his ears. He wrenched a pot from her hand and flung it to the floor, the metal clanging against the tile.

"I don't care about no damn dishes," he said as he reached into the sink, grabbing another pot and two small cookie sheets, throwing those to the floor, as well. "I care about my breakfast. I care about getting some food in me."

"Leave my mother alone!" Farrah screamed, her eyes darting between their captors. "She said she would cook for you. What the hell is wrong with you?"

"Baby girl, don't—"

"This is *our* house. This—"

"You best stop talking little girl, before I come over there and—"

"Before you *what*?" Farrah stuck her chin out. "What are you gonna do to me, Tree? Huh? Rape me again? Slam another bowl in my face? Huh?"

"You gonna wish that's all I do."

Farrah's eyes wobbled as she scanned the room, finally landing, her body coiled, ready to spring loose. Blair looked at her daughter. She was going for the knife block. She leapt across the room as soon as Farrah did and intercepted her, struggling to clamp her arms down to her sides.

"Stop it," she hissed. "It's not worth it."

"You're telling me to calm down? You." Farrah laughed, incredulous. "Are you joking?"

"Yo, you should listen to your mama." Tree coughed. "Wifey knows what's up."

"Farrah, please." Blair closed her eyes, the exhaustion seeping back into her bones. "We just have to get through today. Please."

Farrah slumped against Blair, clearly spent. She held onto her daughter, rubbing her back, whispering to her to calm down. She pulled back and took her girl's face in her hands. "Okay?"

"How touching." Tree laughed, his gaze falling on Cookie. He reached over and snatched her by the ear. "Why you just sitting here? Huh? You ain't got nothing to say? You not gonna defend your man?"

"Don't do that, T—"

He continued to tug on her ear, yanking and twisting it as she screamed. The Gilberts glanced at each other, while Dio looked uncomfortable. Tree pulled Cookie from the chair and she dropped to the ground, cries and screams mingling with each other. Finally, he pushed her away and she lay against the kitchen floor, whimpering like a dog.

Tree banged on the cabinet. "Yo, I'm not going to ask you again. I want my breakfast. Now."

Blair inhaled. "Shut up."

"What?"

"I said I'm making you breakfast." She shuffled over to the stove, fear and exhaustion pulling at her with equal force.

"That's what I thought," Tree said.

She motioned to Farrah to pull pots and pans from the cabinet as she trudged to the refrigerator, glancing at a hunched-over Malcolm, his elbows digging into his thighs as he rubbed his eyes. She knew the fog was descending, curling its way into the cracks and crevices of his brain. What would the fog take today? What pound of flesh would this entire nightmare extract? Would it be a debilitating headache? The dizziness he said made him feel like a spinning top even when he was standing still? Would it be the irritability, the moody petulance that could rival Blair's? The incapacitating fatigue, the only thing, aside from the sleeping pills, that put him to sleep?

She knew what would flush out the fog, though it wasn't likely he was going to get any assistance from these jackasses.

Blair grabbed a K-cup and popped it into the coffee maker. Coffee was a poor substitute for Grade A Kush, but it was all she had.

The coffee maker beeped and Blair grabbed a mug, filling it with steaming Kona gold. She handed the hot mug to Malcolm. He went to reach for it and it slipped through his seared fingers, alarmingly more red than yesterday, sending steaming black liquid across the floor.

"Oh, shi—" Blair jumped back to avoid the splatter. She searched Malcolm's face for signs of a faculty beginning its inevitable decline. The doctors said Parkinson's was a possibility. His eyes could start to go. Dementia could be around the corner.

Instead, Malcolm grabbed her arm, digging his good fingers into her flesh, the still brutish strength surging through him and straight into her. He pressed six sleeping pills into her palm, glancing at their captors and back at her again. Blair clamped her hand over the pink pearls, nodding. Understanding.

"I'm sorry, honey. Let me get you another cup," she said, her heart racing. Should she offer them some coffee and drop the pills into their mugs? Would they dissolve?

"Man, I don't know how you drink coffee. That shit gives me the runs." Tree laughed and made farting noises with his mouth.

So much for coffee. Blair racked her brain. She spied her monster blender on the counter next to the sink. Smoothies. She'd put the pills in a smoothie. Would six be enough? They *were* pretty potent. She'd pour them into small cups. More concentrated that way.

She flung the refrigerator open, pulling out a carton of eggs, a package of bacon, and the bright yellow box of frozen waffles Dio had thrown into the basket yesterday, careful to juggle the pills in her palm to keep even one from slipping. Blair took out a carton of strawberries and blueberries and five cartons of yogurt, plunking everything on the counter. A banana that hadn't made it onto the dining room table stared at her from the bottom shelf and she grabbed that, too.

She dumped the blueberries into the blender and glanced over her shoulder. Cookie had taken a seat next to a wilted Malcolm at the kitchen table, a distraught look on her face. Tree sat hunched over the table, sketching something on a napkin with a pen someone had left behind. Dio had folded himself into a corner, staring down at the floor. Farrah cracked eggs into a bowl, her purple, puffy face impassive.

Blair dropped the pills into the blender, careful not to let any of them clink against the glass. Her fingers shook as she peeled the foil from three cartons of yogurt and dumped them one by one on top of the mound of blueberries, the pills disappearing beneath the pink goo. She plucked the green stems from the strawberries, throwing fruit into the glass jar by the handful, tossing the banana in last.

She hit the power button, her heart thumping as loud as the blender. She watched the jaws pulverize the contents, the hard shell of the pills clinking against the glass as they turned to powder. She bit her bottom lip and took another glance behind her. Malcolm tapped his thumbs against each other, watching her. She pressed her lips together.

Let's see if this works.

He nodded in return.

It has to.

Blair shut off the blender. She placed her hand on the handle of the cabinet where she kept the glasses.

"What the fuck you doin'?" Tree asked. He was looking up from his drawing, scowling.

"Oh my God, I wish you would stop talking," Blair muttered, then froze, forgetting for a split second, where she was, who she was with. What was going on. She sucked in her breath, waiting.

Tree jerked out of his chair yet again, limping across the room with lightning speed. He picked up the blender.

"You want me to stop talking?" he asked.

Blair flinched, the flash of what he did to Farrah yesterday with the bowl careening across her brain. The twitch of awareness ripping through her at the realization she could be seconds away from the same fate.

Instead, he slammed the jar to the floor. Purple sludge oozed out of the broken husk of glass and across the tile. Blair and Farrah jumped back to escape the explosion, clinging to each other.

He picked up the package of bacon and the box of waffles and threw them at Blair, barely missing her. "How about you shut your damn mouth and talk me up some bacon, some eggs, not whatever the hell you were doing. You hear me, Wifey?"

"Tree!" Malcolm yelled across the room, causing the boy to whip his head around.

"What?"

"My wife is going to make you a nice breakfast so will you just calm down?"

"Man, don't you—" He reared back as though he was ready to fly across the room to pummel Malcolm. He sniffed and dropped his fist.

He sauntered back over to the chair and picked up his pen, resuming his drawing.

"Just make the damn bacon and eggs." He propped his bad foot on a chair. "And them waffles. And a big glass of grape pop."

Farrah slunk back to the counter and resumed cracking eggs. Blair looked down, the liquid continuing its exploration of the kitchen floor and held back her tears as she watched yet another escape attempt slither away from her.

FAMILY TIES

Gwen Majors: Oh, man. Their mother. Bibi. Now *she* was a piece of work.

Dreena Harrison Grace: Bibi *said* she was an actress, but I think the only thing she ever really did was six months as a waitress on *As the World Turns* or something.

Elena York: Bibi Johnson was a sometime cocktail waitress, sometime model, and wannabe actress. She was beautiful, but not especially talented. She pretty much floated from one unremarkable modeling job to the next, one bit part to the next, never really making much of a dent in either. The bulk of her modeling gigs were comprised of layouts for those old confessional magazines and ads for things like cigarettes and pimple cream that you'd find buried in the back of girlie magazines. Her acting career consisted mostly of "under five" roles—a coat-check girl, a florist—things of that nature. She always had dreams of making it big in show business but just didn't have the talent.

Dreena Harrison Grace: We only met Bibi a handful of times. It was obvious Blair was embarrassed by her. Bibi would always be saying the wrong thing or doing the wrong thing. You could tell once upon a time she'd been really pretty, but the years had not been good to her. She was tiny, like skin and bones tiny, so her skin would kind of hang off her like a curtain or something. And too much make-up, like this really bright hot pink lipstick that was always on her teeth, which were yellow—like banana yellow—and really cheap, ratty-looking wigs she'd probably had since the sixties that were always crooked.

Gwen Majors: Her clothes were always a mess, too. She'd wear these faux fur stoles that had holes like moths must have lived in them. And these satin dresses. Oh my God those dresses. They were in these really bright colors—blues, greens, reds—they were a mess, too. Full of cigarette burns and grease stains, with the hems coming apart and strings hanging off everything.

Dreena Harrison Grace: It was kind of hard not to feel sorry for Blair for—God forgive me for saying this—being stuck with Bridget for a sister and Bibi for a mother.

Gwen Majors: I'm sorry, but Bibi and Bridget were just straight-up vultures. Those two would eat the carcass.

Dreena Harrison Grace: Blair told me some things, like how her mother, from the time they were little, would leave them alone for days on end with like a loaf of bread and sugar to eat while she chased after the latest loser. Or how, when she wasn't ignoring them, she'd beat them with hairbrushes or her shoe, or play the girls against each other. You know, "Bridget, Blair borrowed your dress. You're not going to let her get away with that, are you?" "Blair, Bridget's so much prettier than you. You'll never be that pretty." Stuff like that.

Jenny Valentine: Blair had hired Bridget as her personal assistant. Well, that's what she was supposed to be anyway, but she didn't do anything except be a pain in the ass. There's something about her that kind of rubbed me the wrong way. The way Bridget pranced around, the way she talked to people, you would think *she* was the famous one.

Gwen Majors: Bridget really took advantage of Blair. Was always using her sister's name for extra perks and stuff, you know like restaurant reservations or to borrow clothes from designers, free tickets to other singers' shows, whatever. Blair just kind of put up with it. Guilt, I guess.

Jenny Valentine: Once we were in Dallas, doing a bunch of promotional stops—radio stations, in-stores, malls, that kind of thing and we were staying at this hotel, a really nice hotel. First, Bridget was going to the spa every day for manicures and facials while she was supposed to be working. Then, the rest of us were at a listening party somewhere, and Bridget said she was too tired to go and was going to stay in her room, order room service. Anyway, she got the most expensive things on the menu—lobster, steak, caviar, champagne. The works. None of us were ordering stuff like that—we were so busy, running all over town, we were lucky if we got a Happy Meal.

I guess she wanted the steak well done and it was medium rare. She went ballistic. Starts throwing food all over the room, smearing it everywhere—the walls, the bed—everywhere—throwing plates and glasses at the poor server. She calls down to the restaurant—"Don't you know who I am? Don't you know who I am?"—before she finally marches downstairs to the restaurant, still screaming about how they're supposed to respect her and how this is the worst hotel she's ever stayed in—barrels her way into the kitchen and stands there while they cook her a whole new steak, a whole new meal. And then sits in the kitchen and makes them watch her eat it.

Gwen Majors: You know, I never told anybody this, but one time, after a show in St. Louis, it was late and Bridget was supposed to be packing up all of Blair's costumes and makeup and everything before we rolled on to the next gig. We were doing an interview with some magazine and it was over, and everyone was just kind of hanging out. I had to run to our dressing room for something—depending on the venue, the three of us would share a room.

Anyway, the door was kind of open and through the crack, I could see Bridget wearing one of Blair's stage outfits and she's in the mirror with a hairbrush and she's pretending like she's being interviewed by the reporter. She's pretending like she's Blair. It was super creepy. I didn't say anything, just kind of backed away from the door. I felt bad for Blair because I'm sure she had no idea.

Jenny Valentine: The room service thing was pretty much the last straw. Management told Blair Bridget had to go. And then she was gone. Even though she never said it, I think Blair was relieved.

Gwen Majors: (Counts off on her fingers) School for cosmetology, fashion design, cooking, interior design, hospitality courses. She was either always in school for something, or getting fired from a job. Always.

Isabelle Ryan: Relationships were another disaster for Bridget. She ricocheted from failed relationship to failed relationship. A few short-lived marriages. Convicts, drug dealers, bums. If there was a bad relationship to be had, Bridget had it.

Skye Stafford: Blair always tried to bring Bridget along, always tried to help her, but Bridget was one of those people who it never worked out for.

Elena York: It was pretty clear that Bridget wanted to be Blair. She wanted her sister's life.

6:45 P.M.

Malcolm's head hung heavy toward his chest. His temples pounded with each inhale.

A whoop of laughter burst from Tree and Dio as they watched a movie—a supposed comedy—startling Malcolm, momentarily slicing through his haze. Cookie lay at the far end of the couch, dozing, drool hanging from the corner of her mouth. Tree took a healthy swig of wine from one of the four bottles he'd pilfered from the wine room, then passed it to Dio.

Sunday had been a virtual repeat of Saturday, sans any escape attempts or violent outbursts. A day of waiting. A long, excruciating day of waiting.

There'd been no unexpected visitors. Tree had kept Malcolm's phone turned off. Blair and Farrah's phones, smashed to pieces. Which meant no texts, no calls. No more threats. No more beatings.

No more rapes.

The kitchen remained a disaster area and they'd all been tied up again and stashed down in the basement. Blair and Farrah had promptly nodded off, falling into each other. Tree and Dio lit up, polishing off the last of Malcolm's stash before they both fell prey to the Sunday afternoon malaise a few hours later, their tumultuous snores like buzz saws. Cookie and Malcolm eyed each other with the by-now practiced suspicion of neither trusting the other not to do anything foolish. Tree had woken up, hungry and demanding, forcing Blair and Farrah yet again to whip up more pizzas, burgers, fries, and whatever other garbage they'd bought at the store yesterday. Blair and Farrah had each managed a few spoonfuls of yogurt, leaving the cartons mostly full. Malcolm had choked down the cup of coffee Blair had handed him that morning. The thought of food turned the Gilberts' stomachs.

Dusk was creeping in. The view outside his picture windows told him it had been a sunny day, though it was hard to discern whether it had been sunny and warm or sunny and cold. He'd seen a breeze ruffle the trees, so it could have been either. His head did a slow swivel toward Blair, who was awake, her gaze focused on the ceiling, Farrah's head tucked into her lap, snoring softly. Tears stabbed his eyes. He'd let them both down in the worst of ways. He'd spend the rest of his life begging for their forgiveness.

"I have to tell you something," Blair whispered.

His eyes drifted shut. "What?"

"Malcolm, if we don't get out of this—"

"Don't say that, BJ."

"If we don't—"

"Blair—"

"You were right, and I'm sorry," she whispered.

Yesterday morning, those words would have been a triumph. Acknowledgment. Recognition. "You were right and I was wrong." What every man wants to hear in an argument with his wife but knows he never will. In this moment, though, the victory was hollow. Like winning the championship because the other team forfeited. You win on the field. Not the penalty box. Their argument was the last thing he was thinking about, the last thing in the world that mattered. Especially not after last night.

"We don't have to talk about this now."

"We have to talk about it now."

"Jesus, BJ—"

"This may be our only chance and I don't want to die without letting you know I was stupid and wrong and I'm just—I hope you can forgive me."

"We're not going to die."

"I still want to apologize."

He sighed, forcing his eyes open, forcing himself to concentrate. "You don't have to apologize," he whispered, his voice drowsy. "It's not important."

They lapsed into silence. The TV still shouted. Dio and Tree still laughed. Cookie still snored.

"I also want you to know I love you," she said, her voice splintering. "I love you so much and I don't know how you put up with me."

"BJ—"

"Because I can be a bitch. A real pain in the ass."

"Stop it, Blair."

"And I've done so much dirt and you've put up with me and I want you to know how much I love and appreciate you, just in case I don't get the chance, just in case I don't get to tell you—"

"You're right. You are a pain in the ass. But you're my pain in the ass."

"I was looking forward to making up with you. You know. How we always do," she whispered.

"We will."

"You know they have to kill us, don't you?"

"Don't say that."

"We've seen their faces. We know enough to describe them."

"Blair—"

"They're going to kill me and Farrah the minute Tree gets his money tomorrow morning. He'll bring you back, you'll see our dead bodies and then they'll kill you."

"Blair, for fuck's sakes."

"They'll set the house on fire. That's how they'll get rid of the evidence. I've seen it on the news a million times—a family, attacked in their home, just like us and they set the house on fire and no one ever finds out who did it. That's what's going to happen. They'll set the house on fire and they'll never get caught. No one will ever know what happened to us."

"You've got to stop this, Blair."

"Malcolm, we have to be prepared. We can't sit here and pretend like our time isn't running out." She returned her gaze to the ceiling. "By this time tomorrow, we'll all be dead."

"Shut up."

"I have to accept it, Malcolm," she said quietly. "And so do you. They're going to win."

"I'm not giving up, BJ. And you can't either. We'll find a way out of this. *I* will find a way to get us out of this. You believe me?"

She sighed. "Malcolm."

"I asked if you believe me."

She turned to him, tears wobbling in her eyes. "If that's what you want me to say, then yes, I believe you."

"But you don't," he said. "Not really."

"I can't believe it anymore, Malcolm. I believed it yesterday. I believed it this morning. But now ... too much has happened."

Malcolm bit his bottom lip and stared ahead. "I'm not giving up, Blair. I can't. I won't."

TICK, TICK

Neely Smith: Well, you know that Bridget was actually the one dating Malcolm first, don't you?

Willie Dalton: "Dating" is a strong word. More like f******.

Ricky Gilbert: Malcolm met Bridget—you know I'm not sure how they met.

Alex Martinez: They met at the club. Malcolm was forever meeting honeys at the club.

Terry Gilbert: It might have been that they met in New York. Bridget was back living in the Bronx at the time and Malcolm was in town to play the Giants.

Willie Dalton: I was there that night, the night he met Bridget. It was the off-season, and Mal had come out to Cali—I actually lived in LA part of the year, 'cause my ex-wife was on a TV show at the time, and he was coming out quite a bit that summer to hang. Anyway, we were at some club on Sunset, the three of us—me, Alex, and Mal. Bridget was there with two of her girlfriends and, we all, shall we say, chose our partners for the night (Laughs). Truth be told, Bridget zeroed in on Mal right away, so she didn't really give him a whole lot of choice (Laughs).

Alex Martinez: You know Bridget was cute. Banging body. I heard once some drug dealer ex-boyfriend of hers had paid for her implants. Yeah, Malcolm hit it. Of course. But, let's be honest, she wasn't the type of girl you brought home to moms, you know what I'm saying?

Chrissy Lennox: We were doing a show at the Hollywood Bowl and Bridget brought Malcolm backstage afterwards. I think she wanted to show off to her sister, you know, "Look at who I'm dating, aren't you jealous?" It was pretty obvious who was more into who, though. I don't think Malcolm looked at Bridget once.

Neely Smith: Oh, Malcolm was definitely flirting with Blair. Definitely. But, she wasn't paying him any attention. She was being nice, but she wasn't like sitting in his lap or anything. She didn't know who the hell Malcolm was, which probably pissed Bridget off even more.

Ricky Gilbert: I think my brother fell in love with Blair like *boom!* Right then. No turning back (Laughs.)

Isabelle Ryan: Well, Malcolm pursued Blair quite heavily. He really began to woo her. Dozens of red roses would greet her at whatever venue Captivate was playing at. He would shower her with expensive jewelry. As usual, he was playing to win.

Chrissy Lennox: She didn't keep any of the stuff he sent to her. She gave away the flowers, sent back all the jewelry, threw all the letters in the trash. I think at first, of course, it was because of the whole Bridget situation. She didn't want to take something else away from her sister. Well, that and Malcolm was a dog (Laughs).

Skye Stafford: Malcolm did what a lot of men do when they're tired of a woman—disappeared. Stopped calling Bridget, stopped communicating with her, just *poof!* Vanished. When he finally realized he wasn't going to get anywhere with Blair, he decided the first thing he needed to do was clean up the mess with Bridget. So, he took her out to dinner, just the two of them, told her he was sorry for the way he had treated her, she didn't deserve that, she was beautiful, she would find a great guy one day. So on and so on.

Elena York: Bridget was just sobbing, because as bad as Malcolm had treated her, he was actually the first guy to show her *any* measure of respect. She thanked him, told him she understood he was interested in Blair and wished him well. She gave Blair her blessing, saying maybe she was meant to bring the two of them together.

Sasha Reid, Friend of Bridget Johnson: Oh, Bridget cried on my shoulder many, many times about Malcolm. Many times. She was so excited when she met him. She really thought he was the one. Even though they only dated like two weeks, *maybe* three at the most, she had all of these dreams of being whisked away to this glamorous, perfect life and instead, it happened to Blair. You have to admit, that kind of sucks.

Chrissy Lennox: Well, I'm sure when Bridget met Malcolm, she saw dollar signs. Then of course, he slipped through her fingers and right into Blair's hands.

Elena York: Blair and Malcolm got married in a small, very romantic ceremony on the beach in Malibu—family, close friends. In hindsight, this wedding seemed to be a harbinger of the trouble to come.

Neely Smith: Well, Bridget sold the wedding pictures to the tabloids, which was, you know, not cool. I mean, this was the biggest football star in the world at that time marrying a pop princess. We— all the Captivate girls—Dreena, Gwen, Jenny, Chrissy, and me—we were all there, a bunch of NFL guys, some NBA players, so yeah, there was pretty high demand for photos of that wedding.

Gwen Majors: Bridget had some guy she was dating—it was

always some guy she was dating—anyway, she begged Blair to let this guy, a so-called professional photographer, take the wedding photos and Blair, of course, gave in. And like a week later—I think Blair and Malcolm were still on their honeymoon in Spain or wherever they were—the photos showed up in the tabloids. Any wedding photos they have are whatever crappy, drunken Polaroids any of us gave them, but no official portraits, no pictures of the wedding party, nothing.

Sasha Reid: It's not an exaggeration for me to say that Bridget hated her sister. Hated. Not, "I love you, but I don't like you," but, "I hate your guts and wouldn't piss on you if you were on fire."

Skye Stafford: Even though Blair forgave her sister, the truth is, dealing with Bridget was hard for her. She managed to keep her distance initially, but then Bibi got sick. Lung cancer. Blair, of course, feels obligated to move her to Highland Park. Except Bibi said she'd only come if Bridget came, too. As usual, Blair felt she didn't have a choice.

Chrissy Lennox: I felt bad for Malcolm. He didn't realize that he wasn't just marrying Blair. Bibi and Bridget were also part of the deal.

Elena York: This went on for two excruciating years, all of them living under one roof.

Skye Stafford: Finally, Bibi dies and Malcolm kicks Bridget out about a week later. He'd had it. He wanted his house back, he wanted his wife back. He wanted his life back.

Jenny Valentine: Bridget's little parting gift on that one, was to steal virtually every item—every album, tape, cassingle, sequin from a gown, button from a shirt, strand of hair from a wig, you name it—anything and everything to do with Captivate—from Blair. Cleaned her out. The only thing she left her with was her original Barbie doll and the only reason she didn't get her hands on it was because she couldn't find it.

Chrissy Lennox: She would have sold the thread off a dress if she could have. Then again, she probably did.

Gwen Majors: Sold everything. Every last thing. And Blair forgave her.

Kim Fletcher: I can remember when I met her, being surprised—shocked, really—that she didn't have all of this really cool memorabilia. I was a huge Captivate fan and let me tell you, she had some great stories and I hung on every word. I just knew she would have all these really great album covers and dresses and pictures and backstage passes and all of that stuff. She didn't have anything. Not one thing. This is a woman who had a room in her house devoted strictly to preserving all of Malcolm's football memorabilia and memorialized pretty much everything Farrah ever did. All kinds of scrapbooks and photo albums and blowing up her finger paintings and framing them. And she had absolutely nothing from her Captivate days. I remember she kind of blew it off, like it wasn't important to her. That was her old life, she gave everything to her sister, blah, blah, blah. Sounded like BS to me. Years later, Malcolm mentioned in passing what had really happened and I couldn't believe it. Who does that?

Elena York: After Malcolm kicked Bridget out, life did settle down for the Gilbert family, and by all accounts, those were really peaceful, really happy years. They raised Farrah, went on vacations. Malcolm built his business, and Blair cultivated friendships and hobbies and volunteer work. Life was good.

Isabelle Ryan: Malcolm forbade Bridget from ever coming to the house again. During those years, the only time the sisters saw each other was on the infrequent trips Blair took to New York. He wouldn't even allow Farrah to have contact with her aunt. That's how much he despised Bridget.

Gwen Majors: Bridget never really went away, though. Still bleeding Blair dry. She'd start with small amounts—a couple hundred here, a couple hundred there. "I'm six months behind on my rent, I need money for a whole new wardrobe for this new job that I'll probably get fired from in six weeks."

Jenny Valentine: Blair had a tremendous, *tremendous* amount of guilt where her sister was concerned. I think if you asked her straight out, she'd deny it. I think if you got a few glasses of wine in her, she'd admit that on some level, she felt like she'd stolen her sister's life.

Neely Smith: And Bridget milked Blair's guilt for every dime she could.

Skye Stafford: About a year prior, Blair gave her sister fifty thousand dollars, claiming she needed a brand new car along with some back rent she owed. Understandably, Malcolm was livid.

Isabelle Ryan: To him, Bridget was a cancer that needed to be cut out. He said if Blair gave Bridget one more dime, the marriage was over. He was leaving.

Elena York: Malcolm actually called Bridget and told her she was cut off, that she wasn't getting another cent from them. Blair was furious he'd called her sister. Incensed.

Isabelle Ryan: However, Blair complied. For a time.

Elena York: And then, Blair did something that tipped all of the dominoes over.

PHONE CONVERSATION
4:30 P.M., FRIDAY, MARCH 31

Call between Blair and Malcolm Gilbert. Malcolm Gilbert is MG; Blair Gilbert is BG

MG: Blair ... I just got a notification that you transferred twenty thousand dollars to Bridget this morning?

BG: What do you want me to do Malcolm Gilbert? Huh? She's my sister—

MG: Blair, you have given—

BG: Loaned—

MG: A loan? Did you say a loan? What loan? Huh? What loan? Blair, you've probably given her millions of dollars over the years. Hell, more. And I don't remember being paid back five dollars, five cents, not even a penny—

BG: Well, what about that money you gave Willie two years ago for his back taxes? Huh? What about that?

MG: First of all, I talked to you about it before I did *anything*, and you said, yeah, you should absolutely help him out. Second of all, he didn't come begging to me with his hand out. Third, he paid me back —with interest.

BG: Well ... I was going to tell you. I just didn't get a chance to. She needed it.

MG: Blair. Blair! Do I have to remind you of how much she has shit on you over the years?

BG: Look, she was in a bad place—

MG: When is she not in a bad place? That's every day! Every damn day of that girl's life is a bad place.

BG: What do you want me to do? Make her give it back?

MG: Hell, yeah, I want you to make her give it back! And don't give her anymore after that, either.

BG: Have you lost your mind, Malcolm Gilbert?

MG: Have you?

BG: (Sniffs). Well, it's already done, so there isn't anything I can do about it.

MG: Blair. Do you remember what I said last year when you gave her fifty thousand?

BG: Mal—

MG: Do you remember what I said last year after you gave her fifty thousand?

BG: Leave me? (Scoffs). Please.

MG: Blair, when you do shit like this, I can't trust you. And when a husband can't trust his wife, that's not a marriage.

BG: Mal—

MG: All right, Blair. All right. I'm giving you one more chance. One more chance. Now listen, because I'm only going to say this once. If that money isn't back in our account by nine a.m. on Monday, I will walk out and I won't be coming back.

BG: Oh, boo hoo. Please. I'll believe it when I see it.

MG: I walked out on you before, Blair. I can do it again.

BG: You came back.

MG: For Farrah. I came back for Farrah that time. She's grown now. What's gonna make me come back this time?

BG: Fuck you.

MG: And who's going to defend your sister when I sue her?

BG: (Gasps). What did you say?

MG: Don't pretend like you didn't hear me. If that money is not back in the bank by nine a.m. on Monday, two things are gonna happen. One, I will walk out that door, and I won't be back. Two, I will be on the phone with Larry two minutes after nine, telling him to get ready to serve Bridget, because I will sue her for every goddamn penny that hasn't been paid back. I will jack her up. She won't be able to buy a toothpick when I'm done. Oh, and Blair? I know about all the little five hundred here, a thousand there. I know you sign over your royalty checks to her, thinking I wouldn't know about it. I know about *all* of it.

BG: You can't do that—

MG: Can't do what? Walk out? Divorce you? Sue Bridget? Blair, I will *happily* do all three.

BG: Are you threatening me? Huh? Is that—You better back that truck up—

MG: No, Blair, *you'd* better back that truck up. No, Blair, this is it. This is *it*. I'm not doing this anymore. You better get your priorities together.

BG: You—

MG: Enough, Blair. Enough. Enough. Do yourself a favor and stop talking

(Line disconnects).

BOOM

Lieutenant Dimitri Cora: Saturday morning, Blair Gilbert gets a phone call.

Detective Andrea Chang: Bridget and Blair's calls—the sisters talked practically every day. These calls would last anywhere from fifteen minutes to over an hour. The calls almost never deviated from that pattern.

Lieutenant Sharon Donahue: One week before, Bridget called Blair and asked her for twenty thousand dollars, claiming she needed it for a medical bill she forgot about. Some cosmetic procedure that she'd had and now owed money on.

Detective Andrea Chang: Bridget's pattern of calls to her sister in the week leading up to the home invasion became more frequent, even for her. The volume of calls doubled from on average, five times a day to up to ten, fifteen or more a day. She was hounding her for money.

Lieutenant Sharon Donahue: On Friday morning after her Pilates class, Blair wired twenty thousand dollars to her sister.

Lieutenant Dimitri Cora: Bridget calls her sister at ten thirty Saturday morning. That call lasted forty-five seconds.

Detective Andrea Chang: They never had calls that short. Ever.

Lieutenant Sharon Donahue: When we ran a dump of the cell phone tower near the Gilberts' house, there was a call to Terrell Winters' burner phone from another burner phone. That call came into his phone just seconds after the call between Blair and Bridget. Terrell attempted to reach that number throughout the day on Saturday and a few times on Sunday.

Detective Andrea Chang: A day never went by without Bridget calling her sister. Suddenly, there's not a peep out of Bridget. After that less-than-a-minute call on Saturday morning, Bridget goes silent. Dead silent.

Lieutenant Dimitri Cora: The area code for that burner phone originated from Long Island City, where Bridget Johnson lived. We called the phone number and discovered it had been purchased at a bodega near Bridget's apartment. In a pure stroke of luck, they had CCTV from the day it was purchased and we saw a man by the name of Jamar Norris making the transaction.

Lieutenant Sharon Donahue: We ran down some more of our phone number profiles and learned that Jamar Norris's cousin is Bridget Johnson's neighbor.

Detective Andrea Chang: Basically, Bridget called Blair Saturday morning to verify she was home, before immediately getting on her burner phone to essentially wave the red flag in Terrell's direction, to execute this horrific plot against her sister.

Lieutenant Dimitri Cora: Blair never knew what was coming.

PART 3

MONDAY, APRIL 3
HIGHLAND PARK, ILLINOIS
THE RESIDENCE
OF
MALCOLM AND BLAIR GILBERT

5:30 A.M.

Farrah woke up slowly, in stages.

First, she was aware of soft snoring.

The groans and strains of the house.

The lingering stink of her mother being sick. Her own BO from not having showered since Friday morning. Tree's sweat and slobber still smeared across her skin. Amazement that any scent managed to find its way through the broken corridors of her nose.

Murmurs. Murmurs? Voices. Those voices didn't sound anything like *those* voices.

The TV. The voices came from the TV. They'd fallen asleep, the TV spitting out yet another movie.

Then the stabbing jolts of a tortured body, stiff and twisted.

The persistent throb of her lips. Her face. Her nose.

The tip of her tongue pushed against her tooth, or what used to be her tooth, now a pulsing, salty black hole, kept company on one side by a jagged edge.

Farrah allowed her eyes to drift open. She blinked several times to adjust to the blinding light of the TV, to search for shapes, familiar and strange, to attempt to get it together, figure out how many hours of misery were left.

They were in the basement. Had been there all day Sunday. Tied up. Gagged sometimes. Gag-free other times. Undone three times to use the bathroom. Undone three times to serve the monster's insatiable appetite. Just for food, thank goodness. He seemed to have quelled his other craving Saturday night—*Saturday night?*—losing interest almost as soon as he took it. Conquest, one and done. Or two and done was probably a better way to put it.

BO Boy was curled onto the floor. The monster was splayed out on the couch, his mouth wide, his eyes closed, his mouth ajar. His bitch was huddled into the recesses of the chaise.

Her mother was slumped next to her, her head lolling from side to side. Muffled wheezes escaped her nose.

Her father. Farrah scanned the space next to her mother, expecting to see his bulk propped up against the wall, thinking she would see the whites of his eyes, the insomnia that had plagued him her whole life, keeping him involuntarily on watch.

Her father.

Gone.

Her father was gone.

The mounds of duct tape that had bound his feet and hands lay in shards on the floor.

She swept her eyes across the room one more time, panic sluicing through the chambers of her heart. She made a mental imprint of every sight, every sound, every piece of furniture.

Nowhere.

Missing.

Gone.

Dead?

"Oh, God," she whispered to herself as she swiveled around, her eyes still searching.

They'd killed him. Killed him while she and her mom were passed out asleep, not knowing, not able to protest, not able to try to stop it. Hadn't heard him scream, hadn't heard the—what?—Gun shot? Stabbing? Beating?

Farrah nudged her mother. "Mom." She cringed at the foreign lisp, the congestion.

Nothing.

She tried again. "Mom," her whisper louder now, more persistent. "Wake up. Please, wake up."

Farrah prodded Blair repeatedly until her mother finally jolted awake, disoriented, her head whipping around like a flag in the wind, her eyes wild with terror.

"What's happening?" Blair mumbled, still disoriented.

"Daddy's gone," she whispered.

"What?"

"Daddy. He's not here. He's gone." Farrah paused, tears pooling in her eyes. "I think they killed him."

"What? No, no, baby, we would have heard something."

"Then where is he?"

Her mother's eyes fell onto the piles of tape that had restrained her father. "He escaped. Somehow, he escaped, which means this is almost over. It's like I told you, Daddy always has a plan." She nodded, her head falling back against the wall. "All we have to do it wait. Daddy is fixing everything."

Farrah nodded reluctantly, terror and uncertainty still racing through her. Her mother inched closer, her fingertips grazing her own. She grasped at them, grateful, for a few seconds anyway, to feel her mother's touch. Farrah kept her ear cocked for any signs of life upstairs. The creak of a floorboard, the soft padding of a foot.

There was none.

Tree grunted from across the room as he rolled over. He flashed a look at Farrah and Blair, about to fall back asleep when he jolted upright and jumped up, stumbling over to them, seething, as he dropped to the floor, his hands running over the carpet, clutching at the tufts, as though he could conjure up Malcolm by touch.

"Where the fuck is he? Huh? Huh?"

Her mother shook her head. "I don't know. We have no idea where he is." Her voice was trembling, like it was on the verge of collapse.

He straddled Blair, his fists pummeling her face.

"Where is he?" Tree said as he continued to rain blows down on Blair's head. "Where is he?"

"I don't know!" Her mother was screaming, choking, gasping.

Farrah swung around as best she could with her restraints, delivering a kick to his leg with her bound feet. He punched her in her eye, knocking her back.

"You want to lose another tooth? Huh? Huh?" He looked over at his two minions once more. "D. Dio! Wake the hell up!"

Dio didn't stir, prompting Tree to hobble over to him and kick him in the leg several times with his good foot, which caused Dio to jerk awake, his limbs flailing like a marionette tossed into the toy box.

"What's wrong?"

"Ol' Boy ain't here," Tree said as he hobbled over to his girlfriend and shook her by the shoulders. "Cookie. Yo, Cookie! Wake the fuck up."

Cookie opened her eyes and stared, not moving from her perch, not struggling to wake from a deep slumber.

"What?" Her voice was calm. Cold.

"Get up. We got to find Mally Mal. He escaped."

"No." She shook her head, still looking up at Tree.

Tree stared at her, his eyes wide, almost as if he couldn't believe what he was hearing. "What you mean, 'no'?"

"Let him go, T," she said, her voice shaking. "Let everybody go."

Tree wrenched her up from the chaise, causing her to yelp. Farrah exchanged a worried glance with her mother.

"What you say?" Tree asked.

"I can't do this." She sobbed, shaking her head. "I can't do this. It wasn't supposed to be like this. You said we was supposed to come up here and get some money—"

"Bitch, if I tell you get up and help me look, you get up and help me look." Tree pulled a kicking Cookie toward the staircase as Dio's head swiveled between them and Farrah and Blair, seemingly unsure of what to do.

Cookie's tiny fists beat helplessly against Tree's chest as he attempted to clamp her hands down and drag her upstairs all at once.

"D, what the hell you doing?" He looked at his minion. "Help me!"

Dio sprang into action at the directive, leaping over to help Tree subdue a now hysterical Cookie.

"I'm through!" she shrieked, her arms and feet flailing against both men. "I'm not doing this no more. I want to go home. I just want to go home." Wails wracked her body.

By now, the two men had wrestled a screaming Cookie to the ground. "You ain't going nowhere," Tree said, still struggling to pin her arms to the ground. Dio held her feet as she continued to kick and strain against them both. "You gonna do what I tell you to do, or I'm gonna beat your ass like you ain't never been beat before."

"I just wanna go home. Please, just let me go home," she cried. "I don't want to do this anymore, Tree, please, I just want to go home."

"You ain't going nowhere, you hear me? Not until I say you can leave. And we ain't leaving. Not until I get my money."

Cookie had nothing to offer but her continued sobs and screams and kicks and flails. Tree yanked his gun out of his waistband and pointed it at Cookie's head. Her sobs were replaced with sniveling.

"You gonna stop all that crying?" he asked.

She erupted into a fresh round of tears.

Tree fired.

Blair and Farrah screamed and fell into each other as Cookie went limp, blood pouring from the crater in her forehead. Tree shot her twice more and waited, staring at her for a moment before he sniffed and tapped Dio's shoulder.

"Yo, she got all that jewelry in her pockets. Help me empty them out."

Farrah trembled, the gun shot reverberating in her ears, the thick, metallic smell of gun powder swirling in the air. She kept her face tucked into her mother's shoulder, unable to look at Cookie, unable to watch Tree and Dio pilfer her mother's jewelry from the dead girl's pockets and stuff it into their own.

Tree sniffed again, wiping the back of his hand across his nose as he looked over at them. He limped over to where they remained huddled and whimpering.

"We gonna tear this bitch apart," he said, almost to himself, as he undid their feet. "We going room to room and we going to find Mally Mal then I'm gonna shoot him. I'm gonna shoot him in his face, and I'm going to enjoy it. I'm going to enjoy watching his bitch ass fall to the ground, smoking, damn brain everywhere." He stopped and looked at Blair. "And you're gonna watch."

"Please. Please don't—"

He smacked her mother across the face and wrenched her up from the floor, commanding Dio to do the same to Farrah. Tree and Dio pushed them up the stairs. Farrah's eyes darted around the dark living room, searching for her father's bulk.

And then she heard the click.

THE LAST HOURS

Lieutenant Dimitri Cora: Here's what happened in the Gilbert house in those final hours.

It's four fifteen a.m. The family is tied up in the basement. Blair and Farrah are asleep, as are Terrell, Courtney, and Lenard.

Malcolm is awake. It's just him, a movie blaring on the TV, and hours to go before the bank opens.

Miraculously, as he's sitting there, he spots a paperclip wedged between the baseboard and edge of the carpet.

He doesn't have time to think about how it got here. It was there and he was going to use it. With his good hand, he manages to poke through the mounds of duct tape at his feet and wrists ready to sneak upstairs for his gun concealed in a hidden safe in a bookcase in his study. He doesn't want what happened the last time to happen again. He wants to be ready.

Just as he gets himself out of the tape, ready to head upstairs, Courtney rolls over and wakes up. She sees he's freed himself. He freezes. They lock eyes for a moment.

Neither one moves. Neither one breathes. Neither one can look away from the other.

Courtney is the one to blink. She rolls over, giving Malcolm permission to leave. She'll keep his secret.

Malcolm sneaks upstairs and retrieves his gun, a twenty-two he was certain Terrell would find on his earlier rampage through the study. The one he told his wife he'd get rid of the year before. She feared his concussion might lead him to blow his brains out, but he secretly kept the gun to prove he wouldn't.

He's about to creep back downstairs to untie Blair and Farrah. He hears the commotion as Terrell and Lenard wake up and discover he's gone. Hears Terrell shoot and kill Courtney.

Terrell and Lenard hustle the women up the stairs. Malcolm aims his gun at Terrell. It's dark. He's seeing double. His hands are shaking. He shoots at Terrell, but misses.

Lenard and Terrell both fire at Malcolm, who ducks behind a couch. Terrell runs out of bullets. Lenard's gun jams. Malcolm gets off another shot, hitting Lenard in the shoulder. Terrell grabs a log from the fireplace and rushes toward Malcolm, who gets off another shot, but misses again.

Terrell smacks Malcolm in the face with the log, sending Malcolm's gun flying.

Blair, her hands still bound with tape, dives for Malcolm's gun. Lenard manages to drag himself to her and stomps on her hands, breaking them both.

Terrell and Malcolm continue to brawl on the floor. Farrah makes a run for the front door. Lenard sees her. He grabs Malcolm's gun.

He fires two bullets into her back.

She falls to the ground.

Lenard fires at Malcolm, hitting him in the thigh. He drops to the floor. Terrell takes the gun from Lenard and aims at Malcolm. Hits him in the stomach. Terrell takes aim a third time. That gun also jams.

Blair drags herself across the room toward her barely-breathing daughter, manages to get her arms around her and holds her.

A bloodied Malcolm struggles to his feet and staggers toward a stunned Terrell.

Terrell aims the gun at Malcolm and pulls the trigger, hoping he can get it going again.

Nothing.

Malcolm continues his advance. Tree's hands are up in the air, his head is wobbling in disbelief.

A shot rings out.

Malcolm falls to the ground, a bullet exploding in his other leg.

It's Lenard.

Malcolm's writhing on the floor. Blair's screaming. Terrell drops his gun and takes Lenard's gun from him.

He stands over Blair and shoots her twice in the chest, just missing her heart.

Terrell rips Blair's necklace from her body, gets Lenard to his feet, says they have to set the house on fire. They grab the rest of Blair's jewelry then run through the house looking for matches, lighter fluid, anything. They settle for dumping a bottle and a half of wine they'd been drinking earlier over the bodies and scattering around some tea lights they found in a kitchen drawer after taking them out of their metal containers. They didn't want to be there when the fire started, so they figured once the candles burned down, the house would go up in flames.

Unbeknownst to them, the Scotchgarding on the rug prevented the candles from igniting. According to Anita Sanchez, Blair Gilbert Scotchgarded the rugs every three or four months.

Fires are pretty common in home invasions, because the perps mistakenly believe it will burn away any kind of forensic evidence. Even if the house had gone up in flames, we would have been able to retrieve DNA. Hair, fibers, blood, fingerprints. It would have made our jobs a lot harder, but not impossible.

Terrell and Lenard light the candles then break a window to escape the house and peel out just as the sun is coming up.

Anita Sanchez comes in a little before eight. Blair and Farrah are dead. Miraculously, Malcolm, shot three times, is alive. Barely.

If she'd gotten there even five minutes later, Malcolm Gilbert would be dead.

She saves his life.

THE FINAL PIECES

Lieutenant Dimitri Cora: As it turns out, we didn't have to fly to New York to get Bridget. She came to us.

Lieutenant Sharon Donahue: Bridget came to town a few days after the murders. She headed straight for the house and immediately tried to gain access to her sister's property, her personal items. But of course, it was all a part of the crime scene and was evidence, so she didn't get anything. She starts sobbing about how she just wants her sister's stuff, how her sister would want her to have it.

Gwen Majors: That didn't surprise me at all. The only thing missing was her pulling up with a moving truck.

Jenny Valentine: Your sister's been brutally murdered and your first thought is, "How can I get my hands on her stuff?" That's who Bridget Johnson is.

Lieutenant Dimitri Cora: We got a hold of Lenard McKinney after his little sister called nine-one-one about the GSW he got during that final shootout at the Gilberts'.

So, we've got Terrell Winters and Lenard McKinney in custody, already knew that burner phone came from Bridget's neighbor in Long Island City. It wasn't too many steps to "She was the one to solicit her sister's murder." We just needed to connect a few more dots.

Lieutenant Sharon Donahue: When Bridget first got to town, she made a point of reaching out to us, offering her help, how she hoped we would catch whoever did this. She gave us her cell phone number, what hotel she was staying at. You know, don't hesitate to call her anytime, day or night. We played along, but meanwhile, we were working around the clock, drawing a line to all of those dots.

Skye Stafford: How this all started was ... Bridget got in touch with one of her drug dealer ex-boyfriends, tells him she's looking for a guy in Chicago to take her sister out, hints there'll be something in it for him down the line if he helps her with this. He connects her with his old cellmate, Traymond Vinson. Traymond and Bridget start to talk, but then he says he can't do it on the day she wants it done, because he'll be out of town. But he knows someone who can, and puts her in touch with the son of his ex-wife's neighbor—Terrell Winters.

Sasha Reid: Over the years, Bridget would joke—usually after a few glasses of wine—that if Blair were out of the way, she could have Malcolm all to herself, that she could reclaim what was rightfully hers. It was always, "That's my house she's living in." "That's my husband she's married to." "That's my life she's living." I didn't think she was serious, of course, because she'd always kind of laugh while she was saying it.

The weekend of the murders, she showed up at my house, asked if I wanted to go to lunch. Insisted we go to lunch. Then she wanted to go shopping. She suggested going back to my place and ordering a pizza and watching a movie. Then she said she was too drunk to drive home and could she stay overnight. Then she wanted to go to brunch the next day. Finally, about three, I had to kick her out. She'd taken up my whole weekend. Now I know it was because she needed me to be her alibi.

Lieutenant Dimitri Cora: We traced a PayCoin account to Bridget where she had purchased a voice changer, real high-tech, real sophisticated stuff. Which is why Terrell always thought he was talking to a man.

Lieutenant Sharon Donahue: We didn't tell Terrell who we suspected of hiring him. Instead, we get Bridget down to the station, just say we want to talk about the murders, that we think there's a way she can help us. She was all too happy to oblige. Meanwhile, we had a search warrant for the hotel room and we seize that burner phone, that voice changer, her laptop. It was a goldmine of evidence.

We set that burner phone we confiscated down on the table. She doesn't even flinch. We have Terrell call it from the other room and it lights right up. We tell her to answer. We cuff Terrell in the front, have him walk in, that phone pressed to his ear. The burner is still ringing. I answer it, put it on speaker, and Terrell's voice fills the room. I think she might have had a heart attack.

She went berserk, just completely off the rails when we arrested her. I've seen a lot, but I thought she was going to spontaneously combust.

Isabelle Ryan: It's been almost ten years and to this day, she insists she's innocent, that she was framed.

Lieutenant Dimitri Cora: Bridget believed, truly believed, that all she needed to do to make her life perfect, was to get rid of her sister. Then, she would swoop in to dry the widower Malcolm's tears, get him to fall in love with her and finally, *finally*, assume the mantle of the life she believed was rightfully hers.

Bridget Johnson would have done anything to be Bridget Gilbert. Anything. Even murder her sister.

Elena York: Perhaps the most horrific thing about all of this, is when Blair gave Bridget that twenty thousand dollars, she had no idea she'd handed over a down payment on her own murder.

PHONE CONVERSATION
8:30 A.M., CST MONDAY, APRIL 3

Call between Terrell Winters and Bridget Johnson. Terrell Winters is TW; Bridget Johnson is BJ

TW: Man, where the hell you been? I been calling you all weekend.

BJ: I told you I wasn't going to be around while it was going down—

TW: We had some problems. A lot of damn problems.

BJ: Problems? What do you mean problems? What kind of problems?

TW: You didn't tell me she was married to Malcolm Gilbert. Malcolm Fucking Gilbert. And that he was gonna be there.

BJ: Malcolm? Wait, Malcolm was at the house when you got there? He was supposed to be playing golf.

TW: (Scoffs). No, Malcolm wasn't playing golf. Opened the mother-fuckin' door.

BJ: Are you—are you serious?

TW: Yeah, I'm serious! Then the damn daughter was there—

BJ: Wait—*Farrah* was there too? What?

TW: It was a damn cast of thousands up in there. I ring the doorbell, expecting Ol' Girl was gonna answer, which is what you *said* would happen and damn Malcolm Gilbert is staring me in the face.

BJ: What did you do?

TW: I mean what could I do? We had to rush up in there and try and take care of business. You wasn't answering the damn phone, so I just had to make a decision quick.

BJ: Okay, but you still haven't told me what you did.

TW: I mean, we came in and he was talking about he'll give me what-ever cash he's got on hand, which wasn't nothin'. Then he says we'll go to the bank for more money, but we get there and the damn bank was closed.

BJ: You still haven't told me—

TW: Man, shut the hell up. I'm trying to tell you what happened.

BJ: (Sighs). All right, go on.

TW: So anyway, now we got to wait until Monday for the bank to open.

BJ: So you stayed there the whole weekend? With Malcolm, Blair, and Farrah?

TW: Yeah, we was all there, all six of us. Had the three of them tied up. All we had to do was make it to Monday—

BJ: Make it to—wait, you didn't kill—I mean Malcolm's not dead—

TW: I had to shoot him.

BJ: What? What? What do you mean you shot Malcolm? What?

TW: Yeah, I had to shoot him. Things got all the way out of hand. I had to do something.

BJ: You killed him? You killed Malcolm?

TW: I mean, yeah, he's dead. He's dead. We had to set the damn house on fire. It's gonna be showing up on the news soon. Like real soon.

BJ: You stupid—

TW: Hey, I did what I had to do.

BJ: You weren't supposed to do anything to Malcolm. You weren't supposed to *touch* him.

TW: How the hell was I supposed to know that? Huh? You didn't tell me what to do if he was there. You didn't tell me nothing. I had to make that shit up as I went along. Should have answered the damn phone.

BJ: I didn't have the phone, all right? Was out all weekend. You weren't supposed to call me until after it was all over. (Silence). I can't fucking believe this.

TW: Look, it wasn't like I could come back, since you said it had to be this weekend, or you weren't going to pay me (Pauses). Why did it have to be this weekend, anyway?

BJ: Today's my birthday. I thought getting rid of Blair would be a good fiftieth birthday present to myself.

TW: Damn. (Several minutes of silence pass). Hello?

BJ: God, I still can't believe Malcolm is gone.

TW: Believe it.

BJ: Farrah, too?

TW: Everybody's dead. We shot everybody, then set the house on fire before we left.

BJ: (Exhales, followed by a long pause.). Farrah, too. Huh. Well ... it's not like she was Malcolm's daughter anyway.

TW: What?

BJ: What time did you leave the house?

TW: Look, you gonna have to throw some more paper my way.

BJ: For what?

TW: I got—man, I got hit, bit—my damn hand, my foot—I can't hardly walk—

BJ: That's not my problem.

TW: Hell, yeah, it's your problem. I done went through all this. You wasn't around to tell me what I should do, so yeah, you need to throw like a bonus or something my way.

BJ: You weren't supposed to kill Malcolm.

TW: But you wanted Ol' Girl gone and she gone. (Sniffs) I did my job. Now you do yours. (Silence). Hello?

BJ: You said you shot her? Blair, I mean.

TW: Yeah, I shot her. I told you, we shot everybody. Had to.

BJ: I'm almost sad you set the house on fire. (Laughs). I thought it would be funny if you dumped her body in a dumpster. Taking the trash out. Well. I wanted her to suffer. I had dreams all weekend that you slit her throat, stabbed her fifty times, bashed her skull in. I guess getting shot and set on fire is suffering.

TW: (Pauses). You must have really hated her. What she ever do to you?

BJ: You don't know the half. (Pauses). Did you get the necklace I asked for at least? The one she was wearing?

TW: Yeah, I got it.

BJ: Well, thank God you got that right, at least.

TW: You want that necklace, give me my money. Thirty thousand.

BJ: Thirty thousand?

TW: Yeah, that's what I said. Thirty G's.

BJ: I'll give you ten. That's what we agreed on.

TW: Oh, you want to act like a bitch now, huh?

BJ: Excuse me?

TW: I need Thirty G's. Otherwise, I'm going straight to five-o—

BJ: Are you threatening me?

TW: I'm just saying you try to cross me, I'm going straight to the police, tell 'em everything I know.

BJ: And what do you think you know, exactly?

TW: I mean, I—I'm just saying—

BJ: How stupid do you think I am? How fucking stupid do you think I am? You don't even know *who* I am. You don't know my name, you don't have my phone number. My actual, real phone number. You've never even met me. You could walk past me on the street and wouldn't even know it. This—you know I have a voice changer on this phone, right? The voice you're hearing? It's not even my real voice. I could be a man, a woman. I could have an accent. I could be from fucking Australia, fucking *Mexico* for all you know. You have no idea. So go ahead. Go run to the police and tell them all about this mysterious person who you did this job for that you've never met, don't know anything about, and that you agreed to kill for (Laughs). Sounds like a fucking TV show.

TW: I mean, they'll track you down, some kind of way. They got all kinds of equipment and—

BJ: (Laughs). I don't think so. Don't worry. You'll get your money. I've got to handle a few things first. In the meantime, don't fuck with me, all right? Don't try one thing, because you don't have me where you want me. I've got you where I want you

(Pauses).

Who's the bitch now?

(Line disconnects).

THE AFTERMATH

Elena York: Terrell Winters and Lenard McKinney waived their right to trial. They pleaded guilty to first degree murder, along with about twenty-five other counts including premeditated murder, kidnapping, and assault. They both received life without the possibility of parole.

Skye Stafford: The judge said they had a blackness in their soul, a stain so dark, so depraved, they almost couldn't be described as human beings.

Isabelle Ryan: When Malcolm gave his victim impact statement, when he described the torture the family was subjected to over those two days, you could have heard a pin drop in that courtroom. And you couldn't ignore the sobs, the cries, the despair from everyone in the courtroom. Except the two defendants. Their faces were dry as a bone.

Gwen Majors: Bridget actually went through with the farce of a trial, if you can believe that—which actually, I could—screaming that she was innocent, demanding her right to a fair trial. It was disgusting. I think she actually thought a jury would buy her bulls**t.

Terry Gilbert: Malcolm didn't attend Bridget's trial or any of the motions or hearings. All his testimony was via video. He said because it's what she wanted, to be in the same room with him. Said he wouldn't give her the satisfaction of ever again being in the same room with him. And in ten years, he never has. And he never will.

Skye Stafford: Bridget Johnson was sentenced to one hundred and thirty four years each for Farrah and Blair. Two hundred and sixty eight years. First chance of parole in one hundred years.

Elena York: In an incredible twist of irony, Blair didn't leave her sister any money.

Skye Stafford: Farrah was Blair's sole beneficiary. Since she and Farrah died together, per Blair's request, all her cash and various other items were donated to different women's and community organizations she worked with.

Elena York: What she did give Bridget was her Captivate Barbie doll. The only thing her will said was, "I know you always wanted this. It's yours."

Jenny Valentine: She probably figured Bridget would sell it anyway, so it was *like* she was getting money, but still ... the irony wasn't lost on anyone. And I loved it.

Sasha Reid: I feel bad, because I—Bridget was my friend. Probably my best friend. I loved her. I know people say she's a monster, and yes, she did a horrible thing—an unforgivable thing. But, you know, deep down, she does have a heart.

Rosemary Stubbs, Lenard McKinney's Mother: I still don't believe my son done what they say. Not for one minute. It's all a setup. They planted all that evidence, forced him to confess. You know, since he's a little slow. Happens all the time. They need a scapegoat and they chose my son. Everybody say I'm crazy, that I'm not wanting to accept the truth. I know the truth! I know he didn't do it. I know in my heart. All I can do is pray, pray that there's some lawyer, some group, or somebody out there who's willing to take this on for my son, who's willing to go up there and fight for him.

Sasha Reid: Bridget ... she was the life of the party, you know? Always up for a good time, always upbeat. Always ready for fun. Just a spontaneous person. She'd be that person on Friday who'd say, "Let's go to Vegas for the weekend," or "I think I'm going to dye my hair pink today." Just a lot of fun. And she loved her little dog, Frito. Oh my gosh. She loved that dog. She'd carry little Frito around in her purse pretty much everywhere she went. She'd feed it rice and vegetables and steak, chicken. Sometimes, I think the dog ate better than she did. (Laughs). I wound up adopting him. I didn't feed him steak, but he ate okay (Laughs). And she was a big movie buff. Name any movie and she could quote it, tell you how many Oscars it won. Watching a movie with Bridget was this totally crazy experience. I miss that girl. I miss my friend.

Wanda Miller, Courtney 'Cookie' Miller's Mother: My husband and I gave our daughter a good life: a nice home, food on the table, two parents. We told her every day we loved her. We told her every day we were proud of her. We did everything right, everything we thought we were supposed to do. And my daughter still walked into someone else's home with a gun and threatened the lives of other people. She knew what was going to happen and said nothing. All because she thought she was in love. How do you fight a teenage girl on that?

I'd like to think she would have come to her senses, would have realized Terrell was no good and left him behind. She'd be a woman now.

A mother. Maybe she would have become a doctor. Maybe she would have found a good man to marry. Maybe. So many maybes. So many nevers.

Skye Stafford: Malcolm pretty much slid from view after the murders. He never stepped foot in the house again.

Isabelle Ryan: Almost immediately, Malcolm left the Chicago area and moved back to California. Through the years, Bridget has tried desperately to find him. In the beginning, she bombarded his parents, his brothers, and his attorneys with letters and phone calls, trying to track him down, proclaiming she was set up, that she'll love him until the day she dies. Eventually, phone numbers were changed and unlisted, and restraining orders were obtained, meaning if Bridget violates that order by attempting to contact anyone in the Gilbert family, she gets more time tacked onto her already lengthy sentence.

Bridget Johnson: I've been saying this for ten years and I'll keep saying it: I had nothing to do with my sister's murder.

Skye Stafford: Bridget keeps filing appeals and they keep getting thrown out or denied. She keeps representing herself because rightfully so, no lawyer will touch this with a twenty-foot pole.

Elena York: She leads a pretty lonely existence in jail. She's kept out of the general population because she's despised. She just sits there, year after year, all alone. The only way she's leaving prison is in a body bag.

Lauren Dean, Realtor: I was able to sell the house pretty quickly. The new owner was an NBA player and he and his wife razed the house almost immediately. They built a new house from the ground up and started fresh. Clean slate.

Mitch Gilbert: Those first few years ... my brother didn't talk about it. Didn't cry. Didn't get mad. Didn't show anything. Was just stone. But you could look at him and see he was haunted. Shattered.

Malcolm Gilbert: I got remarried about three years ago. Chantal. She's amazing. She saved me. She took what was broken and pieced it back together again. She made me laugh.

Nate Gilbert: I'll never forget the first time I heard my brother laugh. It ... it kind of made me jump a little, you know, the shock when I heard it, it had been so long. I didn't think I'd ever hear my brother laugh again.

Malcolm Gilbert: I live a pretty quiet life. I golf a little. Sit on the pier all day and fish. I don't catch much (Laughs). But, you know, I go out there with my little tackle box, my little thing of bait. I'm happy to sit there and cast my line. To be near the water. The sunshine.

Chantal and I, we go to dinner and do jigsaw puzzles together. She, uh (laughs) she keeps me stocked with crossword books. We travel. Have our small circle of friends. She goes to every doctor's appointment, manages all of the medications. She even (laughs), lights up with me once in a while. Medicinal, you know. We're happy.

I actually started a foundation—The Blair and Farrah Gilbert Foundation. It gives music and writing scholarships. I meet with the recipients privately, take them to lunch, get to know them, tell them about my wife and daughter.

I can talk about them now, Blair and Farrah, and smile. I couldn't do that for years. I *wouldn't* talk about them. I can talk about Farrah's ballet recitals; the slumber parties she had; that she was fluent in French and Spanish; how she'd sneak me fast food when Blair wasn't looking. The trips Blair and I took or the voicemails she would leave me. She would sing me little love songs. I'd always seem to get them in the middle of the night when I couldn't sleep. The impromptu picnics she'd plan for us in the middle of the day on a random

Wednesday. Even our fights (Laughs). I can even look back and laugh about our fights.

Isabelle Ryan: Some tragedies are unavoidable. This one wasn't. Terrell and Courtney and Lenard could have stopped it at any time. Terrell could have gone to the police to report this murder he was being asked to commit, this horrifying crime he was asked to carry out. When Terrell rang that doorbell and Malcolm opened the door, they could have turned around and gone home. Even if Malcolm hadn't been the one to open the door and indeed it had been Blair, as they thought it would be, they still could have turned around and gone home. When Farrah came downstairs, they could have turned around and gone home. They had so many opportunities to do the right thing, so many opportunities to walk away.

Lani Jacobs: I miss Blair every day. Even now, I still jog by her house—or where her house used to be—there's a different house there now—but I jog by it, and thinking about her makes me smile. I'll never meet anyone like her ever again. I wouldn't want to.

Jenny Valentine: I always have a Captivate song or two, or a Captivate medley in my shows. And I always sing "The Dream of You," which Blair sang lead on, as a tribute. We—me, Gwen, and Blair used to get together once a year, you know for dinner, drinks. Memories. Gwen and I still do it, but of course, it's not the same. It's just not the same.

Laila Amari: Whenever I read a magazine or a newspaper or a book, I always think of Farrah. She would have been a terrific writer. Some part of me thinks that somewhere, that's exactly what she's doing.

Mitch Gilbert: We don't dwell on what happened. We can't. We just remember how much we loved them.

Bridget Johnson: The worst thing has been not letting me see Malcolm. They've been filling his head with lies all these years, turning him against me, making him hate me. I could have helped him with his grief. I could have been there for him. I would have taken care of him. We could have helped each other. We're both victims. But I'll keep trying. Nothing will keep me from trying.

Until the day I die, I will keep on trying.

Because I will *never* give up on Malcolm.

Want more? You can access six deleted scenes from **WHAT YOU DON'T KNOW** (along with commentary from Bianca) - including the original beginning and ending!

Just visit www.biancasloane.com/what-you-dont-know-deleted-scenes today!

ACKNOWLEDGMENTS

This was such a fun book to write, because it was so different. While I always try to write something new and fresh each time, the truth is, in that pursuit, some books are easier to write than others. This one falls into the category of pure enjoyment.

Thank you First Reader Kathryn for pointing out the flaws (as you do). My Beta Readers, Lanee, Joy, Murry for giving me such great insight, especially when I couldn't see the forest for the trees.

Big thanks to Samantha Bailey (by the way, go, now and buy her awesome book, WOMAN ON THE EDGE). Happy I can say I knew you when and look forward to your continued awesomeness! Thank you, Wendy Janes, for your keen eye and for being so great to work with. Always.

Many thanks to my family for your continued support and encouragement. It means more than I can say.

To the readers of this book, THANK YOU. Whether this is your first Bianca Sloane story, or if you've read them all, I truly appreciate your spending time with me. Here's to many more adventures on the dark side of love.

Hey, Mr. D.—Where's your hammer?

HAVE YOU READ THEM ALL?

"SLOANE HAS A KNACK FOR DRAWING READERS IN."
-OOSA ONLINE BOOK CLUB

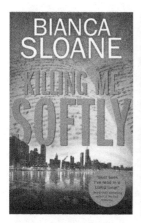

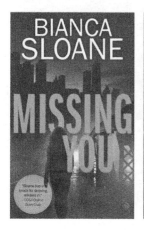

www.biancasloane.com

GET THE SCOOP FROM BIANCA SLOANE!

For updates on new book releases, exclusive content, behind-the-scenes tidbits and more, join Bianca's Book Club at

WWW.BIANCASLOANE.COM

TURN THE PAGE FOR A PREVIEW OF
BIANCA SLOANE'S MIND-BLOWING
PSYCHOLOGICAL THRILLER!

BIANCA
SLOANE

KILLING ME
SOFTLY

"Best book
I've read in a
LONG time!"
- Adam Croft, bestselling
author of *Her Last
Tomorrow.*

*"[A] cross between 'Sleeping with the
Enemy' and a superb murder mystery."*
- a CrimeReadersBlog.Wordpress.com

PROLOGUE

He drove through the night, stopping twice for gas and once to take a piss off the side of the expressway.

During one of the gas station stops, he'd made a phone call, then got back in the car to head toward his destination. He pulled up to the back entrance of the building, feeling good about what he had planned. He just needed to refine it.

He was mildly surprised to see Keegan's gleaming black Mercedes waiting for him. He parked and got out, while Keegan did the same, leaving his motor running. Keegan looked older than he remembered, worn out. Of course, it could have been because he had roused the man from bed in the middle of the night.

Or it could have been that he was just old.

He extended his hand toward Keegan, who kept his hands shoved into the pockets of his long, belted black wool coat. Wisps of salt and pepper hair escaped from beneath the brim of his gray fedora. He looked around, annoyed.

"All right, you got me out here in the middle of the fucking night, so what do you want me to do?"

"Like I told you on the phone, I need you to admit a patient. She's a special case and requires your personal supervision."

"Who is she?"

He sniffed. "That's not important. What is important is that you keep her in solitary away from everyone else."

Keegan scoffed. "That's impossible. I can't be here twenty-four hours a day."

"All right, all right, draft a nurse to help you. But I don't want a parade of orderlies and other people in and out to see her. You're the only one I want handling the case."

Keegan started to shiver. "What is it you want me to do with her?"

"First, there's a drug protocol I'm gonna want you to administer. Second, there's some very specific therapy she'll need, but I'll fill you in on all that later. For now, just keep her sedated, keep her clean, keep her fed. And keep her away from people. That's the most important thing. She'll get hysterical."

"How long am I supposed to keep this up?"

"Until I tell you not to. And you better follow my instructions to the letter. Otherwise—" He made a slicing motion across his neck.

Keegan clicked his tongue and shook his head. "Goddamn, I wish I'd never met you."

He chuckled. "Yeah, well, we can talk about that later. Right now, we need to get her inside." He glanced back at the car. "She's going to be waking up soon and I'll need to explain to her what's going on so she won't be scared."

Keegan turned off his car. He slid into the backseat of his own car and shook her gently. She stirred a little and he smiled.

"Hey, there. How are you?"

She looked around, her eyes drowsy slits in her face. He cradled her and ran a finger across her cheek. "I'm going to take care of everything. I promise. I'll always take care of you."

She moaned softly and her head lolled back against the crook of his arm. He maneuvered her out of the car before he hoisted her up and started to walk toward Keegan, who held the back door open. He ducked into the building, grunting as he adjusted her weight. Happy to be out of the cold, he followed Keegan through the maze of hallways and doors, warmth seeping back into his body. His sneakers squeaked against the shiny tiles, while Keegan's black Crocs made silent thuds. Finally, they arrived at the padded rooms and Keegan instructed Phillip to place her on the bench outside of one.

"I'll have to get a key, so wait here. I'll also need to check her in."

"Don't do that."

"Jesus Christ, I have to account, some way, somehow, for some woman springing up overnight in a padded room. She didn't just wander in off the street."

"All right, all right. Just keep everything close to the vest."

Keegan rolled his eyes. "Yeah, I got it. Can I at least get a name to put on the paperwork?"

He looked down at her and brushed a stray lock of hair from her face. "Paula. Her name is Paula."

1

Sondra stalked across the plush sage green carpet, her bare feet squishing deep into the soft fibers. She went to rake her fingers through her long and tangled black waves, forgetting they had been swept back into a sleek ponytail for the occasion. She let out an irritated sigh and looked for the millionth time at the closed bathroom door.

"Tracy," she called out. "Come on, I need to smoke before all this."

"Just a sec," came her sister's muffled reply from the other side of the door.

Sondra rolled her eyes and began to gnaw on the raw and bloody cuticle of the ring finger of her right hand. Finally, she heard the click of the door and saw a sliver of light slash the carpet. Tracy Ellis stepped into the bedroom and stood with pride in front of her older sister.

"So ...?" she asked.

Sondra stopped her pacing and looked at her sister. Tracy's olive skin, hazel eyes and lush chestnut brown hair had always meant she never wanted for attention—even female at times—but that old cliché about a woman never being more beautiful than on her wedding day was an apt description at that moment.

"Well, you sure clean up nice," Sondra said with a lump in her throat.

Tracy smiled and looked down at her elegant white silk halter dress, smoothing it down the length of her size four waist.

"I can't believe I'm getting married," she murmured, her smile never disappearing. Tracy looked up at Sondra, her face beaming.

"Do you think Phillip will like it?"

"Oh, jeez, Tracy, that's a stupid question."

"Humor me."

"All right, I'll play along. He won't be able to keep his eyes off you. Probably not his hands either."

"Well, that should make for an interesting ceremony."

Tracy turned to look at herself in the bedroom's full-length mirror, examining herself from every angle. "You know why I wanted you to wait, right?"

Sondra chuckled. "I knew something had to be up. All right, spill it."

"My something new. Mommy gave me something blue and borrowed, Cicely gave me the old, so ... that leaves you as something new." Tracy started examining her eye makeup in the mirror. "God knows I don't want anything old or borrowed from you. No telling what trashcan you might have pulled it out of."

"Jeez, you drag one table home from a curb in the eighties and you're branded for life."

"Keep playing innocent. Now, come on, let's go. Cough it up."

Sondra tried for all of thirty seconds to look clueless, before she started laughing. "All right, all right. Yes, I was responsible for the something new." Sondra walked over to pick up her oversized bag from the bed and withdrew a small blue Tiffany box.

"All right, Blackie O, get over here."

"Shut up."

Sondra laughed and held the box out to Tracy, who took it gently from her sister's hand. She looked at Sondra for a moment before she sat on the edge of the bed and began to unravel the signature white bow. Slowly, Tracy lifted the lid off the box and pulled out a small blue cloth pouch. Because her fingers were trembling, it took her a few tries to unsnap it, but when she did, she found a delicate sterling silver necklace inside.

"Oh," she said softly as she let it dangle from her fingers. She ran the tip of her French manicured nail across the lone charm to see what it was. "T," she whispered, her eyes welling with tears at the realization the looped and swirling letter was her initial.

Sondra took the necklace from Tracy's shaking fingers and began to undo the clasp. "We all know you're the pretty little poodle to my mangy, slobbery Saint Bernard," she said as she fastened the necklace around Tracy's slender neck. "So, I thought you should have some-thing princess-y." Sondra stood back to admire her sister and smiled.

"Like I said, you clean up nice."

Tracy turned and grabbed her sister by the elbows, tears sliding down her face, streaking her foundation.

"I love you, Sonny," Tracy said.

The two women hugged each other when suddenly Sondra pulled back and looked at her sister.

"Are you happy?"

Tracy nodded and dabbed at her eyes with the blue handkerchief from her mother. "Happier than I can say."

Sondra gave a quick nod and released Tracy from her grasp. "Okay," she said, fumbling for her cigarettes in her bag, trying to keep her own tears from spilling over. "Okay." She found the box and pulled them out. "That's all I wanted to know. Now. I'm gonna have my smoke and when I get back, we're gonna get you married."

* * *

It was, as days go, a perfect day for a wedding. Though it was early August, it was a balmy eighty-five degrees and there was a slight breeze that just kissed the bare arms and legs of the thirty-some odd guests gathered to witness the union of Tracy Ellis and Phillip Pearson. Tracy's best friend, Cicely, had offered up her spacious Winnetka home for the ceremony, and the attendees were all gathered in her backyard surrounded by fragrant rose bushes and sweet honeysuckle.

Sondra stood at the edge of the white runner waiting for her cue to make her way down the aisle. Though Tracy knew a ton of people, she and Phillip had decided to keep the whole affair small and low-key, inviting only their families and closest friends. Sondra was the lone bridesmaid and a co-worker Phillip was relatively close with, served as best man.

Sondra cocked her head slightly as she looked at her brother-in-law-to-be standing uncomfortably at the altar. He stood stiff as a board in his navy suit, his hands clenched together in front of him. The glare of the sun turned his coke-bottle glasses white, making him look like a character from the old "Annie" comic strip. He licked his lips as he swayed from side-to-side.

Sondra thought Phillip was an odd choice for Tracy. The couple had a whirlwind courtship, becoming engaged four months after meeting and now, six months later, getting hitched. While she got hit on just walking out her front door, time and again, she went for tall, dark and handsome.

Phillip was anything but. Phillip reminded Sondra of Urkel, with his small build, high-pitched voice and dated box-top haircut. It wouldn't have surprised her if he had a pair of suspenders stashed in his closet. However, unlike the madcap and boisterous Urkel, Phillip was painfully shy, introverted and far from a breezy conversationalist. He was a mild-mannered pharmacist, which was in fact how they'd met; he'd filled a prescription for Tracy. Although Sondra had reservations, as far as she could tell, he treated Tracy like gold, which was all that mattered to her; she just wanted her sister to be happy.

The harpist began to play "Ave Maria," giving Sondra her signal. She wobbled a bit in her rhinestone-laden high-heeled sandals, her feet unaccustomed to wearing anything that wasn't a flip-flop or Doc Marten. Her knee-length, size six pink taffeta tank dress made a soft swish as she proceeded down the aisle. She caught her mother's eye and winked as Mimi Ellis gave her a broad smile. Sondra reached the altar and looked down the aisle, waiting for her sister to make her entrance.

As their father gripped his youngest daughter's arm, the guests stood to watch Tracy make her way toward her groom. She couldn't keep the smile or tears off her face as she looked into the eyes of the man who was to be her husband. Phillip let out a breath as Tracy got closer and shook his head a little and Sondra could see him mouth, "so beautiful," to himself as he continued to watch her, wiping his own tears away.

Gordon Ellis kissed Tracy on the cheek, gave Phillip a firm hand-shake before he placed Tracy's hand inside his future son-in-law's, and joined his wife in the front row. Sondra took a deep breath and watched in silent awe as her sister got married.

* * *

The balmy breezes continued to waft through the air as Sondra stood at the end of the driveway enjoying the first cigarette she'd had since the ceremony ended. She had to admit, it had been beautiful. The couple had written their own vows and everyone cried, Sondra included. The first dance had been to "Let's Stay Together," the father-daughter dance to "My Girl." Sondra gave a touching toast honoring her sister and Phillip that brought out everyone's hankies. Tracy's own speech about what a difficult road it had been to get here, but how she would take the trip again if it would lead her to Phillip, made couples snuggle closer and singles hopeful that one day they too would find their true love.

Sondra stubbed out her cigarette and as she made her way to the backyard, she caught sight of her parents and Tracy and Phillip talking, each couple with linked hands. She watched them, taking mental pictures: their statuesque, blonde, blue-eyed German mother, a former Olympic medalist swimmer and now a sought-after swimming coach; their black father, a renowned professor of cultural studies at Stanford and best-selling author of several books examining the influence of blacks on popular culture; and Tracy, a slightly darker version of Mimi, was a TV news producer here in Chicago.

Sondra crossed her arms and let her finger trail up and down along the curve of her own rich, buttery caramel neck, her sable brown eyes misting over. She wanted to hold this moment in her heart and mind for as long as she could, knowing it would be a long time before they were all together again.

Out of the corner of her eye, she saw the cake table and realized she hadn't had any yet. She wiped away the tears and began to walk in that direction when Phillip caught up to her.

"Hey," he said as he touched Sondra's elbow.

"Hi," she replied as she picked up a plastic fork and white Styrofoam plate supporting a small piece of lemon chiffon cake with buttercream frosting and began to nibble.

Phillip shoved his hands into the pockets of his tuxedo pants and smiled. "I just wanted to tell you how much it meant to Tracy that you could be here today."

Sondra swallowed and shrugged. "Where else would I be?"

"Well, I mean, I know you have a lot to do and all with your trip coming up. When are you leaving?"

"Next Friday, so I've got almost a week to get everything together."

"What's your documentary going to be on?"

"Images of beauty around the world. Plastic surgery, rituals, that kind of thing."

"Sounds cool. How long will you be gone?"

"About a year and some change. Then I'll come back and do the editing. It's going to be an intense time."

"Tracy is really going to miss you."

Sondra looked over Phillip's shoulder and saw Tracy bouncing a friend's little girl on her hip while she talked animatedly to another guest. "I'm gonna miss her too. But, you know my cell phone is one of those global things and I'll have access to email, though it may not be the greatest." Sondra put the plate down on the table, only half of the cake eaten. "We'll still be in touch."

Phillip nodded absentmindedly then opened and closed his mouth, seeming to struggle with what to say.

"Listen, I know you think we rushed into this—"

Sondra held up her hand. "Do you love my sister?"

Phillip nodded. "More than I can say."

"Then that's it. As long as you love and take care of her, that's it."

Phillip pursed his lips together into a grateful smile. "Don't worry. I'll always take care of your sister."

* * *

The reception had run well into the night and Sondra was exhausted. She had a seven a.m. flight back to New York, and Tracy and Phillip would be leaving for their honeymoon in Jamaica on Sunday afternoon, so Sondra wanted to make sure she said goodbye to Tracy before the limo took her back to her hotel in the city. She leaned against the jamb of the front door watching Tracy hug the last guest, the straps of her rhinestone sandals slung around her wrist. She waved brightly to them until they climbed into their car and drove away. Tracy's shoulders slumped a little and she looked over at Sondra.

"So, a year, huh?" she said as she walked over to join Sondra in the entryway.

Sondra nodded. "Yup. Will I be an aunt by the time I get back?"

Tracy winked. "I have a pretty good feeling you will."

Sondra's head flipped up. "You're not—"

Tracy giggled. "Oh God no. No, no, but we've talked about starting a family in the next year or so." Tracy hugged herself and closed her eyes. "I can't wait."

Sondra looked down at the front walk in front of her, tracing a pattern with her toe.

"You'll be a great mom." She looked up and smiled. "I can't wait for you either."

Tracy's face grew somber as she looked at Sondra. "You just make sure you come back."

Sondra held up two fingers. "Scout's honor."

"Didn't you get kicked out of Girl Scouts?"

"Yeah, because I flashed my party pants at a Cub Scout."

Tracy playfully pinched Sondra's arm, who went to put her sister in a headlock. The two women stopped laughing long enough to give each other a lingering hug.

"I love you, baby girl," Sondra said.

"Back at ya, Sonny." Tracy smiled. "I'll see you soon."

2

All ten of Sondra's fingers were red, ragged messes. She'd been flying all day and night and, unable to smoke, had nearly chewed each digit to the bone. The pilot announced their initial descent into Chicago and if she could have parachuted in, she would have.

As the plane descended, Sondra flattened her forehead against the window of the plane, searching for the landscape of the city hidden beneath the white swell of clouds, frantic to land, to know ...

Finally, the plane taxied to the gate and Sondra ripped her seatbelt from across her slender waist, waiting for the doors to open. The aisles filled with passengers hauling down luggage, turning on cell phones to check messages and chatting away about emails, business meetings and what restaurants they would dine at while visiting Chicago. Going on with their lives as normal.

Sondra went to turn her own phone back on, before remembering the battery died just as she boarded. She balled her hand into a fist and bit her knuckle in a futile attempt to give her decimated fingers a rest.

She wondered how long it would take the air marshal to catch her if she tried to shove past all these people.

The traffic began to inch forward. The tip of Sondra's tongue caught the saltiness from the perspiration on her upper lip as she folded her lanky frame over the seat in front of her, waiting for her turn in line. Clutching her one carry-on bag, she shuffled her way into the aisle before finally reaching the door.

She tried to keep her cool as she went through customs. She kept a level gaze on the gate agent as he queried her about her time overseas and what she would be doing while in the U.S.

She had to force the tears to stay inside while answering him.

As soon as she was free of customs, she broke into a run, her smoker's lungs protesting the whole time. The soles of her flip-flops slapped against the shiny tile like lit firecrackers as the crowds of arrivals and departures parted once they heard her pound towards them. She knew her feet would freeze, but she didn't care. Tears stung Sondra's eyes and she swatted at them as if they were errant gnats buzzing around her face as she scanned the boards overhead for directions to ground transportation.

Panting, sweating, and nearly hacking up a lung, Sondra found the door leading to the taxis. The doors slid open and the blast of arctic air almost knocked her to the salt-stained sidewalk. Shivering in her thin sweatshirt, Sondra ran her trembling, blood-crusted fingers through her wavy, black tresses as she darted to the taxi stand. She hopped from one foot to the other to keep warm while she waited for yet another slow line to move forward. The fat black dispatcher, dwarfed beneath a dusty black down coat and furry earmuffs, gave her the once over.

"What happened to your coat, young lady? You know this is Chicago in January," he laughed, his breath billowing out from beneath jagged, yellow buckteeth to mock her.

Sondra ignored him and ran to the orange Wolley cab he indicated. She jumped in and gave the driver the address, blowing breath into her hands to revive them. She was about to fish out her cigarettes when she noticed the 'No Smoking' sign taped to the back of the seat. She groaned to herself and sat on her hands, rocking back and forth in a feeble attempt to keep herself calm.

The gray and grit of the city looked repulsive to her on this frigid afternoon. She didn't hear the low murmur of NPR—the universal radio station of cab drivers—as she stared unseeing out the window while smiling billboards sheathed under the sludge of winter, decaying buildings and grimy El trains hissed past her in a haze. After an eternity, the cab turned down her sister's North side street and came to a stop in front of her house. Sondra threw a wad of crumpled twenties at the driver and flung the door open, not bothering to close it. She didn't hear the cabbie yelling after her as she bounded up the front steps of the house and slammed herself against the door to make it open.

The first thing she heard was her mother's pained cries. The first thing she saw was her father's face, and the shake of his head.

Sondra's knees buckled and she crumpled into a pile on the gleaming hardwood floor.

ABOUT THE AUTHOR

Bianca Sloane is the author of the suspense novels *Killing Me Softly* (previously published as *Live and Let Die*), chosen as "Thriller of the Month" (May 2013) by e-thriller.com and a "2013 Top Read" by OOSA Online Book Club, *Sweet Little Lies, Every Breath You Take,* and *Missing You*: A Companion Novella to *Every Breath You Take*). When she's not writing, she's watching Bravo TV or Investigation Discovery, reading, or cooking. Sloane resides in Chicago. To connect with Bianca:

www.biancasloane.com
Bianca@BiancaSloane.com